Collected Short Stories

Collected Short Stories

Michael McLaverty

POOLBEG PRESS: DUBLIN

This collection first published 1978 by
Poolbeg Press Ltd.,
Knocksedan House,
Swords, Co. Dublin, Ireland.

The generous assistance of the
Arts Council of Northern Ireland
in the publication of this book
is gratefully acknowledged.

Designed by Steven Hope.
Cover photograph by Bórd Fáilte

Printed by Cahill (1976) Limted,
East Wall Road, Dublin 3.

Contents

Introduction

Michael McLaverty writes and talks with an artist's passion. When I met him first in 1962, he was headmaster of St Thomas's Intermediate School in Ballymurphy where I was a student teacher. He would come into the English class to conduct, for the benefit of a less than literary 4B, elaborate and humorous conversations about the efficacy of poetry. "Did you ever remark, Mr Heaney," he would enquire, "how when you see the photograph of a rugby team you can always pick out the boys who studied poetry by the look on their faces?" Faithfully and fallaciously, I would reply, "Yes, Mr. McLaverty," and "There you are now," he would say to them, closing the case triumphantly, then leaving the room with a warning: "Work hard and when you leave school, don't end up measuring your spits on some street corner!" He had them in the palm of his hand. They rejoiced in the way his talk heightened their world of football teams and street corners and they were affected by the style of his sincerity.

But Michael was as concerned to educate the taste of this young graduate as he was successful in enlivening the imaginations of those veteran pupils. "Look for the intimate thing," he would say, and go on to praise the "note of exile" in Chekov, or to exhort me to read Tolstoy's "Death of Ivan Ilych", one of his sacred texts. For if fidelity to the intimate and the local is one of his obvious strengths as a writer, another is his sense of the great tradition that he works in, his contempt for the flashy and the topical, his love of the universal, the worn grain of unspectacular experience, the well-turned grain of language itself. "Don't be reading newspapers, they'll only spoil your style," he would advise me, more than half in earnest.

I wish this book had been available then. His achievement in the short story had been greeted and praised by editors and critics such as Middleton Murry and Edwin Muir, but by the early sixties both *The White Mare* (published in a small edition by Richard Rowley's Mourne Press in Newcastle) and *The Game Cock,* a fuller collection issued by a commercial publisher in 1947, were out of print, as were the novels. It is sad to reflect that for two decades most of his exemplary work was unavailable, but heartening to find audiences in the seventies responding so strongly to *Call My Brother Back* when it was reissued by Riverrun, and to Poolbeg's selection of the stories, *The Road to the Shore,* published in 1976. The purity of the art, the sureness of touch and truth of vision, all grow clearer as the mastery in his voice is discerned behind the modesty of its pitch.

Michael McLaverty has been called a realist, and we can assent to that description. The precision with which he recreates the life of Belfast streets or Rathlin shores or Co. Down fields and the authenticity of the speech he hears in all those places — this affords us much pleasure. But realism is finally an unsatisfactory word when it is applied to a body of work as poetic as these stories. There is, of course, a regional basis to McLaverty's world and a documentary solidity to his observation, yet the region is contemplated with a gaze more loving and more lingering than any fieldworker or folklorist could ever manage. Those streets and shores and fields have been weathered in his affections and patient understanding until the contours of each landscape have become a moulded language, a prospect of the mind.

What McLaverty said of a wordy contemporary could never be said of his own stories: "Exciting at first blush, but not durable." His language is temperate, eager only in its exactitude. His love of Gerard Manley Hopkins is reflected in a love of the inscape of things, the freshness that lives deep down in them, and in a comprehension of the central place of suffering and sacrifice in the life of the spirit — never in that merely verbal effulgence that Hopkins can equally inspire. His tact and pacing, in the individual sentence and the overall story, are beautiful: in his best work, the elegiac is bodied forth in perfectly pondered images and rhythms, the pathetic is handled as carefully as brain tissue.

A contemporary of Patrick Kavanagh and, like him, a Monaghan man by birth, sharing the poet's conviction that God is to be found in "bits and pieces of everyday", that "naming these things is the love-act and its pledge", but averse to the violence of Kavanagh's invective and satire, McLaverty's place in our literature is secure. It is time that it was vaunted.

SEAMUS HEANEY

The Prophet

BRENDAN STOOD on the big stone near the byre, letting the rain splash on his bare head and dribble down his face. It was cold standing barefooted on the stone, but he didn't seem to mind, for now and again he'd stick out his tongue to catch the tickling drops. The byre door was open and the dark entrance showed the rain falling in grey streaks; it stuttered in the causeway and trickled in a puddle around the stone carrying with it bits of straw and hens' feathers. Beside him was a steaming manure heap with a pitchfork sticking in the top, its handle varnished with the rain. Under a heeled-up cart stood hens, humped and bedraggled, their grey eyelids blinking slowly with sleep.

Brendan shouted at them and laughed at the way they stretched their necks and shook the rain off their feathers. He waited until they hunched again to sleep and then he let another yell followed by louder laughs. A white duck clattering from behind the byre caught his attention. It stopped, looking from side to side, then it flapped its wings and quacked loudly. Brendan thought this was a sign for the rain to stop and he clodded the duck with a few lumps of turf. He looked up at the sky and out to sea. The sky was grey: the Mull of Kintyre was smothered in fog; and turning round he saw a tonsure of mist on Knocklayde. He smiled at the prospect of more rain.

Presently, a latch clicked and his mother flung out a basin of water which splashed on the cobbles, the sleepy hens awakening and racing towards it. For a moment the woman leaned on the half-door, looking at her son, at his brown jersey black with rain around the shoulders, his tattered trousers clinging to his wet-pink knees, and his bare legs streaked with mud.

"Brendan, boy!" she shouted. "What in under Heaven are ye doin' there? Come in out o' that this minute or ye'll be foundered."

Brendan hopped off the stone, and as he entered the house he ducked when his mother made a clout at him. Inside he stood near the hearth with the steam rising from off his clothes and the rain trickling darkly on the stone floor.

"Dry yerself with that cloth, you silly boy: do ye want to go like yer Granda?"

Brendan didn't speak; he sat down on a stool near the fire, rubbing his head with the cloth, and thinking of Granda – poor Granda that died last month! If his mother only knew, it was like Granda he wanted to be; not to be dead, but to be able to tell the weather. His Granda could always tell when it was going to rain or snow.

Brendan pictured him sitting at the corner of the hearth, leaning forward on his stick, and the red handkerchief with the white spots sticking out of his pocket. He saw his brown beard and moustache, and the dark toothless mouth that reminded him of a thrush's nest. In his mind he heard his Granda groaning and saying: "There's bad weather in it, Brendan me son; there's bad weather coming for I feel it in my bones."

"And how do you feel it, Granda?" Brendan would ask.

"When you're old like me, me son, it's maybe you'll feel it too, but God grant you won't. Standin' out on the mountainside with the sheep and it rainin' heaven's hard, and you without another coat to your back. And out at the fishin' at night with the cold wind and the frozen lines, and your trousers clammed to your knees. Your boots squelchin' in the shughs after divils of cows, and may be not a bite of shop's meat from one year to another. In water and out of water, in shughs and out of shughs; 'tis them things, Brendan, that'd make you feel it; 'tis them things. . . ."

12

"Under Heaven, Brendan," shouted his mother interrupting his thoughts, "you're scorchin'!"

Brendan became aware of the biscuity smell of scorched clothes and felt his damp legs and knees sticky with heat. He still held the cloth in his hand.

"Gimme that," said his mother, taking the cloth and vigorously rubbing his head. "Get up to bed now for ye have me heart scalded this blessed day."

Brendan asked for a piece of bread and went up to the room off the kitchen. His younger brother Bob was already asleep. Brendan stood at the little four-paned window, eating his piece, and looking out. He could hear the Lighthouse rockets shattering the rain-cold air and he knew the mists were thickening on land and sea. It was getting dark. The hens had left the shelter of the cart and gone to roost, the manure heap still steamed, and Prince, the sheep-dog, nosed around the byre with soaking paws and his hairy tail corded with rain. Brendan wondered could Prince tell the weather for he was always in water and out of water, in shughs and out of shughs.

He turned from the window and knelt on the bare, boarded floor to say his prayers. He prayed to his Granda to help him to tell the weather, and his mind wandered to the school and to the boys asking him what kind of a day will it be tomorrow. He glowed at the thought and snuggled in beside his warm brother. He put his cold feet on his back and Bob wakened and threatened to shout to Mammie if he wouldn't lie over.

"All right," said Brendan. "I was going to tell you how to tell the weather, but I'll not do it now."

"Ach, no one could tell the weather only Granda," replied Bob sleepily.

"Couldn't they? Granda told me the secret and I can tell it."

Bob didn't reply and tried to sleep again. But Brendan lay awake and thought he felt something, felt his shoulders cold, and wondered if that's what Granda felt.

"Bob," he said, putting his cold feet on his brother

13

again, "there's going to be rain tomorrow."

Bob heard him, but didn't speak, and soon the two boys fell asleep.

In the morning they set off for school, Brendan taking his little brother by the hand. It wasn't raining, but the air was cold and damp. The sky was grey like the evening before, and water lay in the cart-ruts along the road. Below them the sea lay calm with dark paths zig-zagging across it, while the hills around were sodden and beaten into cold, shrivelled shapes. As their bare feet slapped the wet road, Brendan kept telling his brother how he had foretold the weather, and little Bob listened with great belief and pride. Now and again they'd stop and look at the imprint of bare feet on the rain-softened road trying to guess what boy had passed along before them.

When they got into the one-roomed school there was an air of restless gaiety, for tomorrow was to be the School Sports. Bob was full of his big brother's magic, and began telling everyone how his Brendan could tell the weather. Then one little boy put up his hand saying, "Sir! Sir! he says his brother can tell the weather."

The master looked over at Brendan whose toes were twitching under the desk.

"Can you forecast the weather?" asked the master. Brendan's face got red and the master smiled. "I never knew we had a prophet in the school before. And what kind of a day will it be tomorrow?" he added. But Brendan never spoke.

On account of the Sports the school was let out early, the scholars gushing from the door in all directions. Brendan and Bob were not alone now. The three Lighthouse boys were with them chaffing about the weather.

"What'll it be like for the Sports?" says one. "Oh, Prophet of Israel," says another, imitating the master's voice, "what will there be tomorrow?" Brendan walked on in silence and they laughed and chanted:

"Oh, the prophet!

14

The prophet!
The rick-stick-stophet!"

Then Brendan stopped, and felt, felt something. "I'll tell
ye — " he says, "if ye want to know. There'll be rain
tomorrow, bucketfuls and bucketfuls of it."

"And how do you know?" they all said together.

"It's me Granda that learned me before he died."

A great silence came on them.

"Tell me how to do it and I'll give you a puffin's egg
and I'll show you me robin's nest," asked one earnestly.
Brendan didn't answer and they walked beside him, looking at him as if he were a black man.

He turned into the house and his companions walked on
for a while in silence.

"I bet you a million pounds he can't tell the weather,"
ventured one.

"You're right," said another, "for doesn't Father
McKinley get us to pray for a good day when the Bishop is
comin' for Confirmation."

"We'll see tomorrow anyhow; but mind you his Granda
was a quare ould fella and me Da often said he was an ould
witch," replied the eldest.

From the kitchen window Brendan watched his three
companions disappear down the road and he knew that
they were talking about him. He clenched his fists and
wished with all his might for rain tomorrow, while his
Granda's words, like an old rhyme, ran through his mind —
"in water and out of water, in shughs and out of shughs,
'tis them things that make you feel it!"

After the dinner he went off with Bob to the lake to sail
boats. Brendan's was a Norwegian schooner, a flat,
pointed stick with two big goose feathers. A nail with a
piece of cord was stuck in her stern so that she could tow
Bob's little, one-masted vessel. Brendan watched his boat
crinkling the water, leaving a trail behind it like a swim-
ming duck. With his trousers rolled up he waded out as far
as he could go, following his boat and chanting — "in

water and out of water, in shughs and out of shughs,"

Coming home he was wet to the skin, but there was great joy in his heart for he felt now there'd be rain tomorrow.

That night he prayed for a long time, prayed to God and to his Granda to bring on the rain, and in bed he thought he felt whatever Granda felt. At one time he was sure he felt the rain at the window, but it was only the fuchsia leaves brushing against the pane. He lay for awhile thinking of wet days with the rain sizzling in the lake, the hens hunched up under the cart, the ducks suttering in the shughs, and Prince running across the kitchen floor with wet paws. And from such thoughts sleep came.

In the morning he awoke and lay listening, listening for the sound of rain. But outside the birds sang and in the window a large fly buzzed. He raised himself on his elbows and stared around. A blue sky was framed in the window. The sun was shining and a leafy shadow of the fuchsia bush trembled on the white-washed bedroom wall. The birds' songs came clearer now to his keener wakefulness. He looked at his sleeping brother. Then he lay back on the pillow, and dripping drearily into his mind came thoughts of his companions jeering and shouting — *The Prophet! The Prophet!*

Pigeons

OUR JOHNNY kept pigeons, three white ones and a brown one that could tumble in the air like a leaf. They were nice pigeons, but they dirtied the slates and cooed so early in the morning that my Daddy said that someday he would wring their bloody necks. That is a long while ago now, for we still have the pigeons, but Johnny is dead; he died for Ireland.

Whenever I think of our Johnny I always think of Saturday. Nearly every Saturday night he had something for me, maybe sweets, a toy train, a whistle, or glass marbles with rainbows inside them. I would be in bed when he'd come home; I always tried to keep awake, but my eyes wouldn't let me – they always closed tight when I wasn't thinking. We both slept together in the wee back room, and when Johnny came up to bed he always lit the gas, the gas that had no mantle. If he had something for me he would shake me and say: "Frankie, Frankie, are you asleep?" My eyes would be very gluey and I would rub them with my fists until they would open in the gaslight. For a long while I would see gold needles sticking out of the flame, then they would melt away and the gas become like a pansy leaf with a blue heart. Johnny would be standing beside the bed and I would smile all blinky at him. Maybe he'd stick a sweet in my mouth, but if I hadn't said my prayers he'd lift me out on to the cold, cold floor. When I would be jumping in again in my shirt tails, he would play whack at me and laugh if he got me. Soon he would climb into bed and tell me about the ice-cream shops, and the bird-shop that had funny pigeons and rabbits and mice in the window. Someday he was going to bring me down the town and buy me a black and white mouse, and a custard bun full of ice-cream. But he'll never do it now because he died for Ireland.

On Saturdays, too, I watched for him at the backdoor when he was coming from work. He always came over the waste ground, because it was the shortest. His dungarees would be all shiny, but they hadn't a nice smell. I would pull them off him, and he would lift me on to his shoulder, and swing me round and round until my head got light and the things in the kitchen went up and down. My Mammie said he had me spoilt. He always gave me pennies on Saturday, two pennies, and I bought a licorice pipe with one penny and kept the other for Sunday. Then he would go into the cold scullery to wash his black hands and face; he would stand at the sink, scrubbing and scrubbing and singing "The Old Rusty Bridge by the Mill", but if you went near him he'd squirt soap in your eye. After he had washed himself, we would get our Saturday dinner, the dinner with the sausages because it was pay-day. Johnny used to give me a bit of his sausages, but if my Mammie saw me she'd slap me for taking the bite out of his mouth. It was a long, long wait before we went out to the yard to the pigeons.

The pigeon-shed was on the slates above the closet. There was a ladder up to it, but Johnny wouldn't let me climb for fear I'd break my neck. But I used to climb up when he wasn't looking. There was a great flutter and flapping of wings when Johnny would open the trap-door to let them out. They would fly out in a line, brownie first and the white ones last. We would lie on the waste ground at the back of our street watching them fly. They would fly round and round, rising higher and higher each time. Then they would fly so high we would blink our eyes and lose them in the blue sky. But Johnny always found them first. "I can see them, Frankie," he would say. "Yonder they are. Look! above the brickyard chimney." He would put his arm around my neck, pointing with his outstretched hand. I would strain my eyes, and at last I would see them, their wings flashing in the sun as they turned towards home. They were great fliers. But brownie would get tired and he would tumble head over heels like you'd think he was going to fall. The white ones always flew down to him, and Johnny would go wild. "He's a good tumbler, but he won't let the others fly high. I think I'll sell him." He would look at me, plucking at the grass, afraid to look up. "Ah, Frankie," he would say, "I won't sell him. Sure I'm only codding." All day we would sit, if the weather was good, watching our pigeons flying, and brownie doing somersaults. When they were tired they would light on the blue slates, and Johnny would throw corn up to them. Saturday was a great day for us and for our pigeons, but it was on Saturday that Johnny died for Ireland.

We were lying, as usual, at the back, while the pigeons were let out for a fly round. It was a lovely sunny day. Every house had clothes out on the lines, and the clothes were fluttering in the breeze. Some of the neighbours were sitting at their backdoors, nursing babies or darning socks. They weren't nice neighbours for they told the rent-man about the shed on the slates, and he made us pay a penny a week for it. But we didn't talk much to them, for we loved our pigeons, and on that lovely day we were splitting out sides laughing at the way brownie was tumbling, when a strange man in a black hat and burberry coat came near us. Johnny jumped up and went to meet him. I saw them talking, with their heads bent towards the ground, and then the strange man went away. Johnny looked very sad and he didn't laugh at brownie any more. He gave me the things out of his pockets, a penknife, a key, and a little blue note-book with its edges all curled. "Don't say anything to Mammie. Look after the pigeons, Frankie, until I come back. I won't be long." He gave my hand a tight squeeze, then he walked away without turning round to wave at me.

All that day I lay out watching the pigeons, and when I

got tired I opened the note-book. It had a smell of fags and there was fag-dust inside it. I could read what he had written down:

```
Corn        ........................  2-6d
Club        ........................   6d
3 Pkts. Woodbine       .........   6d
Frankie     .....................   2d
```

He had the same thing written down on a whole lot of pages; if he had been at school he would have got slapped for wasting the good paper. I put the note-book in my pocket when my Mammie called me for my tea. She asked me about Johnny and I told her he wouldn't be long until he was back. Then it got late. The pigeons flew off the slates and into the shed, and still Johnny didn't come back.

It came on night. My sisters were sent out to look for him. My Daddy came home from work. We were all in now, my two sisters and Mammie and Daddy, everyone except Johnny. Daddy took out his pipe with the tin lid, but he didn't light it. We were all quiet, but my mother's hands would move from her lap to her chin, and she was sighing. The kettle began humming and shuffling the lid about, and my Daddy lifted it off the fire and placed it on the warm hob. The clock on the mantelpiece chimed eleven and my sisters blessed themselves – it got a soul out of Purgatory when you did that. They forgot all about my bed-time and I was let stay up though my eyes felt full of sand. The rain was falling. We could hear it slapping in the yard and trindling down the grate. It was a blowy night for someone's back-door was banging, making the dogs bark. The newspapers that lay on the scullery floor to keep it clean began to crackle up and down with the wind till you'd have thought there was a mouse under them. A bicycle bell rang in the street outside our kitchen window and it made Mammie jump. Then a motor rattled down, shaking the house and the vases on the shelf. My Daddy opened the scullery door and went into the yard. The gas blinked and a coughing smell of a chimney burning came into the kitchen. I'm sure it was Mrs. Ryan's. She always burned hers on a wet night. If the peelers caught her she'd be locked in jail, for you weren't allowed to burn your own chimney.

I wish Daddy would burn ours. It was nice to see him putting the bunch of lighted papers on the yard-brush and sticking them up the wide chimney. The chimney would roar, and if you went outside you'd see lines of sparks like hot wires coming out and the smoke bubbling over like lemonade in a bottle. But he wouldn't burn it tonight, because we were waiting on Johnny.

"Is there any sign of him?" said Mammie, when Daddy came in again.

"None yet; but he'll be all right; he'll be all right. We'll say the prayers, and he'll be in before we're finished."

We were just ready to kneel when a knock came to backdoor. It was a very dim knock and we all sat still, listening. "That's him, now," said Daddy, and I saw my mother's face brightening. Daddy went into the yard and I heard the stiff bar on the door opening and feet shuffling. "Easy now: Easy now," said someone. Then Daddy came in, his face as white as a sheet. He said something to Mammie. "Mother of God it isn't true — it isn't!" she said. Daddy turned and sent me up to bed.

Up in the wee room I could see down into the yard. The light from the kitchen shone into it and I saw men with black hats and the rain falling on them like little needles, but I couldn't see our Johnny. I looked up at the shed on the slates, the rain was melting down its sides, and the wet felt was shining like new boots. When I looked into the yard again, Daddy was bending over something. I got frightened and went into my sisters' room. They were crying and I cried, too, while I sat shivering in my shirt and my teeth chattering. "What's wrong?" I asked. But they only cried and said: "Nothing, son. Nothing. Go to sleep, Frankie, like a good little boy." My big sister put me into her bed, and put the clothes around me and stroked my head. Then she lay on the top of the bed beside me, and I could feel her breathing heavily on my back. Outside it was still blowy for the wind was kicking an empty salmon-tin which rattled along the street. For a long time I listened to the noises the wind made, and then I slept.

In the morning when I opened my eyes I wondered at finding myself in my sisters' room. It was very still: the blinds were down and the room was full of yellow light. I listened for the sound of plates, a brush scrubbing, or my big sister singing. But I heard nothing, neither inside the house nor outside it. I remembered about last night, my sisters crying because our Johnny didn't come home. I sat up in bed; I felt afraid because the house was strange, and I got out and went into the wee back room.

The door was open and there was yellow light in it, too, and the back of the bed had white cloth and I couldn't see over it. Then I saw my Mammie in the room sitting on a chair. She stretched out her arms and I ran across and knelt beside her, burying my face in her lap. She had on a smooth, black dress, and I could smell the camphor balls off it, the smell that kills the moths, the funny things with no blood and no bones that eat holes in your jersey. There were no holes in Mammie's dress. She rubbed my head with her hands and said: "You're the only boy I have now." I could hear her heart thumping very hard, and then she cried, and I cried and cried, with my head down on her lap. "What's wrong, Mammie?" I asked, looking up at her wet eyes. "Nothing, darling: nothing, pet. He died for Ireland." I turned my head and looked at the bed. Johnny was lying on the white bed in a brown dress. His hands were pale and they were joined around his rosary beads, and a big crucifix between them. There was a big lump of wadding at the side of his head and wee pieces up his nose. I cried more and more, and then my Mammie made me put on my clothes, and go downstairs for my breakfast.

All that day my Mammie stayed in the room to talk to the people that came to see our Johnny. And all the women shook hands with Mammie and they all said the same thing: "I'm sorry for your trouble, but he died for his country." They knelt beside the white bed and prayed, and then sat for awhile looking at Johnny, and speaking in low whispers. My sisters brought them wine and biscuits, and some of them cried when they were taking it, dabbing their eyes with their handkerchiefs or the tails of their shawls. Mrs. McCann came and she got wine, too, though she had told the rent man about the shed on the slates and we had to pay a penny a week. I was in the wee room when she came, and I saw her looking at the lighted candles and the flowers on the table, and up at the gas that had no mantle. But she couldn't see it because my big sister had put white paper over it, and she had done the same with the four brass knobs on the bed. She began to sniff and sniff and my Mammie opened the window without saying anything. The blind began to snuffle in and out, the lighted candles to waggle, and the flowers to smell. We could hear the pigeons cooing and flapping in the shed, and I could see at the back of my eyes, their necks fattening and their feathers bristling like a dog going to fight. It's well Daddy didn't hear them or he might have wrung their necks.

At night the kitchen was crammed with men and women, and many had to sit in the cold scullery. Mrs. Ryan, next door, lent us her chairs for the people to sit on. There was lemonade and biscuits and tea and porter. Some of the men, who drank black porter, gave me pennies, and they smoked and talked all night. The kitchen was full of smoke and it made your eyes sting. One man told my Daddy he should be a proud man, because Johnny had died for the Republic. My Daddy blinked his eyes when he heard this, and he got up and went into the yard for a long time.

The next day was the funeral. Black shiny horses with their mouths all suds, and silver buckles on their straps, came trotting into the street. All the wee lads were looking at themselves in the glossy backs of the cabs where you could see yourself all fat and funny like a dwarf. I didn't play, because Johnny was dead and I had on a new, dark suit. Jack Byrne was out playing and he told me that we had only two cabs and that there were three cabs at his Daddy's funeral. There were crowds of peelers in the street, some of them talking to tall, red-faced men with overcoats and walking sticks.

Three men along with my Daddy carried the yellow coffin down the stairs. There was a green, white, and gold flag over it. But a thin policeman, with a black walking stick and black leggings, pulled the flag off the coffin when it went into the street. Then a girl snatched the flag out of the peeler's hands and he turned all pale. At the end of our street there were more peelers and every one wore a harp with a crown on his cap. Brother Gabriel used to fairly wallop us in school if we drew harps with crowns on them. One day we told him the peelers wore them on their caps. "Huh!" he said, "The police! the police! They don't love their country. They serve England. England, my boys! The England that chased our people to live in the damp bogs! The England that starved our ancestors till they had to eat grass and nettles by the roadside. And our poor priests had to say Mass out on the cold mountains! No, my dear boys, never draw a harp with a crown on it!" And then he got us to write in our books:

"Next to God I love thee
Dear Ireland, my native land!"

"It's a glorious thing," he said, "to die for Ireland, to die for Ireland!" His voice got very shaky when he said this and he turned his back and looked into the press. But Brother Gabriel is not in the school now; if he was he'd be good to me, because our Johnny died for Ireland.

The road to the cemetery was lined with people. Little boys that were at my school lifted a fringe of hair when the coffin passed. The trams were stopped in a big, long line –

it was nice to see so many at one look. Outside the gates of the graveyard there was an armoured car with no one peeping his head out. Inside it was very still and warm with the sun shining. With my Daddy I walked behind the carried coffin and it smelt like the new seats in the chapel. The crowds of people were quiet. You could hear the cinders on the path squanching as we walked over them, and now and again the horses snorting.

I began to cry when I saw the deep hole in the ground and the big castles of red clay at the side of it. A priest, with a purple sash round his neck, shovelled a taste of clay on the coffin and it made a hard rattle that made me cry sore. Daddy had his head bowed and there were tears in his eyes, but they didn't run down his cheeks like mine did. The priest began to pray, and I knew I'd never see Johnny again, never, never, until I'd die and go to Heaven if I kept good and didn't say bad words and obeyed my Mammie and my Daddy. But I wouldn't like Daddy to tell me to give away the pigeons. When the prayers were over a tall man with no hat and a wee moustache stood beside the grave and began to talk. He talked about our Johnny being a soldier of the Republic, and, now and then, he pointed with his finger at the grave. As soon as he stopped talking we said the Rosary, and all the people went away. I got a ride back in a black cab with my Daddy and Uncle Pat and Uncle Joe. We stopped at "The Bee Hive" and they bought lemonade for me and porter for the cab driver. And then we went home.

I still have the pigeons and big Tom Duffy helps me to clean the shed and let them out to fly. Near night I give them plenty of corn so that they'll sleep long and not waken Daddy in the morning. When I see them fattening their necks and cooing I clod them off the slates.

Yesterday I was lying on the waste ground watching the pigeons and Daddy came walking towards me smoking his pipe with the tin lid. I tried to show him the pigeons flying through the clouds. He only looked at them for a minute

and turned away without speaking, and now I'm hoping
he won't wring their necks.

Aunt Suzanne

THE McKINLEYS all went down to the station to meet their Aunt Suzanne, who was coming to take care of them now that their mother was dead. Mary, the eldest, was fifteen; Annie was eleven; and wee Arthur was nine. They boarded a tram at the foot of the street, and after much pleading and hauling, Arthur got them to go up on top. He loved the top of the tram, to kneel on the ribbed seat, and to feel the wind dunting his face or combing his hair.

To-day he leaned over the iron railings looking down at the top of the driver's cap: the cap was shiny and greasy, and a large lump knuckled up in the centre. Arthur tried to light a spit on it when Mary wasn't looking, but at last she spied him, slapped his hands, promising that never again would she come on top with him. The kneeling on the seat had imprinted red furrows on his knees, and he fingered them till a sandwich-man caught his eye. He stood up, staring at the walking triangle of boards, watching the legs of the man and wondering how he could see out. When he asked Mary how the man could see, Annie chimed in: "You're a stupid fella! Did you not see the peep-hole in the board?" Arthur made up his mind there and then that he would be a sandwich-man travelling round and round the streets, just like a motor-car.

At the station they had to wait, Mary telling and retelling Arthur not to be forgetting his manners, occasionally taking his hands out of his pockets, and pulling down his jersey. Overhead arched the glass roof, pigeons cooing along the girders and sparrows chirping in and out. Three taxi drivers sat on the running-board of a motor reading a newspaper, and near them a cab horse fed wheezily out of a nosebag. There was plenty of time, and Mary put a penny in a chocolate machine, letting Arthur pull out the drawer. The chocolate was neatly wrapped in silver paper, but when she went to divide it, it was so thin that it crumbled in her hands.

As Arthur ate his chocolate he was fascinated by a huge advertisement — a smiling girl poised on a white-rigged bottle that splashed through the sea. He could read some of the words, and Annie helped him to read others, but when he asked unanswerable questions about the bottle, Annie told him to look out for the train and play at who-would-see-it-first coming in along the shiny lines.

A bell began to ring somewhere, and the taxi drivers got up, dusting their clothes. Mary moved along the platform, the steel bumpers and the noisy trucks of the porters filling Arthur's mind with terrifying wonder. Presently there came a thundering rumble and the train came panting in, smoke hitting the glass roof with all its might.

Mary fidgeted: "Now you two, hold on to me tight. Don't get lost! Look out for Aunt Suzanne! She's small; she'll be in black! She has a . . . She has a . . . She has a . . . Oh, I see her! There she is!" People hurried past, brushing roughly against wee Arthur till he was ready to cry from fright, but Mary's gleeful shouts sent a breathless weak excitement over him. And then, as if she had jumped out of the ground, he was looking up at Aunt Suzanne.

She was a small woman, not as tall as Mary, with a black plush coat, a yellow crinkly face, and a black hat skewered with enormous hat-pins. But as he looked down below her coat, he saw something funny: he saw one boot, and where the other should have been was a ring of iron. Mary nipped him: "Aunt Suzanne's speaking to you."

"And who's this?"

"That's Arthur."

"A lovely little boy. God bless him," she said, touching his cheek with a cold hand.

"And what book are you in?" she added.

"Third," Mary replied for him.

"Third! Well, now, isn't that a great little man! ... And this is Annie. Well, well, she was only a wee baby when I saw her last – a lovely, wee baby. Tut, tut, tut, how the time flies!"

Annie relieved her of a band-box; Mary took her black, glossy bag, and linking her by the arm they began to move off along the platform. Occasionally Aunt Suzanne would stop and say: "Well, well, it's just like old times again!" But the clink of the iron foot on the pavement made Arthur twist and turn so that he could see how it moved. When Mary saw him gaping she scowled at him, and for the moment he would look in front, fixing his gaze on a horse or a tram, but always there came the clink-clink of iron on stone, and always he would turn his head and stare at the foot, then the iron, the boot again, and then the . . .

"Walk on a minute, Auntie. Arthur's boot's loosed," and Mary pushed Arthur to the side and began to untie his laces and bow them tightly again, until Aunt Suzanne and Annie were out of hearing. "Now!" she said, pointing a threatening finger at him. "If I-get-you-looking at Auntie's leg, there's no telling what I'll give you. Do you hear me? Come along and be a good boy. You'll never get out with us again! Never!" She tightened up his tie and pulled him along by the hand.

Into a tram they got, Annie and Arthur sitting opposite Mary and Aunt Suzanne.

"No, no, child, dear, I'll get them," said Aunt Suzanne when the conductor came along. Mary handed the tickets to Arthur, but he only turned them over in his hand, and then his eyes swivelled to the iron foot that didn't reach the floor. And then he looked up at his Auntie's face and stared at it fixedly. Below her hat were two wings of grey hair, and from the corners of her buttony nose were two deep lines, making a letter A with her mouth. There were a few white hairs on her chin, and her eyes were brown and sunken. Suddenly the eyes narrowed, and Arthur returned his Auntie's smile. He decided that he was going to like her, but he hoped he hadn't to sleep with her because of her iron leg.

Passing up the street he felt that all the wee lads would be gazing at his Auntie with her clop-clink, clink-clop. If she'd only cover it with a stocking and put pasteboard inside it, nobody'd hear it or know what it was. Suddenly he left them and ran over to three of his companions who were standing with their hands behind their backs looking at a baker's horse. To show off before his Auntie he ran under the horse's legs and out by the other side.

"Holy misfortunes, what a child!" said Auntie Sue, frightened to a standstill.

"Arthur!" yelled Mary.

Arthur came running back and Mary gave him a stinging smack on the jaw. "You've been working for that this day!"

All the way to the house and into the house, he sobbed and sniffed: "Wait'll me Da comes home till ye see what ye'll get!"

"That's just it," said Mary. "Me father has him spoilt!"

"Sh-sh-sh, big little mans don't cry. Tut-tut," pleaded Auntie Sue. "Give me my bag till you see what I have for you — and none for the rest," she added, casting a wink at Mary and Annie. When Arthur heard the happy rustle of paper, his sobs became less frequent, and when he received a piece of sugarstick coloured like a barber's pole he sat on the fender sucking contentedly, and even suffered Mary to wipe his face with a damp cloth.

Aunt Suzanne rested on the sofa looking with admiration at the clean tiles of the floor, the white-scrubbed table, and at the mantelpiece where two delph dogs guarded a row of shining brassware: horseshoes, two candlesticks, a rigged ship, and a three-legged pot containing a bunch of matches. "Yiv the place shining," she said proudly. "Did you do it all by yourself, Mary? . . . You and Annie. Och, och, but it's nice to see two sisters agreeable."

Mary took the band-box and the glossy bag and put them in a room off the kitchen, and while she poked the fire to hurry on the kettle, Annie spread a clean newspaper on the table and laid down the cups and saucers; Aunt Suzanne stretched herself out on the sofa, and wee Arthur was sent out to play till the big people had finished their tea.

From the table they could see, through the curtain on the window, the red-bricked houses on the opposite side of the street; and many a question Mary had to answer about the neighbours – the gossipy ones, the friendly ones, and the borrowing ones.

Just when they had finished their tea, Arthur came crying into the yard and battered impatiently at the scullery door.

"What's up now?" said Mary, letting him in. He didn't answer, but ran to Auntie Sue. She took him in her arms and nursed him, but he scratched his cheek on a brooch in her breast and cried all the more.

"What's wrong, my pigeon? What's wrong, my darling? Tell your Auntie Sue."

"The wee lads called you iron-hoof and cork leg," he whimpered.

"There's a cheeky lot of gets about this place," said Mary. "Wait till I get my hands on some of them."

"And what did you say to them?" Auntie asked, shaking him to and fro.

"I said you hadn't a cork leg," he replied, bursting into more tears.

"There, there!" consoled Auntie.

"Maybe God'll give some of them a bad leg before very long," put in Annie.

"God forbid, child dear; sure, they're only childer and mean no harm."

They were relieved when Arthur stopped whimpering, for they never knew at what time their father would step in on them and find wee Arthur in tears. It was late that night, however, when he came home from work in the flour mill, and they had all gone to bed except Auntie Sue.

Whilst he shaved in a looking-glass hung to a nail in the

mantelpiece, his face under the gaslight, he kept up a chat with her. Later, he talked about old times and about Armagh, where Susie came from; then he fell silent, looking at the flames nodding and leaping in the fire and the flakes of soot shivering in the wide chimney. She, too, fell silent with her hands joined on her lap, looking at the wrinkles of flour in his boots, and thinking of his poor wife, her own sister. And then, without preface, he turned to her: "Tell me, Susie, are you off the bottle?"

"Off the bottle!" she started. "Not a drop of strong drink has wet my lips this many a long year. I forget the taste of it — that's the God's truth, Daniel."

"I'm glad to hear that. It's the divil's own poison. Poor Katy, God be good to her, would be here now only for it."

"Aye, aye," she sighed, taking a handkerchief and dabbing her eyes.

He looked at her awkwardly for a minute and said: "You'll be dead tired after your journey. . . Be good to the childer, Susie, and keep a tight eye on wee Arthur. . . Good night, now!"

After the first week or two Arthur and Auntie became great friends. He no longer stared at her iron-leg, and no longer paid heed to its stamping up the stairs or its clinking across the tiles. Auntie Sue was good to him and paid him halfpennies for gathering cinders. With a battered bucket, a piece of cardboard covering the hole in the bottom, he would go out to the waste ground at the back of the small houses. There the neighbours flung out their ashes, cabbage stalks, and potato-skins. He would squat for hours on his hunkers, rummaging with a stick for the blue cinders, until the bucket would be nearly filled. Then up with him carrying the bucket in front with his two arms under the handle. Aunt Suzanne would open the yard door at his knock. "That's the man! Them'll make a grand fire. There's nothing like cinders," and out would come the black purse, and a penny or a halfpenny would be squeezed into an eager hand.

Then, one warm day, when Annie and Mary were down the town, Arthur wanted to earn a penny for the pictures, and, as usual, he took out the bucket to gather cinders. The cinders were hot under the sun, and near him bare-footed boys sat with pieces of mirror glass, reflecting the sunlight into the cool corners of the houses. Men, waistcoats unbuttoned, sat with newspapers over their heads, and on the yard walls thrushes in their cages sang madly in the sun. Dogs lounged about with hanging tongues and heaving sides. But Arthur worked on.

The sun scorched down on him and a creak came in his neck, but only a few cinders lay in the bottom of the bucket. He sighed, wiped the sweat from his face with the sleeve of his jersey, and hoked on.

He felt thirsty and came into the yard, where the tiles burned under his bare feet. All the doors were open, but the air was still. Two fly-papers covered with flies hung from the clothesline in the kitchen. He padded around for Aunt Suzanne and pushed open her room door; and there she was sitting on the bed with a black bottle to her mouth.

"Aw, give's a slug."

"Merciful God, where did you come from? You put the heart out of me!" She twisted the cork into the bottle and slapped it tight with the heel of her hand. "Pwt-th-t!" she said in disgust, making a wry face. "Rotten medicine! Worse than castor, but poor Auntie has to take it."

She went to the sink in the scullery, the splashing tap spilling coolness into the air. Arthur held the wet cup in his hands and drank noisily. He drank it all and finished with a sigh. She gave him a halfpenny. "Don't tell your Da that poor Auntie has to take medicine, he'd be vexed to hear it. Now go and gather your cinders."

Later he returned with an almost empty bucket and found Aunt Suzanne snoring on the sofa. He started to sing loudly so as to waken her, and she got up and vigorously poked the fire which the sun had almost put out.

"Give's a penny for the pictures?"

33

"If I had a penny I'd frame it, and you with no cinders."

"Go'n," he whimpered, "or I'll tell me Da about your medicine."

"Get out of my sight! Do you think I'm made of money!" she said crossly, watching the dust from the fire settling on the mantlepiece.

"Go'n!"

She lifted the poker in anger, and Arthur raced into the yard. He barricaded himself in an old hen-shed and started to sing:

> "Boiled beef and carrots,
> Boiled beef and carrots,
> And porter for Suzanne."

He was innocent of the cruel implication, but it riled Auntie Sue, and she hammered at the door with the poker and flung jugfuls of water in at him through the slits in the boards. "The divil has the hold of you, me boyo! Wait'll your Da hears this and you'll catch it!"

He yelled louder; and, thinking of the neighbours, she went in and left him. He heard the bar shoot with finality in the scullery door and her last words: "You'll not get in the night! Go on, now, about your business."

All the evening he was in the dumps and sat far out on the waste ground at the back of the house. Annie and Mary came out with sweets in their hands and coaxed him in, assuring him that Auntie Sue was not going to touch him. And sure enough she had a Paris bun for his tea and jam on his bread. Then she stroked his head, kissed him, and packed him off to bed early.

That night the father returned to the nightly ritual of family prayers, which had been upset by the arrival of Suzanne in their midst. All knelt except Auntie Sue, who sat on a low chair with her rosary beads twined round one hand, the other resting on her lap. She closed her eyes as she answered the responses, and when she opened them there was always something to distract her: a new seat needed in Daniel's trousers, a stitch needed in Annie's dress. Then she fell to dreaming as she gazed at Mary's two plaits, tied at the ends with green ribbon – hair like her poor mother, God rest her. And then Annie's one plait with a broken ivory clasp – that's what she'd buy them at Christmas, two nice clasps, and maybe brooches with their names on them. A creak from Daniel's chair brought her mind back with a start, and she asked God to forgive her for such distraction as she turned to her beads again. But when he said solemnly: "All now repeat the Heroic Offering after me," she felt weak, and her heart pounded so loudly she thought they would all hear it.

For Thy greater glory and consolation, O Sacred Heart of Jesus . . . God forgive me for telling lies to that saintly man . . . *For Thy sake to give good example* . . . and wee Arthur saw me swilling it . . . *To practise self-denial* . . .and me with a bottle under a board in the room . . . *To make reparation to Thee for the sins of intemperance and the conversion of excessive drinkers* . . . God forgive me, God forgive me for being a hypocrite! I can't repeat the next of it . . . *I promise to abstain from all intoxicating drinks for life.*

She listened to the end of it with tightened lips, afraid to profane the sacred words, and thankful for the way the children almost shouted it. And later she was glad to get into the comforting darkness of her room, where she lay twisting and turning for a long time before sleep came to her.

After that she was cautious and always had a secret drink behind a locked door, and kept bottles under a loose floorboard. It was Arthur she feared: he was always appearing at surprising moments stalking her, playing at Indians, pretending to himself that she was a squaw on horseback, her iron-ring reminding him of a stirrup. But Annie and Mary were the sensible children! They looked forward to Arthur's bedtime, for with their father at some Sodality meeting they had their Auntie to themselves. They would ply her with questions about her schooldays, and about Armagh and the games she played when she was young. And Auntie sitting on the sofa between them, Annie hugging one arm and Mary the other, would turn to one and then the other, looking down at their anxious eyes as she told them scraps about her life. Before Daniel would come in she would sing for them verse after verse of *Lady Mouse*.

"Lady Mouse, are you within?
Hm, hm-m-m-m-m-m-m-m-m-m.
Lady Mouse, are you within?
Yes, kind sir, as she sat and spun,
Hm, hm-m-m-m-m-m-m-m-m-m."

They had it by heart now, and all three hummed the hm-ms that ended each verse. Sometimes the hm-ms would be so prolonged by Annie or Mary till one or other would burst out laughing, and Auntie would hold her sides: "I'll be kilt laughing, I'll be kilt."

She sang for them songs of the countryside, courting songs and songs of Ireland's heroes and Ireland's traitors, and sometimes she gave them riddles and phrases to say quickly: "Three grey geese in a green full of grazing, grey were the geese and green was the grazing." She taught them how to knit and how to crochet, and of a Sunday she would read to them out of her prayer book, and though the print was as big as that in a child's primer, she always followed the words with her finger.

In the long November nights, when the pains would come into her legs she would go off to bed early, and then Annie and Mary would come slipping into the room with a mug of hot tea for her and two big slices of griddle bread. They would light the candle and sit on the edge of the bed. While Auntie would be sipping the tea and dipping the bread in it, her eyes would travel round the holy pictures that she had tacked to the wall. "I have a quare squad of them around me, and there's none of them like that fella there," she would say, pointing to a picture of St. Patrick banishing the snakes. "A decent fella, a real gentleman, many's a good turn he done me."

Up through the long winter nights she drank little, and now and again at the family prayers she was on the verge of promising to abstain for life, but something told her she'd never keep it. Christmas came and she taught the children how to make a plum pudding; and she bought them brooches like her own with the words *Annie* and *Mary* in silver-white stones, and for Arthur a tram-conductor's cap and a ticket-puncher.

Then one cold winter's day when the snow had fallen and Annie and Mary had gone for messages, Auntie Sue was in the house alone. The coalman hadn't come, and there was only a fistful of cinders for the fire. She felt cold. She closed all the doors, but still there seemed to slice through every crevice in the house a wicked, icy draught. Her teeth chattered and she lifted the wrinkled quilt off her bed and put it round her shoulders, looking miserably through the kitchen window at the white street and the light fading from the sky. Her thin blood craved for a drop of warmth – and not as much as a thimbleful of "medicine" in the house to wet her lips or make a drop of punch. Without waiting to talk it over in her mind, she left four shillings on the kitchen table for the coalman, put on her black plush coat and hat, took an umbrella, and out with her.

The hard snow lay deep in the street, yellowed by cart-ruts and blackened by coal-dust. In the sky a few stars were coming out. She put up her umbrella, though the snow wasn't falling. She passed neighbours cleaning their doorways with shovels, and now and again heard the wet, sad sloosh of a brush. A few snowballs thudded on top of her umbrella and she hurried on, her iron-ring cutting circles in the snow. Then Arthur came running up with a snowball in his hand and she blew his nose for him and gave him a penny to buy sweets for himself. She turned the corner on to the main road, saw rags of snow clinging to the wheels of a cart, and the rich glow on a coalman's face as he lit his swinging lamp. The snow slushed in her boot and she shivered.

She went into The Bee Hive and sat in a snug near the stove. There was dry sawdust on the floor, a smell of new varnish, and a great glow of heat. She'd have a nice drop of punch. She held out her hands to the heat and smiled sweetishly as she heard the tight scringe of a cork coming out of a bottle.

That night the children were long in bed and Auntie Sue had not returned. Daniel was seated on the sofa in the firelight, a pair of his trousers drying on the back of a chair, the children's wet boots in a row on the fender. A quilt of snow fell from the roof into the yard. A knock came to the front door. Daniel lit the gas, and when he opened the door there was Aunt Suzanne hanging between the arms of two men. They linked her into the kitchen and on to the sofa, her skirt and coat dripping wet, her hat feathered with snow. She sang to herself pieces of *Lady Mouse* and began to hum. "Three gay grease," she said. "No, that's not it. Poor Auntie Sue can't say, 'Thee geese geen.'. . ."

Daniel stood in the middle of the floor staring with rising anger at the miserable woman on the sofa. She looked up at him with half-shut eyes and mumbled: "As dacent a man as ever walked in shoe-leather."

He went into her room and bundled all the things he could find into her band-box. He opened the door and looked up and down the street. A gramophone was playing and a child crying. The snow was falling and drifting quietly on to the window sills and the shut doors. Over the white, silent roofs the cold sky was sprayed with stars. A man with bowed head passed and said: "That's a hardy night," and Daniel heard him knock the snow off his boots and close his door. He came inside. Auntie Sue had leaned back on the sofa, her hands listless, her eyes shut. He took his trousers from the back of the chair, threw an overcoat over the huddled figure, and put out the gas.

In the morning Auntie Sue was leaving, and they all went down on the tram to see her off; Arthur knelt on the seat looking out, and no one chastised him when he pursed his lips against the window. They spoke little. They could find no words to say to each other.

At the station, before getting into the carriage, Aunt Suzanne gave him a penny, and her eyes were wet as she held Annie's and Mary's hands and stroked them lovingly. They couldn't look up at her, but stood awkwardly swaying to and fro. The train slid out and they lifted their arms and waved them wearily, tears filling their eyes. Arthur stood watching the back of the receding train. Then he plucked at Mary's coat. "Come, on quick," he said, but they didn't seem to hear him, and he ran on in front to the chocolate machine with the penny Auntie Sue had given him.

Stone

A SMALL flame trembled above the turf on the hearth, shrivelled and disappeared, leaving a cord of smoke ravelling itself in the wide chimney. Old Jamesy Heaney sitting with his hands on his knees, his shoulders drooped forward, waited for the fire to light. At his feet lay his black and white collie, her forepaws in the ashes, a wet nose on the flags. The closed door was slitted with light, and through the nests of cobwebs on the deep window came a blue wintry brightness. It was cold.

The old man prodded the fire with a twig and presently it fluttered into life. He'd made a sup of tea before going to the village and while the tin boiled he'd get ready his eggs. He stood up and hobbled to the dresser. The dog got up too, leaving a damp mark on the stone where her nose had lain. She yawned and sat back on her haunches watching the slow fumbling movements of her master.

He was a small grasshopper of a man, withered and worn, and cold to look at. His clothes were patched and tattered, and round the loose soles of his knobbly boots he had lapped coils of wire which now and again rasped on the stone floor. As he lifted a can from a nail in the wall the dog jumped around him and ran towards the door. Old Jamesy paid no heed to her, and went on wrapping hen-eggs carefully in paper and placing them in the can. He had only seven eggs this evening: the frost must have put the hens off their laying. He'd have another look outside; maybe there'd be one or two more.

An icy wind blew into the cottage as the collie crushed out in front of him, sending panic into the fluttering hens.

Jamesy yelled at her in a voice that broke sharp on the lean hollows. He crossed to the hen-shed; it was a rickety place patched with the coloured lids of tin-boxes. Near it was an ash tree trodden bare round the trunk where the hens and goat lay of a hot summer day under the quivering shade from its little leaves. Now it was deserted, a red flannel rag caught on the black twigs, making a leafy sound as the wind strummed the branches. Jamesy shrugged his shoulders as he looked at the frost on the rag and at the misty vapour that smothered the nearby sea; the devil take it for frost, good hot mate given to the hens — and no eggs. When he came out from the shed they began clustering at his feet and he whished them away from him.

"It's the last yellow male ye'll get for awhile, me ladies. Content yerselves on the nest or go and scrape and fend for yerselves. Be off now!"

The black tin was spluttering and hissing on the fire when he came inside. He gripped the handle with his coat and snuggled the tin on top of a hot, crushed turf.

Jamesy lived alone and made his own meals. He was the last of the Heaneys left on the island. Sitting now with the mug between bony hands, his grey beard on his chest and his long hair fringing his coat collar, he looked like an ancient prophet. The dog nuzzled under his arm and awakened him from a dream, whereupon he threw the dregs of tea at the back of the fire and lifted his can and stick.

He turned the key in the door, tried the latch a few times, and clattered across to the road. From the first crest on the road he would stop and look back at his cottage. From there he would see the smoke tearing itself from the stump of a chimney; the loose black thatch with the eaves as ragged as an old brush; and the tree near the gable where he himself sat in the cool of a summer's evening enjoying the hush around him and the sleepy stir of the sea. And from these his gaze would slowly turn to the potato patch, black and bare now with withered stalks strewn about.

It filled him with pride to look down at the closed cottage impersonally, as if the house belonged to someone else and he envying the owner as he passed on the road. It was a wild, draughty place surely, but it was far from the villagers with their taunts and jibes; and he loved it, loved every stone of it. And then it was his own; there was sweet comfort in that thought.

Gripping his stick he turned his back reluctantly. His old goat, shrunken with cold, me-eh-eh-ed as she saw him disappear over the hill. Jamesy walked firmly on his heels, knees slightly bent, his stick jabbing the road. The air was keen and blue, long streamers of cloud frozen to the sky, the scattered bushes naked and empty of birds. A frost-fringed stream trickled darkly at the side of the road, and now and then the ice that patched the hoofmarks splintered under Jamesy's stick. He wore no overcoat and as he walked along his shoulder blades knuckled under his jacket. He kept an even pace. Once the dog thudded after a rabbit, and returning licked Jamesy's hand, and trotted proudly in front.

At the top of the graveyard hill he stopped for the second time, his breath gusty and misty in the air. Satisfied that there was no one about he shuffled over to the rusty iron gate of the graveyard and lifted the loop of wire that held it. The dog waited on the road beside the can.

Jamesy didn't go in to pray. He stood a short distance from the gate looking thoughtfully at the wind-streaked grasses, and at the lumpy graves with their small wooden crosses and slabs of rock. There was only one headstone; a large Celtic cross of blue granite, its panelled arms and shaft decorated with an interlacing design. On its thick base in large block letters was the name of one man, McBride; a bachelor like Jamesy himself. With head to the side Jamesy looked at the gravelled grave with its neat plinth and iron-railings, and then up at the huge stone dusted with frost. Everyone in the island referred to it as the McBride monument, and they talked about it from time to time. A sadness chilled Jamesy. It was a lovely grave; a sweet grave, near the road and looking down on the fistful of houses that was the village. But as he walked over to his own naked patch of ground warmer feelings began to stir within him.

Last week he had bought the site from the priest, a piece of ground eight feet by twelve, and he smiled to himself as he recalled the priest's words: "It'd take less than that to hold your bones, Jamesy. You'd think you had a big family;" and his own reply: "There's nothing' like havin' a roomy place when a body's dead." Poor Father Brady, little did he know what he wanted it for; little did he know!

As he measured the plot with his stick grunts of satisfaction came from him, and occasionally he would glance furtively over the low graveyard wall. He stood back, screwing up his watery eyes to the sky where his imagination etched the stone that would mark his own grave. It'd be two feet higher than the McBride stone; he'd see to that.

Out on the road again his mind began to play with the familiar thoughts, and an exultant feeling flamed within him. It would be his stone that the people'd talk about when he'd be gone; and visitors to the island would look at it and read the name, JAMES HEANEY; a great man they'd whisper amongst themselves! He rolled the thought over in his mind, holding on to it. His body quivered as the solid reality of the stone possessed him. And then he stopped dead in the middle of the road, and the dog, ears cocked looked up at him sideways. Crashing into his mind there came something more than the talk of the people about his headstone; his name was going to live; it would live forever in solid stone.

"Stone is the only lasting thing in life," he breathed aloud; it bates all he never thought of that before. He held his breath, as if to calm his mind, to allow it to gather the sweet breeze of thought and unfold its joys to him. Stone is lasting: all life ends in death, but stone lives on. It was more lasting than all their children. They needn't chaff him any more about his name dying with neither chick nor child to leave behind him! They needn't mock him any longer! There they were as usual the three of them – Joseph McDonnell, John Joe McQuilkin, and Johnny John Beg. He'd have it out with them this evening.

The three old men were smoking in the lee of a gable, watching the sea break on the shore, and the children playing. They were silent, their jigging feet knocking chips of limewash from the wall. But when Jamesy approached, the children raced off into their houses, and the old men began to talk excitedly amongst themselves. In his pride Jamesy walked past them into the shop.

Quietly he placed his can on the counter and sat down on an empty onion-box. There was a great sense of ease and comfort in the box-cluttered shop, with its fat meal bags, the clock ticking, and a warm smell of baking bread coming from the kitchen. He sat still, drawing a sweet warmth from it, afraid to budge lest the shopkeeper would come at once to serve him; it was like being under a clucking hen, he thought. Presently a chair moved and the clip-clop of feet approached; Jamesy tapped the counter with feigned impatience.

The shrivelled shopkeeper entered, her hands white with flour.

"That's a sharp evenin', Jamesy," she greeted.

"Tis that; we're goin' to have a hard winter, I'm thinkin'."

She looked over the counter at his face; his eyes were blurred, and the left one had a red, drooped lid, with water dribbling from it making a streak in his white beard.

"You're eye's brave and angry lookin' the day," she sympathised. "Why don't you try the boracic; a tuppenny packet would make it as clean as a whistle."

"Ach, I'll not bother now, sure it's no trouble to me at all; and in the good weather me eye's as dry as withered seaweed. Anyway the sight'll be soon leavin' me."

"Them that talk about dyin' are the longest to live. . . . But here give me your eggs and less of this ould blether."

She began unwrapping the few eggs; he always changed

44

them for tea, sugar, or bread, and what with his pension coming to him every week, digging his own spuds, and fishing off the rocks, he was able to make a good living.

He delayed in the shop as long as he could, and only when the early dusk began to crush the light from the window did he make to go.

"The right ould miser," the shopkeeper said to herself as he stooped out.

He blinked his eyes in the greyish light and joined the old men at the gable; they always spent their evenings arguing about ships that came ashore or about the placenames of their island. John Joe was the patriarch of the company and no one doubted his word. They all noticed something jaunty about Jamesy's step, the shrug of his shoulders, and the cock of his head. John Joe fidgeted and coughed loudly; what had Jamesy in his mind! What was he going to ask them?

"Comin' along the road I had the queerest thought," he began slowly. They all held their pipes, waiting. "I was thinkin' there's nothin' lastin' in this life except wan thing. D' any of yez know what that is?"

The three men looked perplexed at Jamesy, their slow-moving old brains seeking for an answer. John Joe spat out and tucked the tails of his muffler under his oxters. Jamesy grunted.

"D'ye know what it is? . . . I'll tell ye . . . it's stone that is lasting . . . Stone! Stone!" and he hammered out the words with his stick.

"How so?"

Like someone performing an ancient rite he slowly raised his stick; it trembled for a moment on the graveyard, and then slowly turned to Croc-na-Screilean, a small hill gathering a skirt of darkness from the falling night.

"D'ye see Croc-na-Screilean," he said, his voice quavering. "Is there any change in it since we were childer? It hasn't changed, man, no more than the colour of the sea . . . why? . . . Because it's stone. Stone, the only lasting thing on this earth!"

They all stood silent; McDonnell and Johnny John Beg turned puzzled eyes to John Joe. John Joe took the pipe from his lips.

"'Tisn't the hill that is lasting, but the memories that belong to it," he said, pointing the shank of his pipe at Jamesy.

"That's the truth you're sayin'," put in McDonnell.

"It's the hill that's lasting, because it's stone," Jamesy stamped back.

John Joe's mind was working quickly.

"A hill is only a hill if it has no memories; it has no life!" And then in excitement he raised his voice: "I declare to God when I look at Croc-na-Screilean tisn't a hill I see at all, but our people – the McDonnells, the Mc-Curdys, the McQuilkins, and the rest – fightin' the invaders in the hollow, and our women and children screamin' and shoutin' at them from the hill. 'Tis that what the hill means to me."

"Aren't all them people dead and gone and the hill's the same", Jamesy answered.

"They're not dead!" they shouted at him in chorus.

"Aren't their children's children here still? Aren't we the same stock?" added Johnny John Beg.

"And where'd we all be if our people hadn't married and made life. Where'd the island be? It'd be a rocky desert, a place for rabbits and wild birds and no one left to talk about Croc-na-Screilean and the stories that belong to it; it'd be only a hill – a dead hill!"

"And when you're dead yourself, Jamesy, you're dead forever with no child to bear your name."

They all added taunts about his childless life. He laughed at them.

"Where will yez all be in a number of years? Yez'll all be dead and rotten and forgotten and Croc-na-Screilean will be there without a change." His eyes travelled to the graveyard: "Stone is lasting! The name of Heaney will last!" With this he left them, his dog jumping up at him, glad to be on the road again.

"He's daft," said John Joe, looking after him. "Crazy! That's what living alone has done for him. And his slutthery old sod of a house that even a swallow would turn up its nose at."

Jamesy laughed as he trudged away from them, his mind aflame with the vision of the headstone.

"Dead!" he said aloud to himself. "Dead! Little do they know!"

The blue of the sky was darkening and a few stars were coming out. Behind him the oil-lamps in the village were turning the windows to gold and doors were being shut against the chill air. The road was blackening. The frost had thawed on the scraggy bushes and drops of water had formed on the bleak thorns. His step rang sharp on the road. The goat bleated and came to meet him, rubbing her teeth against his side.

Once back in the house he locked the door, hooked the blind to the window, and took a box from the roof-tree. By the light of a candle he looked at his money, his pension money, that he had saved for years. Next week he'd take it all to the mainland and arrange about the headstone.

He brewed more tea for himself, cut big slices off the loaf, and bruised a fresh slice for the collie. He was happy. He stretched out a hand and patted the dog. Smoke blew down the chimney and smarted his eyes.

In bed he lay awake looking through the window at the star-sprinkled sky with its rags of cloud skimming past the moon. The cross-sash of the window cast its blurred shadow on the bed. The old man's mind rehearsed the proposed visit to the stonecutter's, and when the first blast of an approaching storm ploofed on the roof like a bedtick he curled himself in the blankets. He dozed for awhile but the rising wind and his excited mind kept sleep away from him.

His rusty bait-can scringed against the wall outside and then he heard it being lifted from its nail and sent clattering across the street. The wind continued to rise; it raked and roared in the tree at the gable and swished across the thatch like a mighty wave. The roar of it made him cower in his bed and the loud grumbles of it in the chimney set the dog barking. Jamesy shouted to her to lie down, but she continued to bark as the wind dunted against the walls and made them shake. Fear seized Jamesy; he felt as if the scraw of a roof would be lifted from off his head. He got out of bed and stood on a chair to get his box. The wind whistled sharply in the slits of the door and groped under the threshold. Wisps of cold air whirled around him. He put the box under the bed and let the dog into the room.

The crackling of sticks made him turn to the window and by the light of the moon he saw his hens fluttering wildly from the streaming wreck of the shed. He clutched at his beads; if he should die before he had the arrangements made for his Stone! He trembled; but the leaping thoughts of his headstone, sparking and burning in his brain, took his mind from the prayers. He'd wait no longer; next boat-day he'd be off to the mainland.

The sea rose with the wind; the thundering waves pounded the rocks and the spray speckled the window. His thorn tree bent to the flood of the storm like an old woman with flying hair. The straw of his hen-shed was swirled high by the wind.

Another crash made Jamesy sit upright. His mouth hung open with fear. He found himself looking at the moon through the branches of a tree. His tree was down! Its bare twigs scraped the window. A cold sweat broke out on him; it was safer to stay inside; he covered his head with the clothes.

As the night advanced the storm broke into intermittent gusts and by dawn it had blown itself out, and Jamesy, exhausted lay in a deep sleep, the collie curled up beside him. It was the dog, licking his brow, that wakened him to the morning. It was clear and cold, filled with the noise of the sea. The land was scoured clean, but around the cottage the storm had played itself.

When he opened the door the scene saddened him. The wreckage of the shed was strewn up on the hill; the street

48

littered with straw and twigs, the thatch combed to one side like the grass on a flooded river-bank. He looked at the tree lying on the ground, its bony roots clawing the air. Life the tree had, and now it is dead: stone has no life, but it lives! He'd have something for John Joe this evening.

All day he chopped at the branches of the tree and hammered the remanants of the shed together. It was useless to build a shed of timber; stone's the thing, he said to himself. From a hill near the house he dug up the scraws that patched the rocks, the dead heather roots tearing dryly under the spade. He built them around the bottom of the shed and all the while the goat lay at the gable chewing unconcernedly, the hens bunched around her.

In the early evening he struck off for the village with his dog. He was contented with himself and the work he had done. His mind clung to the things he had ready for his three companions; the strong ash hurled to the ground; the wooden-shed; and the withered heather clinging for life to the barren rocks. From the crest on the road his house, bare of the outspreading arms of the tree, looked desolate. Looking at it Jamesy became sad and regretful; awakened memories of the tree's companionship arose within him and made him linger on the hill. But the shouts of playing children came to him faintly on the calm chill air and he grinned to himself cunningly and strode off towards the village.

Outside the graveyard on the hill he halted. Slyly he walked to the gate and entered. And then his eyes bulged and he stiffened with awe. He looked for the McBride stone; it was gone; a great vacancy held the sky. The monument lay in fragments on the top of the grave and crosses were tilted or blown down.

Slowly Jamesy backed away. His eyes stared at the great carnage of stone. He left the gate open and made off for home again. The dog stood sideways on the top of the hill, waiting for him to turn, but he went on and on, going quickly, afraid to look back, while behind him the children screamed in delight as they gathered the sticks washed up on the stormy shore.

The Priest's Housekeeper

IT WAS young Father Doyle's third change in seven years, and as he wearily watched his furniture being carried into his new quarters he wished with all his might that the bishop would allow him to remain here for the customary six years. He was tired of moving, and even though this new place was never praised by his colleagues still he would make the best of it. It was a lonely place surely, and it was damp into the bargain, and in the evenings mists stole up from the lough and camped in the fields until early morning. And his nearest neighbours, he was told, wouldn't give him any trouble for they were at rest in the graveyard and separated from his house by a few chestnut trees and a thick hawthorn hedge.

His parish priest lived five miles away in a less lonely part of the country, and as the pieces of furniture were carried in Father Doyle went to the phone to ring him up. The old priest wished him well and was about to hang up when Father Doyle asked him about the housekeeper he was to get for him.

"Has she not turned up yet?" the old priest said in surprise. "There was only one reply to my advertisement and I answered at once and told her when to report for duty. That's bad news. But she'll turn up, never fear. Do the best you can in the meantime, and if you ever feel peckish just give me a tinkle and I'll get Bridget to put an extra plate on the table. It'll be no trouble at all, at all. You must guard against malnutrition. One can't pray and work if one's not properly fed."

Father Doyle thanked him and put down the receiver.

He didn't like bothering people, not even a priest's housekeeper; he'd be able to manage for awhile without one. But the main thing at the moment was to keep warm, and he moved quickly from room to room directing the removers where to place the furniture. And when the last piece was carried in rain fell heavily and he tipped the men generously and apologised for not having a cup of tea ready for them. They thanked him, touched their caps, and climbed into their heavy van. Presently it set off along a road that gleamed like a river in the rain and soon it had disappeared over a hill, leaving nothing behind it except two parallel tracks made by the wheels. Father Doyle shrugged with the cold, turned into the house, and closed the door.

He had two electric heaters and he switched one on in his sitting-room and plugged the other in the kitchen which was as cold as a vault. All his perishable foodstuffs lay on the table: bread, meat, eggs, butter, and a cooked chicken. He had made a list before setting out on his journey and he was pleased he had forgotten nothing, not even a box of matches. He stored most of the things in the fridge and began to light the stove to drive out the cold that had settled in the house.

Wearing his heavy overcoat he made his way upstairs to his bedroom where the furniture removers had screwed up his bed and unrolled his mattress. The window looked out upon the chapel, a rectangular building of grey stone and blue slates, and the rope of an exposed bell hanging down to a ring on the outside wall. Each day he would make sure to ring the Angelus or get the housekeeper to ring it should he be absent. He had great devotion to that prayer since the day a Protestant clergyman praised it as the loveliest of all our Catholic prayers.

The kitchen was filled with smoke when he came downstairs and he opened the draught-door of the stove and heard in a few minutes the healthy roar of the fire. He opened a window and watched the smoke burl out to the cold air. He took a light snack and was making his way to the chapel to read his breviary when a bus stopped at his gate and out of it, stepping backwards, came a solitary passenger. She stood on the roadway, a suitcase in her hand, looked irresolutely about her, and then moved towards the priest's house. Father Doyle walked down to meet her.

"Good evening, Father," she said. "Am I in the right place?"

"You're in the right place, I think. I'm Father Doyle."

"But it was a Father O'Loan I wrote to."

Father Doyle smiled: "It's me that needs you."

She was thin, wore thick spectacles, and her grey hair stuck untidily beneath her hat. She sniffed continually, but whether this was an incipient cold or an ingrained habit he had yet to find out.

He lifted her suitcase and noted that the metal fastenings were unsprung and the case kept closed by two loops of stout string. He'd buy her a new one at Christmas should she turn out to be satisfactory.

"It's a chilly house, Father," she said in a thin, squeaky voice. "I hope I won't get my death."

"I hope you won't," and he checked himself from making a joke about the nearness of the graveyard. At this stage he must be reserved, a bit aloof, until he had found his bearings. He escorted her to her room. It hadn't been touched since her predecessor had vacated it a few days ago. It was narrow, but it was above the kitchen and it should be warm.

"This room's as cold as a railway station," she complained. He explained that no fire had been lighted in the house for the past three days and that he himself had just arrived a short while before her. He placed her case on the only chair in the room.

"I'll bring you an electric heater. I've one in the kitchen and it'll not be needed while the stove's in operation. There's plenty of stuff in the fridge so make yourself a good meal."

"You wouldn't need a fridge in this house, Father," she said, gazing out the window at the wet coal and turf stored in a doorless shed.

He turned from the room without a word. She was going to be a grumbler by all accounts, but as he was glad to get her he wasn't going to cross her if he could help it. More of his weakness, he supposed, more of his misunderstanding of the nature of true meekness.

He crossed to the chapel and finished his office under one light he had switched on near the sanctuary. Darkness had fallen over the country when he came out, stars pincushioned the sky, and lights from the scattered homes shone weakly across the fields. His own house was lighted up like a government office, and he presumed his housekeeper was getting into her stride. There was nothing like bodily activity to keep the circulation in trim this cold weather, he mused.

His car, splashed with mud, was in the yard and he pushed it into the garage out of the cold. A cat meowed at his heels. Parochial property, no doubt; and he went in by the back door to get her a saucerful of milk.

His housekeeper was seated at the stove, the oven door open, and her feet held close to it. She still wore the coat she had travelled in; and the remains of her meal littered the table, and a loaf of bread was cut unevenly as if she had chopped it with a hatchet.

"What's this now your name is?" he asked gently.

"Mary. Mary Carroll."

"Well, Mary, there's a cat out there could do with a little nourishment."

"I don't like cats about the place," she said, swiping a finger across each side of her nose and remaining seated.

"I suppose it could take up its quarters in the coal-shed."

"Proper place for it."

He put milk on a saucer and carried it carefully across the yard, the cat following him, its tail erect. He switched on his car lights, and placing the saucer in the driest corner he called the cat and she lowered her tail, put her head to the milk and lapped greedily.

Father Doyle returned to the house by the front door.

He crouched close to his electric-heater and filled his pipe. Later he'd have a little of the cold chicken for his supper.

He could hear Mary coughing, the stove being raked, and coal being shovelled on to it. He glanced at the clock on the mantelpiece; it had stopped and he wound it up and set it at the right time by his wristlet watch. It was near eight. He had had a tiresome day and he would't stay up late.

Behind him mist crept round the windows and covered them. He rubbed his hands together and thought of a colleague who warned him that this place would drive anyone to drink. He smiled and stared at his closed cabinet that contained bottles of whiskey, brandy, and sherry – all for passing visitors and old missioners whose blood required a little stimulant. Never copy the Mercy Nuns, he had been warned, for they were the very divils for offering an old priest tea. He hadn't, he knew, offered a glass to the van-men, but that was understandable. Their van was clumsy, the roads narrow, and anything could happen – he needn't accuse himself of lack of hospitality on that score. As for himself, thank God, a craving for drink had never yet possessed him. He had his books, he had his work, and he was content. He had also brought his three hives of bees and they were sheltered now from all winds by the trees and thick hedges in his garden. What would they do, he mused, when the first warm rags of sunlight coaxed them from their winter sleep. Would they try to make their way back to their old home, over the mountains to the parish in south Down that he had just left. He supposed they hadn't the instinct of homing pigeons and that, like cats, they would speedily adapt themselves to their new surroundings. Attachment to persons was scarcely a characteristic of bees.

The phone rang and he crossed the room to answer it. It was his mother ringing from the city to inquire if he had settled in. Yes, he was nicely settled, he told her. Yes, the housekeeper had arrived. About sixty, he'd say. No, not too robust, but better than nothing.

He paused while his mother took over and launched into her usual litany. He mustn't be too soft with this one, must be strict with her and keep her in her proper place from the word go. She reminded him that he had more than his share of the wrong sort. But it was good to hear that she was an elderly person: she was likely to be a stay-at-home and not a flighty gadabout or one of those harpies that would be demanding half-days off three times a week. But on no account must he keep her if she happened to be an indifferent cook or slatternly in her ways.

"All right, mother. Now don't be worrying." He smiled into the phone. "I've every comfort and I'm in fine form. Good night now, mother. . . . Good night," and he just had the receiver down when a loud sneeze broke from him. He returned to his arm-chair, and once again he sneezed, muffling the explosion in his handkerchief. If his mother had heard his sneezes there'd be no peace until she had motored down from the city for a personal inspection.

At nine o'clock Mary came and announced that her poor feet were perished and she was going to bed. She didn't mention his supper and he was too diffident to ask about it.

"Them tea things on the table, Father; I'll wash them up first thing in the morning. It's too cold for me to stand at that sink in the scullery; I'd get a founder. You understand."

Yes, he understood.

"It's a cold snap of a place this," she went on. "There's frost on that window in the scullery and this only the month of November."

"It's nice here in the springtime, I believe."

"That's a long way off."

"It'll not seem so long when you get into your way of going and get to know the people."

"The people! What do I want with people I'd dearly like to know. I'm a person who keeps herself to herself. I mind my own business."

Father Doyle, realising he couldn't make contact with her, began to outline her duties for each day. He would say

55

Mass at eight and would have breakfast at nine, dinner at 1.30, a light snack at 4.30, and supper at eight until further notice. She was to light a fire in the sitting-room each day during the winter months.

"That will be all right, Father. That'll be all right."

"Good night now, Mary."

She closed the door, and he heard her coughing as she ascended the cold stairs.

If she got sick on his hands, he'd be in a nice pickle, he told himself, and turning up the collar of his overcoat he refilled his pipe and pressed his back into the cushions in the arm-chair. Once more the phone rang. His mother, he presumed, remembering some other item on her agenda.

He lifted the receiver. It was Father O'Loan. A sick-call had come through, and as the house was nearer Father Doyle's end of the parish it would be more convenient for him to go. Father O'Loan proceeded to give him precise instructions how to reach the place. He was to set out immediately by the main road and take the second turning on the right. This was a narrow road, pitted with pot-holes like a battlefield, and he was to drive very carefully. He was to close all the car windows because the briars from the hedges hung out like fishing-rods and were apt to scratch the face off him. A mile along that road on his left he would meet two stone pillars but no gate. He was to stop there and sound the horn and wait. Somebody would come forward and pilot him up the stony path that led to the sick-woman's house. This sick-call, Father O'Loan assured him, would give him an opportunity to know his people — the first requisite for any young priest in a new parish.

The night was clear and frosty when he set out, and he had no difficulty in finding the road and no difficulty in finding the gateposts. He sounded the horn, and, as in a fairy tale, a man arrived with a lantern and led him up the narrow, slippery path to the house of the sick-woman.

The house was as warm as an oven. Two oil-lamps hung on the walls and a mound of turf burned in a hearth as wide as a Christmas crib. Three grey-haired women welcomed him, all sisters he discovered when he had introduced himself. A door off the room was open, and the old mother, now in her eighty-eighth year, was in bed, a tiny oil-lamp on a table beyond her reach, and pictures of the Sacred Heart, the Blessed Virgin, and Robert Emmet on the walls. About an hour ago she had taken a terrible fit of coughing and they were sure she was going to go on them, but she rallied, thank God, and was now resting peacefully, her black roasry in her hands. Father Doyle felt her pulse, and holding her hand lightly he sat down on a chair beside the bed and chatted to her.

She had given them all a quare fright, she told him. But, thank God, she was ready to go. Her three daughters were all good girls, she went on, and always did their best for her and never gallivanted about the countryside looking for a husband. And her boy Patrick – the man who led Father Doyle to the house – was a biddable boy, none better in the whole county of Antrim. Oh, a great worker: he could cut and clamp more turf in a week than six strong men could do in a month. There was no need to worry about the girls when they'd Patrick to look after them. She could die in peace.

Yes, Father Doyle thought, they'd all die in peace, and their place would fall in ruins and the briars join fingers across the slippery path and defy all entrance.

After hearing her confession he rested his hand on her forehead and told her he'd call again in the morning and not to worry about anything. She smiled with her lips closed. A lovely young priest, she thought, an ornament to the parish. She wouldn't like to die yet – indeed she would not!

He returned to the kitchen and sat by the fire, glad of the thick warmth that wrapped round him. They made tea for him in a shiny brown teapot that rested on the hot ashes at the side of the hearth. He wanted to take it in his hand by the fire but they insisted on his going to the white-clothed table. And there the tea was served to him in their best china, and the table was laden with home-made bread and jam and salted butter, the measure of their hospitality. The tea warmed him and dispelled a gloom that had come over him whilst talking to the old woman. Good strong daughters and a strong son and not a child amongst them! And yet the old woman would die content!

He took his leave and the son with his lantern helped him to turn his car at the gateposts, and presently he was crunching over the potholes that were paned with ice and arrived back at his own house with the moon shining on it and the windows misted over like tissue paper.

At nine in the morning after he had said Mass, Mary carried in his breakfast. The porridge was lumpy and unsalted, and the fried bacon cracked like a biscuit under his fork and bits fled over the carpet. He told her he'd much prefer cornflakes to porridge if she didn't mind.

"That's all right with me, Father," she agreed. "It'll lighten my work."

And for dinner that day and throughout the whole week, except Friday, she gave him fried steak, potatoes, and onions, and for dessert jelly and milk. Father Doyle, with a certain conscious levity, inquired if she never got tired of steak and onions.

"No, Father, not a bit of me. It's a wholesome dish."

He endured the monotony for another while and recalled how his mother had admonished that he who overcame monotony without complaining had overcome the world. He held his patience. He bought a cookery book, and one night after she had gone to bed he left it on the windowledge in her kitchen. But she didn't change except to substitute sausages for steak. He complained to Father O'Loan and he advised him to get rid of her.

"Yes, get rid of her! Get rid of her!" he thundered. "Yes, young man, have no mistaken notions about the meaning of charity. Give her a fortnight's notice. That's the usual procedure. And stand no blasted nonsense. She might weep, but woman's tears were come-easy, go-easy, and you must not soften at the approach of a deluge."

58

Neighbours who had brought presents of chickens and eggs to the young priest she turned away. She'd have them all know that neither she nor Father Doyle lived on charity. She made no friends and didn't want any. Even the cat mysteriously disappeared. The people regarded her as odd, and it was whispered to Father Doyle that she was never seen at Mass on a Sunday, neither at first Mass nor at the second. And on days when he wasn't at home she didn't ring the Angelus bell.

She was a failure and Father Doyle waited for an opportunity to give her her notice, and one day when she carried in his plate with the onions still crackling on it (for she had kept it on top of the oven till the last moment) he coughed and said:

"Where's this now you said you were before coming here?"

"I never said I was anywhere, Father."

"I mean, Mary, where were you employed?"

"I was employed in the kitchen of a hospital."

"Cooking?"

"No, Father, washing up."

"Maybe, Mary, you'd like to go back to that work?"

"No, indeed; I like it here, Father. The language in that hospital kitchen was something my ears couldn't stand. My soul would be in jeopardy if I returned."

Father Doyle wished at that moment it were in Picardy or anywhere a hundred miles from his own kitchen, and before he had time to make her realise he wasn't satisfied with her she had glided from the room. However, he had made the first onslaught, and he thought then of bringing in Father O'Loan to give the final push. After all, it was Father O'Loan who had engaged her and by right he should dismiss her. But how was he to suggest such a plan to Father O'Loan. Father O'Loan would probably round on him, scoff at him as a spineless curate, and order him to dismiss her by a certain date. Father Doyle shuddered: it was better to let the hare sit for awhile and pretend that there were certain signs of improvement.

Towards the end of February his mother and sister were to visit him and as he told Mary of the impending visit she carefully inquired the day and the time and then announced it would be a convenient opportunity for her to take a day off, reminding him she hadn't taken one solitary day to herself since she came into his employment.

"But what will they do for a meal, Mary? They're motoring all the way from the city."

"They aren't invalids, are they? Surely two able-bodied women can look after themselves for one afternoon."

"But wouldn't it be nice if you gave *them* a free day?"

"The two ladies will understand when you explain how the land lies."

"That's all right, Mary," he said unwittingly plagiarising one of her favourite phrases.

"And that will be all right with me, Father," and left the room.

There and then he resolved that before another week had fled he would get rid of her. And with the days on the turn, the early lambs in the fields, he would have brighter prospects of getting another to take her place. He would discuss all with his mother, and, perhaps, it was better after all that Mary would have that day off.

His mother and sister arrived in the early afternoon. Mary was out and they were free to tour the house from top to bottom. They couldn't believe their eyes. It was like a pig sty. The slut hadn't swept under the beds: there were perfect rectangles of fluff for all who cared to see. One can get accustomed to dirt, unfortunately. And did he not realise he was aiding and abetting in another person's sin – the sin of sloth, one of the deadliest! And how miserable he looked: ill-nourished and pale and gaunt as Lazarus. It wouldn't do. Not another priest in the diocese would tolerate her for a single hour. And how long had he put up with her – fifteen weeks, if you please. Was he trying to practise martyrdom or was this Mary Carroll trying to make a saint out of him! If he didn't act and act quickly she herself, being his mother, would pay a visit to the bishop.

Indeed she would! And she besought him, with tears in her eyes, to get rid of this dreadful harridan. He promised he would, and after they had driven away he was so dejected he regretted about having complained so much. But he had promised to get rid of her and get rid of her he would! He would not flinch.

He stiffened himself for Mary's arrival, and as she laid his supper tray on the table he said without looking at her: "Mary, I'm sorry to say you don't suit me. You can take a fortnight's notice or, if you prefer, you can leave tomorrow with a fortnight's wages in advance."

Without a word she left the room. He smiled and congratulated himself. He was a fool not to have spoken bluntly long ago. Polite implication was lost on people like this. The cold truth is the only language they understand.

He turned on the radio. A band was playing a few Irish reels. The mood of revelry appealed to him. The door was knocked on and Mary entered. She stood with her hand on the door-knob. He turned down the radio.

"Father, you said something to me a wee while ago. I came to tell you I'm not leaving. I like it here."

She closed the door before he had time to say a word. He switched off the radio and sat still. His heart was thumping. He began to have doubts about her sanity. There was always something queer about her. There was no doubt about that. She couldn't cook; she was slovenly in her habits; she had alienated the good people of the parish; she had disobeyed his instructions time and time again, and she, a priest's housekeeper, didn't even attend Mass on Sundays or major feast days. The whole set-up was absurd. Was it a case for the bishop? No, the bishop would probably declare it was too localised, too petty, for episcopal interference.

It was better not to decide anything until he had discussed it with Father O'Loan. Father O'Loan was old and he was wise and he was endowed with a voice that would waken the heaviest sleeper from the back of a cathedral. Yes, he would follow Father O'Loan's advice, and the following morning after breakfast he went to see him. He told him how he had given her a fortnight's notice or a fortnight's wages in advance and how she had refused both.

"Perhaps as a last resort I should call in the police?"

"To have her evicted, you mean?" Father O'Loan spluttered. "No, no, that wouldn't do at all. History dies hard in these parts. You'd make a martyr of her in the eyes of the people. They'd become friends of hers as quick as you'd crack your fingers. It would never do to bring in the police. Some quieter method we must pursue. Here today and gone tomorrow like snow off a ditch – that's what we want. It must all go unnoticed, if you know what I mean. Let the hen sit for a day or two."

"Whatever you say," Father Doyle said, only too willing to agree. "I'm sorry for causing this trouble."

"You didn't cause it. She caused it, but I'll end it! Do you know I'm just beginning to enjoy it. Life here can be very dull. This will give me something to think about. I'll call; I'll call tomorrow and I'll make her do the hop-skip-and-jump in true Olympic style."

The following afternoon he called as promised. Father Doyle was alone and he told him that her ladyship was in the kitchen redding up the few dishes.

Father O'Loan coughed loudly: "Just leave her to me and you stay here in the sitting-room."

Father Doyle left the door ajar, and in a few minutes he heard Father O'Loan's voice thunder from the kitchen; then there was silence and a squeaky voice raised to breaking point. There followed a rapid rumbling from Father O'Loan, a deep silence and then his heavy step along the hallway to the sitting-room. He slumped into an armchair.

"That's a dreadful woman, a holy terror! Give me a little spirits to steady my nerves. Never in the long history of the parish did the likes of this ever happen. She won't go! And who is she, may I ask." He took a sip of brandy. "How do you keep your pledge with a woman like that about the place? Drink can be a comfort as well as a curse." He took another sip at his glass, ran a finger round the inside of his collar, and breathed loudly. His face was red. "She won't go, eh! Well, she will go if it's the last thing I do in this mortal life. We could file a lawsuit. No, I'll not do that. That's out of the question." He finished his drink. "I think I'll let her have another broadside before I go. Make it hot and heavy for her and she'll be glad to flee."

"Don't distress yourself any further. I'll put up with her for another while. We'll think of something in due course."

"Not a word to anyone about this. We'd be the laughing-stock of the diocese if it leaked out. Oh, no, not a word about this to a living soul."

But word did leak out amongst the priests of the diocese and each morning Father Doyle had an amusing letter from a colleague; one even sent a postcard with an ink drawing of the house, a plane overhead, an armoured car at the gate, and steel-helmeted soldiers on the lawn. He showed it to Father O'Loan and he, in turn, showed him a piece of satirical verse from an anonymous source. Oh, he had a good idea who composed it though. But he'd end it, and in quick time too.

That night he wrote a long letter to the bishop, explaining in detail the disruption caused by the said Mary Carroll in his little parish, and humbly requesting from his lordship direction in the matter.

At the end of the week the bishop invited him to call, and Father O'Loan finding him in jovial form began to entertain him with dramatic renderings of the whole affair.

With a hand cupped to one ear, because he was discreetly deaf, the bishop listened with controlled amusement.

"Well, my Lord," Father O'Loan concluded, "that's the cleft stick I'm wedged in."

"Well, well," the bishop said slowly. "Most unusual circumstances. But lift up your heart. For the good of Father Doyle's health and for your peace of mind a change is clearly indicated. You'll be pleased to hear that I am appointing Father Doyle chaplain to the Poor Clare Convent here in the city. He can live with his mother until his health is built up."

"But Mary Carroll, my lord?"

"She comes into the picture too. I am transferring Father Brannigan from Lower Mourne to take his place. He has a faithful housekeeper by all accounts; she is a native, I believe, of your own parish and I'm sure she'll be glad to be amongst her own people again."

"But, my lord, that Mary Carroll one is still in residence."

"Mary Carroll's services, as far as we are concerned, are terminated. You'll find she'll plague you no longer." He looked at Father O'Loan with a knowing smile. "Where you have two women quarrelling at the one sink and quarrelling over the one bed things should end in our favour."

The following morning early Father Doyle's furniture was on the move again – this time to be put in storage in the city. In the afternoon Father Doyle left for his mother's house in the city. He didn't see Mary before he left for she had suddenly turned religious and was up in the chapel saying her prayers. He had already paid her a fortnight's wages in advance and so he could set off with a free heart and leave her to Liza, the new housekeeper to deal with.

They had their first meeting in the kitchen when Mary was seated at the table taking tea and a boiled egg. Without a word Liza took command. She raked the stove vigorously, filled the kettle, and in a firm quick voice told Mary to hurry or she'd miss her bus.

"I like it here and I'm not going on no bus," Mary said.

"I like it here also for I was born and bred here and I'm glad to be back as Father Brannigan's housekeeper. Your duties are ended here and it would be better for you to go to Nazareth House in the city and stay there till work turns up."

"I'm going to no Nazareth House. I'm independent."

"I'm glad to hear it and would dearly like to believe it."

She glanced at the clock. "You've exactly fifteen minutes to get ready. Your case is in my room and I'll fetch it for you."

"You'll lay no hand on my case."

"I'll stand no more of your oul guff! Take yourself off quietly before I ring for the police."

"This is Father Doyle's kitchen."

"It was Father Doyle's but he has gone off to live with his mother and sister. The kitchen is now Father Brannigan's and mine, and I must hurry and get the place in order for his arrival." She folded her arms and looked out the window at three people standing at the bus stop. "The bus will be along any minute now. If you miss it you'll have to hoof it – them's my last words to you," and lifting the brush she began to sweep the kitchen, watching Mary out of the corner of her eye.

Suddenly Mary pushed back her chair from the table, squeezed the eggshell in her fist and threw the bits into the fire. She left the kitchen, and in a few minutes Liza heard her pounding across the room above her head.

Liza looked out of the window again. The three people had increased to five.

"Miss Carroll, Miss Carroll," she shouted up the stairs, "hurry like a good woman, the bus will be along any time now."

Mary came downstairs with her case tied with loops of string. She sniffed as if she had a cold, and without a word she slipped out by the side-door.

Liza watched from the window. She saw her mount the bus and saw the bus move off, some withered leaves scampering at its heels.

"Thanks be to God she's gone," and she turned to make herself a cup of tea to steady her nerves.

Uprooted

IN THE large flat field that lay between the sea-road and the farm-house the O'Briens were at the spring sowing, wasting no minute of the lovely spell of weather that had at last driven out the winter's cold from the soil. Jim, the married son, worked the horses and the plough, and his young wife dropped the potato seed on the manure that the old father was forking into the furrows. Two little boys, bread crumbs on their jerseys and jam on their cheeks, were occasionally carrying boxes of seed to their mother or pausing to watch their granda and telling him they wouldn't eat potatoes that grew on such smelly stuff.

"Ah, me boys, you'll be glad to eat anything if this accursed war lasts much longer," he said to them, stuck his fork in the manure and took out his pipe. He blew through the shank and told the boys not to be lazy and to go and help their mother.

It was a fine April day, the sky a thin blue, larks loosening their throats in it, and a clean wind sweeping freely in from the sea and flattening the smoke from the fires of weeds and twigs that were burning in many of the fields around.

"There's great heart in that soil, Jim," the old man called out as the son passed up field with the plodding horses.

"Ach, father, if there was some heart in the horses we'd have the field finished long ago."

"They'll do us rightly till the war is over and then we'll get the tractor. We'll get it, son, never fear. Our name is down for one, high up in the list," and he smiled as he watched the good-natured soil curve like brown water from the shining blades of the plough. "They're pulling fine, Jim, and this weather will hold up."

"If we'd the tractor we wouldn't worry what kind of weather it was. McKeever has three fields done and here we are plodding away with a pair of old horses."

"Don't condemn the horses till she's delivered. Next spring, please God, the war will be over and we'll have the tractor."

"McKeever knew to get one before the war started," the son said, urging on the horses. "We're always late!"

"We'll drive her when she comes — won't we, granda?" one of the little boys said.

"You will, my lads, indeed you will. In a short while you'll be big lumps of fellas and you'll be able to give your granda a long rest," and he spat on his hands and lifted the fork to do another spell of work.

"They were fine grandchildren, fine biddable boys," he said to himself; "and Jim had God's blessing about him when he married their mother. She's a good wife, a good daughter-in-law, a good worker — a whole trinity of goodness." And he raised his head and looked across at her, bent over the drills, her wellingtons browned with clay, and her red head-scarf lifting in the wind. Beyond her was their comfortable farm-house and the baby's washing fluttering whitely on the clothes-line in the garden.

Everything looked lively, sheep calling to their lambs in the adjoining fields, gulls flying inland to the turned up soil, the twigs crackling in the fire at the foot of the field and the smoke taking the sting from the air. The sheepdog lay on an empty sack at the side of the hedge and the boys were piling the empty boxes at each side of him to make a kennel. Now and again they started in the direction of the fire, yearning to throw twigs on it. But they were forbidden to go near it, for yesterday some sparks had fallen on their jerseys and had burnt brown holes in them.

For devilment they threw pieces of sod at their granda when his back was turned, and when he looked towards their mother and not at them they began to laugh. They raised their heads and spied out the larks like crumbs of clay against the blue sky. They tried to count them but were forever losing sight of them or counting ones they had already counted before. Then a screeching of brakes made them turn their eyes to the sea-road where an army car with a canvas cover had pulled up.

"Soldiers!" the boys shouted.

"They'll shoot the pair of you," the granda called out as he saw them scamper to the foot of the field, the dog after them.

The granda rested his arms on the fork and saw five men, three in uniform, come out from the back of the jeep. They stretched their arms, stamped their feet on the road, and lit cigarettes. "Nothing like the army for laziness," he said to himself; "if they'd wield this fork for an hour or two it'd slacken the hide on them." The men gazed seawards, swung their arms back and forth to warm themselves and leisurely returned to the car and took things from the back of it. The old man spat out and eyed them with intense but puzzled curiosity. Two of the men paced the road, stretching a steel tape-measure that flashed in the sun like a live eel. They were up on the fence now, scanning the fields. The dog was barking at them, and the sheep in the nearby field were moving towards a grassy mound, the only hump to be seen in all that flat countryside.

The car moved some perches along the road and again the men got out, carrying with them a white pole with black and red markings.

Jim halted the horses when his father asked him what he thought the army men might be doing.

"God knows, father, what they're up to. They mightn't know themselves. Maybe they're going to plant a gun on top of the mound or make stores for bombs."

"They'll plant no gun or no bombs on my land!"

They saw the strangers enter the sheep-field and close the gate behind them. They saw one place the white pole near the foot of the mound and another erect a gadget on a tripod, stoop and peer through it, his hands resting on his thighs.

"Divil's own cheek!" the old man said, and throwing down his fork he crossed the potato field and shouted across a narrow stream that divided it from the sheep-field.

"Eh, eh, what is it you're wanting there?"

"Surveying, old man, surveying!" one said and wrote something in a notebook he carried in his hand.

"Surveying what?"

They didn't answer him but lifted the tripod and marched off round the mound as if they knew the lie of the land as one reared on it.

All enthusiasm for his work drained away from the old man as he watched them disappear behind the small hill. He had heard of land being taken over by the army in other parts of the county but had hoped that nothing like that would befall him. Not a square foot would he give them! Let them go and seize some boggy stretch that's no good for beast nor crop! He spat into the stream and buttoned his coat. He saw them come round from the back of the hill, saw them take the path past Dan Mullan's old house and heard Dan's old dog raise its hoarse bark. Horses had halted in other fields, and nothing moved now but gulls on the turned-up soil and the warm smoke from the fires drifting inland and hazing the distance.

In about two hours' time the strangers returned to the road and when their car had driven off the old man kept mumbling to himself, debating with his uneasy thoughts and urging Jim to quit for the day. He'd have no peace of mind till the meaning of this sudden trespass upon his land had been unravelled.

"Och, father, forget about them. We might never see light or sight of them again. They're probably some young officers learning about War."

"And what kind of war could they learn about in an old field that grazes sheep? And why didn't they answer me civilly when I spoke to them? 'Surveying' they said and walked off as if I was an old stump of a tree you'd strike a match on."

"You needn't blame them. They're only carrying out orders."

"I don't like it, Jim. They're up to no good. I don't like it I tell you!" and he stuck the fork in the ground and told him to unyoke the horses.

And that evening he urged his son to hurry at his supper and cycle into the village to see if there was any talk about the strangers.

Old Dan Mullan came over for his usual visit. He knew nothing; the strangers had said nothing to him, didn't even bid him the time of day but marched on past his house with maps and strange-looking gear. No, they had no guns with them as far as he could see. Both agreed that it boded no good.

It was late that night when Jim came back and there was no one in the kitchen except the old man smoking at the fire and Mary smoothing the clothes at the table.

"There was talk and rumours of talk," the son said as he hung up his cap at the back of the door.

"Aye."

"No one knows for certain what's afoot. Some say they're going to build barracks of some sort."

"But they can't build on a man's land without permission. Are all rights to be choked and smothered because there's a war on?"

"The government, they say, can do whatever they damn well like. They say they can seize a man's land and pay him compensation."

"Nothing can compensate a man for the loss of his land!" the old man shouted and rose from his chair.

Mary looked towards the room where the children slept and the old man lowered his voice and told of the number of years the O'Briens had worked and tilled and improved that land outside. And do you think he was going to hand it over to any government to hack and ruin! He was not!

"No use, father, crossing a bridge before you come to it. There mightn't be a grain of truth in any of the rumours."

70

"Sure if they were going to take over a field or two you'd be the first to hear of it, granda," Mary said and brought him a light for his pipe that had gone out.

"I suppose you're right, Mary, I suppose you're right," and he lifted a lamp and went out to have a look at the cows.

"Not a word to him, Mary," Jim said in a low voice. "But the sergeant in the village was saying he heard on good authority they were going to build an aerodrome in the flat of the land."

During the next few days the car came again and the strange men in uniform were seen, crossing and recrossing neighbouring fields, and in the evenings they were gone leaving no traces behind them except the rib-marks of the car's tyres on the grassy side of the sea-road. And in the farmers' minds they left a disquieting curiosity that seized on every rumour and magnified it.

At the end of three weeks after showers of rain and the green potato tops struggling into vigorous life on the drills the postman handed a letter to Mary O'Brien.

"I've a fine handful of these letters with me this morning," he said. "I've even one for Dan Mullan."

She looked at the letter, closed the door, and handed it to the old man. He opened it, saw the strange typescript, and gave it to his son to read. He read it slowly, and slower still came the realisation of what it contained. They were ordered to leave their farm and have all goods and chattels thereon removed within three months. Compensation would be agreed upon by the parties concerned.

"I'm not going!" the old man shouted. "I'm not stirring hand or foot from the land that reared me!" He strode about the kitchen, stamping his feet, and gazing out the window, his fists resting on the table.

"Sit down and take your breakfast, granda," Mary said.

"I'll not eat till I come back. I'm going out."

Jim and Mary stared at him, afraid to ask him where he was going. They saw him take his stick and go out along

71

the sea-road, the dog at his heels.

The old man saw nothing, heard nothing, not even the plunge of the sea breaking on the stones below the road. He turned to the left, disappeared behind the grassy mound and headed for the priest's house. The priest had just finished his breakfast, the housekeeper clearing away the dishes when the old man rang the bell at the door. The housekeeper ushered him into the sittingroom where he sat, his eyes fixed on the chair-dents that were like paw-marks in the polished linoleum.

He gave the letter to the priest, and though the priest already knew what it would contain he read it slowly. A month ago he had already written a letter of protest about the prospective aerodrome and had pointed out that a grave-yard lay in the vicinity. His protest did not postpone the prepared plans and they assured him that the graveyard did not come within the boundaries of the commandeered territory.

"It's bad news, Tom," he said folding the old man's letter. "And it's hard news!"

"But surely, Father, they can't drive a man from his own land. Drive him out on the road like a pack of worthless tinkers."

"They could drive me from mine if it stood in their way."

The old man stared at him, uncomprehending, enraged at an unseen force against which priest nor man had any power.

"What's to be done, Father? We've no place to turn to. All our lives we've worked honestly, paid our debts, and buried our dead when their time came."

The priest explained that there were others in the parish, all those in the hollow, who would get their notice to quit. He said something about the cruelty of war, about suffering, and about the cruel inhuman element that emerged from war's preparation and war's prolongation. He spoke of countries ravaged by war, countries where not one farmer or two farmers but thousands were driven out on the roads with nowhere to lay their heads. The old man listened, but everything the priest was saying seemed far away, like something out of a history book, something that bore no relation to him or his family.

"We can do nothing, Tom, but will what God wills," and he rested his hand on the old man's shoulder. "Make up your mind to go and get ready at once. And get a high valuation put on your land. That's my advice to you," and he told him of the letter of protest he had written, and that there was no human feeling, no mercy, in officialdom.

"But maybe, Father, the war will end in three months."

"It's not likely to end in three months – it may take years."

"Then we'll have to go, Father. There's no hope anywhere."

The priest nodded his head aware of the foolishness of tethering the old man's mind to a hopeless hope.

"I'll bide by what you say. We'll go, but we'll try not to go far afield. A man of my years can't live far away from his own people. My people that lie at peace under the sod outside."

"You have great courage, Tom, and God gives His grace to the courageous."

The priest watched him go out, and from the window he watched him move among the mounds in the graveyard and kneel down, one hand resting on a headstone above the graves of his own people.

When he arrived home all fight had gone out of him as he sat at the table.

"Were you away to see about the tractor, granda?" one of his grandsons asked him.

"Tractor, son, what tractor?"

"Give your granda peace to take his breakfast. Run out and play yourselves like good boys."

"Leave them alone, Mary, when the heart's cold the voice of a child can warm it," and as he took his breakfast he told Jim to sell the sheep, then the cattle, but to leave the horses to the last.

A shower of rain fell, scoring the window pane with streaks of silver, and washing the dust from the potato leaves in the large flat field. There'd be a rich harvest there, but there'd be no one to harvest them, and in a short while no smoke would rise from the farmsteads and at night no comforting light shine out from Dan Mullan's across the wide fields. The larks would be free in the sky, but soon there wouldn't be the bark of a dog in the fields, and where children once played there would be nothing but huts peopled with strangers who had no wish to be there.

At night the old man went out alone with his dog, wandering the roads and calling in with Dan Mullan to shred his worries in useless talk. And then home again when the sky was a harvest of stars and the sea-waves breaking in unchanging sound upon the stones on the shore.

In June Dan Mullan went away. The O'Briens helped him to flit, his few stick of furniture piled and roped on a cart, and Dan sitting on top of the old door. Easy for one man to leave and set up house again. Any old four walls that were still standing would do him. All he needed was to fling a few sheets of corrugated iron over them to keep out the rain. And that's what Dan did. He took possession of an old ruined house about two miles along the coast, patched the walls with cement, put down a new floor of concrete and had the two windows repaired. He placed his bed in a corner well away from the sparks of the fire and he often sat on it when Tom called to see him.

"There's one blessing in it all," he said to him one day, "that they didn't order me out in the winter time. By the time the days harden this old place will be warmed up. It's not much of a place with the smell of rotten seaweed at your door – still it'll do me my days. And I've enough money from the old place that'll keep me out of debt."

"The man who owns less is the best off."

"Wherever you go, Tom, you'll always have the comfort of a family. A man can't have everything in this life and he must be content. Jim will find a good farm for you all with the compensation money."

"Not with the war bringing high prices for sheep and cattle farmers are loth to sell their land. And I don't want to go far from here. You can't transplant an old bush. It'll wither in the richest soil."

"In a short while you'll be coming back here to tell me of your good luck. You'll see that I'm right."

But the O'Briens hadn't the luck Dan expected. There were no farms for sale and Jim didn't try hard to fine one. His mind was set in starting a shop in Downpatrick, a town where his children would have schools at their own doorstep. But his chief difficulty was to coax his father into his way of thinking. And one evening when his father came in from Dan's Jim told him that the only farms to be had were in the county of Antrim.

"Antrim has cold, clabbery land — heavy land that'd kill them not used to it," the father said. "It's not like the dry loose soil of our own county. You may drop all notion of going there, Jim. Wherever we go it mustn't be far away from our own people."

"What people, father?"

"Your own people that's at peace in the graveyard beyond."

Jim paused, paused until he was sure that his memory and its associations had sunk below the present moment.

"What if we settled for a while in Downpatrick, father? It's only ten miles away."

"You can't farm the streets of a town."

"I was thinking we could start a shop there."

"A shop!" and his father stared at him and spat into the fire.

"I mean we could start a shop and when the war's over we could sell it and come back here."

"Come back here! But, son, the house will not . . . ."

"I've heard tell of them opening roads in other places, making plans, and then calling a halt to them."

"I pray God they'll give this up. Maybe, Jim, they'll blot it all out. Maybe after all it was foolish to sell the sheep in haste."

It wasn't the answer the son anticipated and he added quickly: "McKeever, I hear, is ready to leave by tomorrow. We'll be the last."

"McKeever!" and the old man took the pipe from his lips. "If McKeever goes we may go. I never knew that man to make a mistake."

"He's going to live in the city from what I hear."

"That'll be the first mistake he ever made in his life."

"We'll never go there, father. Downpatrick's bad enough," he hedged. "Still it's a friendly wee town and the fields and the hills wash up close to it."

"I couldn't end my days in it."

"Nor could me and Mary. But there's nothing else for us in the meantime but to buy a shop. That's the best proposition I can think of," and he told his father how they'd need his advice on their buying and selling. "Whatever we do we must stick together and help one another. We must agree about this while there is still time to do something — no matter how poor it is."

The old man nodded his head: "Whatever you do may the good God guide you in it. You have your life to live, and what you think will be good for Mary and the children will be good enough for me." It was no use at his age, he thought, struggling against his son when there was a coarser authority struggling against all of them.

Within two weeks the son had bought a place in Downpatrick and after removing most of the furniture from the farmhouse he brought in his wife and children. The old man spoke little to anyone.

One day remained to him and he tramped the fields for the last time. The silence of the grave lay over them. Scaffoldings of new huts were being erected on the sea-road, heaps of shavings like the shearings of sheep were blown against the hedges, and the strokes of the men's hammers sounded to the old man like the pulse of his own blood. He reached Dan Mullan's deserted house and as he crossed the threshold, that had no door, a swallow flew out past him.

Strange he never noticed them arriving this year, and he now gazed at them skimming swift and sure over the sunny fields. Inside in the house ashes lay on the hearth, and stones and glass littered the floor where schoolboys had broken the windows when taking a short cut across the fields. Up in a corner clung a grey nest of the swallows. They, too, would be cleared out, nothing was safe, nothing left undisturbed. Foolish birds, he said to himself, why didn't you go to the hills, anywhere but here. They'll not let you rest.

On his way back two lorries were pulled up on the sea-road and men were unloading warm-smelling timber. He greeted nobody and nobody greeted him. He looked out to the sea, to black jagged rocks where he often fished years ago. There was no change in them. The rising sea could do nothing to them except wear them smooth. Someday, please God, he'd be here again, indeed he would. The accursed war would be over, the strange huts and the strangers in them would be gone, and tractors would move quickly over the barren fields and crops rise again.

When they were settled in Downpatrick, the shop closed in the evenings and the father gone to bed, the son used to talk to his wife of the last journey they had made from the house, how his father had padlocked the gate, had his last look at the dark windows of the house, the trees in leaf in the garden and how he had spotted the clothesline and nothing would do him but open up the gate again and go back for that old bit of rope. They worried about him for he didn't go out much except to leave the two boys at the school in the morning and call into the church beside it. The sheep-dog, too, was listless, its coat lost its shine, and its nose was dry and cracked like a piece of black rubber.

At night the streets were dark and few lamps lighted, and before going to bed the old man listened to the news on the radio, news that might tell him of the war's end.

And the mornings were cold and silent. Few lorries or cars were on the roads because of the scarcity of petrol, and it was only on fair days that the old man would rise early on hearing the knocking of farm carts descending to the town and see from his window the sheep on the road with their breaths hanging above them like a sudden fall of sea-mist. And he would hurry on with his breakfast to get out among the lots of sheep that were being sold, the dog barking madly and the old man searching for a familiar face among the groups of farmers. And the seldom time he did spot a friend it was to inquire about the changes that had taken place beyond. Dan Mullan's old house was levelled, he was told, for they were making a road that way. And there were as many new huts about the place as would house an army.

The old man would tell his son about these changes, and tell him that the house must still be standing for nobody had said a word about it. And God would keep her standing he would say to reinforce his faith.

And it was at one of these sheep-fairs that he unexpectedly met Dan Mullan. All day he had been moving around the fair and was returning despondently to the shop when he saw Dan leaning against the counter talking to Jim.

"It's Dan!" the old man shouted, putting an arm on his shoulder and gripping his hand. "And how are you at all at all?"

"Never better in my life, thank God. And Jim's after selling me as much tobacco as'd do me for a year of wet Sundays."

"When there's tobacco in the shop there's nobody we'd gladder give it to than yourself."

"There's not a grain of tobacco to be had in the old place. It was well worth the journey to get it."

"And how did you get here, Dan?"

"I walked a bit and then got a lift in a cart, and the same man's giving me a lift back."

"And your old house is tumbled, I hear?"

"She is. Right through her is a tarred road as shiny as the back of a herring. A runaway they call it."

"I suppose there's great changes everywhere?"

Jim knew what was coming but he had Dan well-primed.

"Aye," Dan said, staring across the counter at bottles of sweets. "Big changes everywhere."

"New huts and sheds?"

"Aye, huts and sheds."

"I'd hardly know the place?"

Dan took the pipe from his lips, prodding the bowl with his finger and struck a match.

"And our house, Dan? Is she — is she in bad shape?"

"No," Dan said, staring at the lighted match above the bowl of his pipe. "She's in fine health."

"Maybe the villains won't touch her. You'll see us back in her some day."

"It could all be," Dan said, not looking at him, while Jim stooped below the counter pretending to rummage for something.

"I must be on my way," Dan said. "But I'll be back soon again."

"You're not going till you get something to eat."

"Eat! Mary gave me a feed that'd do a regiment."

The old man saw the guilty look in his son's face and scarcely listened to him as he said: "When Dan called, father, we searched everywhere for you but couldn't find you."

"That's all right," he said, with a limp wave of his hand.

The old man went out with Dan. They had a quick drink together in a pub, then saw Dan climb into a farmer's cart and set off out of the town.

There was another month to the next fair for he had marked the date on a calendar that hung in the shop. But he didn't intend to wait that length of time till he'd see again, or maybe not see, someone from his part of the country. Maybe if he walked a mile or so out of the town he'd get a lift in a cart and see the changes that Dan talked about. It didn't matter how he'd get back – he'd get back somehow, he felt.

He said nothing to Jim or Mary, and about two weeks later when the children were in school and the sun shining frostily on the roofs of the houses he set off, the dog with him. He climbed the hilly road above the town and in front of him saw the uneven fields that merged into the hazy distance. He felt in fine form. A fresh breeze was blowing and the falling leaves hopped and flittered like mice, and his dog rubbed the itch off itself against the grassy banks that edged the road, ran back and sniffed his trousers and scampered ahead again.

He had gone nearly two miles when a cart overtook him and left him down a mile from the sea. The sun was setting and the long shadows of trees stretched across the road and bent up on the grassy banks at the other side. The air became colder. He could smell the salt in it and he could hear the dull roar of the sea.

In front of him over familiar fields were the outlines of many buildings he had never seen before. But he kept to the road and it brought him among low timbered-huts, huts that swarmed around him on all sides. Concrete paths branches off the road, and at each path was an arrow-shaped signpost with printed letters that made no sense. He was in a strange place, but the road led somewhere, and close to a bend in it that he should know so well there was a single-storey building with many windows and doors. Two of the doors were open and the rest were closed, and a man with an aluminium kettle passed by, and another man with shaving-cream on his chin shouted something and closed his door. And now all the doors were closed. But somewhere to the back of that building was his own house and the road to it, but the road that led to that road he could not find. He trudged on, past piles of drainpipes and heaps of sand, and past machines that were like tractors, silent machines tattered with clay and splashed with cement.

And then suddenly he found himself in the cold open air

amidst the rushing noise from the sea. He halted and to his left saw the long tarred road Dan had mentioned, and there was a flock of gulls on it, and far beyond them were the church and the graveyard, places he had never seen from this part of the sea-road. And then he saw that the sheep-mound was levelled and everything made as flat as the sea. The dog ran away from him and he saw it lapping up water from the stream, the stream that used to flow at the side of his potato field. The dog barked, and with wet paws raced along the smooth tarred road. He followed it till he left the buildings behind him, and then he stopped and gazed towards the place where his house should stand. But it was no longer there, not a stone of it to be seen. There was nothing but a windy plain with neither tree, nor bush, nor cow, nor sheep upon it. Nothing but vacancy, and the sky where the sun had set was a red patch like the glow of a fire on a hearthstone. The dog barked at the gulls and they arose from the black road and passed overhead out to sea. The dog ran back, licked the old man's hands and bounded to the stream again. The old man didn't seem to see it. He trembled and gripped the stick in his hand, his eyes resting on the church and the white headstones in the graveyard.

The Game Cock

WHEN I was young we came to Belfast and my father kept a game cock and a few hens. At the back of the street was waste ground where the fowl could scrape, and my father built a shed for them in the yard and sawed a hole in the back door so that they could hop in and out as they took the notion. In the mornings our cock was always first out on the waste ground.

We called him Dick, but he was none of your ordinary cocks, for he had a pedigree as long as your arm, and his grandfather and grandmother were of Indian breed. He was lovely to look at, with his long yellow legs, black glossy feathers in the chest and tail, and reddish streaky neck. In the long summer evenings my father would watch him for hours, smiling at the way he tore the clayey ground with his claws, coming on a large earwig, and calling the hens to share it. But one day when somebody lamed him with a stone, my father grew so sad that he couldn't take his supper.

We had bought him from Jimmy Reilly, the blind man, and many an evening he came to handle him. I would be doing my school exercise at the kitchen table, my father, in his shirt sleeves, reading the paper. A knock would come to the door, and with great expectancy in his voice my father'd say, "That's the men now. Let them in, son."

And when I opened the door I'd say, "Mind the step!" and in would shuffle wee Johnny Moore leading the blind man. They'd sit on the sofa; Jimmy Reilly, hat on head, and two fists clasped round the shank of the walking stick between his legs; and Johnny Moore with a stinking clay pipe in his mouth.

As soon as they started the talk I'd put down my pen and listen to them.

"Sit up to the fire, men, and get a bit of the heat."

"That's a snorer of a fire you've on, Mick," would come from the blind man.

"What kind of coals is them?" says Johnny Moore, for he had my father pestered with questions.

"The best English; them's none of your Scotch slates!"

"And what's the price of them a ton?"

"They cost a good penny," my father would answer crossly.

"And where do you get them?"

The blind man's stick would rattle on the kitchen tiles and he'd push out his lower lip, stroke his beard and shout, "They're good coals, anyway, no matter where they're got." And then add in his slow natural voice, "How's the cock, Mick?"

"He's in great fettle, Jimmy. He's jumping out of his pelt." And he'd tell how the comb was reddening and how he had chased Maguire's dunghill of a rooster from about the place. And the blind man would smile and say, "That's the stuff! He'll soon have the walk to himself; other cocks would annoy him."

With a lighted candle I would be sent out to the yard to lift Dick off the roost. The roosts were low so that the cock wouldn't bruise his feet when flying to the ground. He'd blink his eyes and cluck-cluck in his throat when I'd bring him into the gas-light and hand him to the blind man.

Jimmy fondled him like a woman fondling a cat. He gently stroked the neck and tail, and then stretched out one wing and then the other. "He's in great condition. We could cut his comb and wattles any time and have him ready for Easter." And he'd put him down on the tiles and listen to the scrape of his claws. Then he'd feel the muscles on the thighs, and stick out his beard with joy, "There's no coldness about that fella, Mick. He has shoulders on him as broad as a bulldog. Aw, my lovely fella," feeling the limber of him as his claws pranced on the tiles. "He'll do us credit. A hould you he'll win a main."

My father would stuff his hands in his pockets and rise off his heels, "And you think he's doing well, Jimmy?"

"Hould yer tongue, man, I wish I was half as fit," Jimmy would answer, his sightless eyes raised to the ceiling.

And one evening as they talked like this about the cock and forthcoming fights, Johnny Moore sneaked across to the table and gave me sums out of his head: *A ropemaker made a rope for his marrying daughter, and in the rope he made twenty knots and in each knot he put a purse, and in each purse he put seven three-penny bits and nine half-pennies. How much of a dowry did the daughter get?*

I couldn't get the answer and he took the pipe from his mouth and laughed loudly, "The scholars, nowadays, have soft brains. You can't do it with your pencil and paper and an old man like me can do it in my head."

My face burned as I said, "But we don't learn them kind of sums." He laughed so much that I was glad when it was time for him to lead the blind man home.

A few evenings afterwards they were back again; the blind man with special scissors to cut Dick's comb and wattles. Jimmy handed the scissors to my father, then he held the cock, his forefinger in its mouth and his thumb at the back of its head.

"Now, Mick," said he, "try and cut it with one stroke."

When my sisters saw the chips of comb snipped off with the scissors and the blood falling on the tiles they began to cry, "That's a sin, father! That's a sin!"

"Tush, tush," said my father, and the blood on his sleeves. "He doesn't feel it. It's just like getting your hair cut. Isn't that right, Jimmy?"

"That's right; just like getting your toenails cut."

But when Dick clucked and shook his head with pain, my sisters cried louder and were sent out to play, and I went into the scullery to gather cobwebs to stop the bleeding.

In a few days the blood had hardened and Dick was his old self again. The men came nearly every night and talked about the cock fights to be held near Toome at Easter. They made plans for Dick's training and arranged how he was to be fed.

About a fortnight before the fights my father got a long box and nailed loose sacking over the front to keep it in darkness. Dick was put into this and his feathers and tail were clipped. For the first two days he got no feed so as to keep his weight down. Then we gave him hard-boiled eggs, but they didn't agree with him and made him scour. The blind man recommended a strict diet of barley and barley water. "That's the stuff to keep his nerves strong and his blood up. A hould you it'll not scour him."

Every morning we took him from his dark box and gave him a few runs up and down the yard. Johnny Moore had made a red flannel bag stuffed with straw, and Dick sparred at this daily, and when he had finished my father would lift him in his arms, stroke him gently, and sponge the feet and head. Day by day the cock grew peevish, and once when he nebbed at me I gave him a clout that brought my father running to the yard.

The night before the fights the steel spurs were tied on him to see how he would look in the pit. "Ah, Jimmy, if you could see him," said my father to the blind man. "He's the picture of health."

The blind man fingered his beard and putting a hand in his pocket, took out a few pound notes and spat on them for luck. "Put that on him to-morrow. There's not another cock this side of the Bann nor in all County Derry that could touch him." Even Johnny Moore risked a few shillings, and the next morning before five o'clock my father wakened me to go to Toome.

It was Easter Monday and there were no trams running early so we set off to walk to the Northern Counties Railway to catch the half-six train. The cock was in a potato bag under my arm, and I got orders not to squeeze him, while my father carried the overcoats and a gladstone filled with things for my Granny, who lived near the place where the cocks were to fight.

The streets were deserted, and our feet echoed in the chill air. Down the Falls Road we hurried. The shopblinds were pulled down, the tram lines shining, and no smoke coming from the chimneys. At the Public Baths my father looked at his watch and then stood out in the road to see the exact time by the Baths' clock.

"Boys-a-boys, my watch is slow. We'll need to hurry." In the excitement the cock got his neb out and pecked at me. I dropped the bag, and out jumped the cock and raced across the tram lines, the two of us after him.

"Don't excite him, son. Take him gently." We tried to corner him in a doorway, my father with his hand outstretched calling in his sweetest way, "Dick, Dick, Dicky." But as soon as he stooped to lift him, the cock dived between his legs, and raced up North Howard Street, and stood contemplating a dark-green public lavatory.

"Whisht," said my father, holding my arm as I went to go forward. "Whisht! If he goes in there we'll nab him."

The cock stood, head erect, and looked up and down the bare street, Then he scraped each side of his bill on the step of the lavatory and crowed into the morning.

"Man, but that's the brazen tinker of a cock for you," said my father, looking at his watch. And then, as if Dick were entering the hen-shed, in he walked and in after him tiptoed my father, and out by the roofless top flew the cock with a few feathers falling from him.

I swished him off the top and he flew for all he was worth over the tram lines, down Alma Street and up on a yard wall.

"We'll be late for the train if we don't catch him quick, and maybe have the peelers down on us before we know where we are."

Up on the wall I was heaved and sat with legs astride. The cock walked away from me, and a dog in the yard yelped and jumped up the back door.

"I'm afraid, Da, I'm afraid."

"Come down out of that and don't whinge there."

A baby started to cry and a man looked out of a window and shouted, "What the hell's wrong?"

"We're after a cock," replied my father apologetically.

The man continued to lean out of the window in his shirt, and a woman yelled from the same room, "Throw a bucket of water round them, Andy. A nice time of the morning to be chasing a bloody rooster."

Here and there a back door opened and barefooted men in their shirts and trousers came into the entry. They all chased after Dick.

"Ah, easy, easy," said my father to a man who was swiping at Dick savagely with a yard-brush. "Don't hit him with that."

By this time the cock had walked half way down the entry, still keeping to the top of the yard walls. Women shouted and dogs barked, and all the time I could hear my father saying, "If we don't catch him quick we'll miss the train."

"Aw," said one man, looking at the scaldy appearance of the cock. "Sure he's not worth botherin' about. There's not as much on him as'd set a rat-trap."

My father kept silent about Dick's pedigree for he didn't want anyone to know about the cockfights, and maybe have the police after us.

We had now reached the end of the entry and Dick flew off the wall and under a little handcart that stood in a corner. Five men bunched in after him, and screeching and scolding the cock was handed to my father.

"I can feel his heart going like a traction engine," he said, when we were on the road again. "He'll be bate. The blind man's money and everybody's money will be lost. Lost!"

We broke into a trot, I carrying the gladstone, and my father the cock and the overcoats. Along York Street we raced, gazing up at the big clocks and watching the hands approach half-six. Sweat broke out on us and a stitch came in my side, but I said nothing as I lagged behind trying to keep pace.

We ran into the station and were just into the carriage when out went the train.

"Aw-aw-aw," said my father, sighing out all his breath in one puff. "I'm done. Punctured! That's a nice start for an Easter Monday!"

He took off his hard hat and pulled out a handkerchief. His bald head was speckled with sweat and the hat had made a red groove on his brow. He puffed and ah-ee-d so many times I thought he'd faint, and I sat with my heart thumping, my shirt clammy with sweat, waiting with fear for what he'd say. But he didn't scold me.

"It was my own fault," he said. "I should have tied a bit of string round the neck of the bag. He'll be bate! He'll be bate!"

He took the spurs from his pocket and pulled the corks off the steel points. "I might as well strap them on a jackdaw as put them on Dick this day, for he'll be tore asunder after that performance."

As the train raced into the country we saw the land covered with a thin mist, and ploughed fields with shining furrows. The cold morning air came into the carriage; it was lovely and fresh. My father's breathing became quieter, and he even pointed out farms that would make great "walks" for cocks. It was going to be a grand day: a foggy sun was bursting through, and crows flew around trees that were laden with their nests.

Dick was taken from the bag and petted; and then my father stretched himself out on the seat and fell asleep. I watched the telegraph wires rising and falling, and kept a lookout for the strange birds that were cut out in the hedge near Doagh.

When we came to Toome my father tied the neck of the bag with a handkerchief and sent me on in front for fear the police might suspect something. The one-streeted village was shady and cool, the sun skimming the housetops. Pieces of straw littered the road, and a few hens stood at the closed barrack door, their droppings on the doorstep.

We passed quickly through the silent village and turned on to the long country road that led to my Granny's. Behind us the train rumbled and whistled over the bridge; and then across the still country came the dull cheer of the Bann waterfall and the wind astir in the leafing branches. Once my father told me to sit and rest myself while he crossed a few fields to a white cottage. It wasn't long until he was back again. "I've got the stuff in my pocket that'll make him gallop. The boys in Lough Beg made a run of poteen for Easter."

When we reached my Granny's she was standing at the door, a string garter fallen round her ankle, and a basin in her hand; near her my Uncle's bicycle was turned upside down and he was mending a puncture. They had great welcome for us and smiled when my father put the poteen on the table. He took tumblers from the dresser, filled one for my Granny, and in another he softened a few pieces of bread for the cock.

My Granny sat at the fire and at every sip she sighed and held the glass up to the light. "Poor fellas, but they run great risks to make that. None of your ould treacle about the Lough Beg stuff . . . made from the best of barley."

As she sipped it she talked to me about my school, and the little sense my father had in his head to be bothering himself about game cocks and maybe land himself in jail; and when the car came up for him she went to the door and waved him off. "Mind the peelers," she shouted. "Ye'd never know where they'd be sniffing around."

During the day I played about the house and tormented the tethered goat, making her rise on her hind legs. I went to the well at the foot of the field and carried a bucket of water to my Granny, and she said I was a big, strong man. Later my Uncle brought me through the tumbled demesne wall and showed me where he had slaughtered a few trees for the fire. I talked to him about Dick and I asked him why he didn't keep game cocks. He laughed at me and said, "I wouldn't have them about the place. They destroy the hens and make them as wild as the rooks." I didn't talk any more about game cocks, but all the time as we walked to the Big House I thought about Dick and wondered would he win his fights. The Big House was in ruins, crows were nesting in the chimneys, and the lake was covered with rushes and green scum. When I asked my uncle where were all the ladies and gentlemen and the gamekeeper, he spat through the naked windows and replied, "They took the land from the people and God cursed them."

When we came back my Granny was standing at the door looking up and down the road wondering what was keeping my father. A few fellows coming from the cockfights passed on bicycles, and soon my father arrived. He was in great form, his face red, and his navy blue trousers covered with clay.

The cock's comb was scratched with blood, his feathers streaky, and his eyes half shut. He was left in the byre until the tea was over. While my father was taking the tea he got up from the table and stood in the middle of the floor telling how Dick had won his fights. "Five battles he won and gave away weight twice."

"Take your tea, Mick, and you can tell us after," my Granny said, her hands in her sleeves, and her feet tapping the hearth.

He would eat for a few minutes and he'd be up again. "Be the holy frost if ye'd seen him tumbling the big Pyle cock from Derry it'd have done yer heart good. I never seen the like of it. Aw, he's a great battler. And look at the morning he put in on them yard walls . . . up and down a dozen streets he went, running and flying and crowing. And then to win his fights. Wait till Jimmy Reilly hears about this and the nice nest egg I have for him. The poteen was great stuff. A great warrior!" And he smiled in recollection.

I was glad when he was ready for home and gladder still when we were in the train where I made the wheels rumble and chant: . . . *They took the land from the people* . . .

God cursed them.

It was dark when we reached Belfast and I carried Dick in the potato bag. We got into a tram at the station; the lights were lit and we sat downstairs. The people were staring at my father, at the clabber on his boots and the wrinkles on his trousers. But he paid no heed to them. In the plate glass opposite I could see our reflections; my father was smiling with his lips together, and I knew he was thinking of the cock.

"He's very quiet, Da," I whispered. "The fightin' has fairly knocked the capers out of him."

"Aw, son, he's a great warrior," and he put his hand in his pocket and slipped me a half crown. "I'll get his photo took as soon as he's his old self again."

I held the money tightly in my hand, and all the way home I rejoiced that Johnny Moore wasn't with us, for he would have set me a problem about a half-crown.

In the kitchen I left the bag on the floor and sat on the sofa, dead tired. My father got down the olive oil to rub on Dick's legs, but when he opened the bag the cock never stirred. He took him out gently and raised his head, but it fell forward limply, and from the open mouth blood dripped to the floor.

"God-a-God, he's dead!" said my father, stretching out one of the wings. He held up the cock's head in the gaslight and looked at him. Then he put him on the table without a word and sat on a chair. For awhile I said nothing, and then I asked quietly, "What'll you do with him, Da?"

He turned and looked at the cock, stretched on the table. "Poor Dick!" he said. And I felt a lump rise in my throat.

Then he got up from the chair. "What'll I do with him! What'll I do with him! I'll get him stuffed! That's what I'll do!"

After Forty Years

IN SPITE of the hard rain that struck against the windows the air in the compartment was warm and comfortable, and as the almost empty train rattled and shrugged through the night-dark countryside the woman in the corner seat persisted with her knitting, and her husband, whose eyes were at their fading stage, tried to read, the book shuffling on his knee despite his efforts to steady it. They were alone, and in the rack above them were two suitcases, a man's tweed hat and a fishing rod in a brown canvas cover. They spoke little to one another, but when the train would draw up at a station the woman would raise her head from her knitting and say: "Where are we now John?"

Her husband would glance at his watch and tell her, and a few minutes later the porter, passing outside on the platform, would confirm in a loud voice the name of the station John had already announced. Then the guard's whistle would flare into the night and with a jolt the train would move off again, the lights from the platform shining for a moment into the passing compartments.

The woman would again take up her knitting, the man his reading, their reflections in the dark windows keeping abreast of them.

The train gathered speed, and the book balanced on the man's knee shook so unsteadily that he turned down a page at the corner, closed it, and folding his arms leaned back against the headrest. His wife looked across at him, at his white hair, and at his pale face that would, after a couple of weeks' fishing, turn to the brown colour she loved to see on him. It would be their first holiday together since he retired from teaching, a holiday she allowed him to arrange without even one suggestion from herself. And to her delight he chose the last week in August and the first week in September. The hotels would be quieter then, and their sleep undisturbed by the restless holidaymakers who crammed the hotels from July to the middle of August. Yes, the hotels, like the train, would be comfortably empty.

The train slowed down, and when it stopped the man awoke and heard the rain slapping from the roof of the carriages and strolling down the pane. He yawned and rubbed his eyes.

"Where are we now, John?"

He didn't answer, but with a folded newspaper wiped away some mist on the window and peered out at a dreary platform where rain-soaked advertisements glistened in the lights from the train. He waited for the porter to call out the name of the station, but evidently, the train being almost empty, the porter didn't consider it worthwhile.

He stood up to open the window and his wife ordered him to put on his hat or he'd catch cold. He obeyed her, crammed it on his head, and on opening the window a few drops of rain flew into the compartment. The air was cold against his face, the wet platform deserted except for the guard and porter, and beyond the white arrowpointed palings that marked the end of the platform a red light of a signal glowed in the darkness.

The train hissed, the guard raised his flag and blew his whistle, and as the train slowly passed the end of the platform John saw the name TOOME in large white letters against a black rectangle. For a moment he caught sight of the lights in the village and he continued to lean out, his wife calling to him to close the window at once. But he didn't seem to hear her, and in a minute the train was thundering over the bridge across the river and a solitary light on its bank scribbled its reflection on the cold water.

"John!"

His wife rose, pushed him to the side, and heaved up the

window on its leather strap.

"Do you want to get your neuralgia back again?"

"That was Toome!"

"I don't care if it was Buckingham Palace. You'd no call to stand there so long. Such a miserable place to be gazing out at!"

"I once lived there myself, Margaret," he said quietly.

"No," she said, incredulous, looking across at him.

"Yes, but only for a short spell. It was my first teaching post."

"You never mentioned that before. And how long have we been married — 40 years. Well, well, why did you never tell me you taught there?"

"No reason whatsoever, Margaret. It just didn't occur to me — that's all."

"Come now, John. You must have had some reason. What was it?"

She had suddenly become animated, and she rolled up her knitting and put it inside a magazine beside her.

"There's some reason why you have kept it from me all these years. Come now — out with it like a good man!"

The train whistled sharply and sped on into the night, and the man, no longer interested in his book, closed his eyes, a sad expression aging his face.

His wife leaned forward and touched his knee.

"What made you leave? Was it too lonely for you?"

"It wasn't lonely. I liked it. I loved the fishing and the boating. I used to spend hours on that river we're after crossing."

"And you left because you liked it. That doesn't make sense to me. Come now: why are you so secretive about it? I must know."

"There's nothing to tell, Margaret," he said, giving a sad smile. "It's over 40 years ago since I was there and there's really nothing to tell."

He shrugged his shoulders and leaned back against the seat.

"Were you in love — is that it?"

"I don't think it was that."

Over the long flat stretch of land the train stretched out eagerly, their shoulders jogged and swayed, and the back of the man's head rubbed against the leather headrest. Toome was a long way behind now, the Toome that he had known: its river that unrolled like a web of ice over the falls and then broadened itself into little lakes which he had explored in the long days of a summer gone by.

"John, there's something on your mind about that place and I must know."

"Wouldn't it be better to let the past lie? Please, Margaret, don't go on."

"So you have a past! And all our married years I have never known."

He smiled and remained remote from her, wrapped up in his own secret memory.

She opened her handbag, touched up her face, and for a moment the compartment smelt like a bathroom. They had no children and in spite of her years she wore young clothes to set off a figure that was still attractive. The train would be late arriving in Derry where they would spend the night before setting out for Donegal in the morning.

"And she was handsome — this early sweetheart of yours?"

"I didn't say she was a sweetheart. It's you that has said it."

"I suppose she was handsome if you fell in love with her. Was she a teacher in the same school?"

"She was. She was a few years older than I was and she was the principal. It was a two-roomed school."

"And you proposed to her and she refused and you left in affront."

"No, Margaret, she was already married."

"That makes it more interesting."

"It makes it more sad."

"Why are you so aggravating? You want me to tell what I know nothing of."

"You're making a brave hand at it, I may tell you. . . .

Sure it doesn't matter now. It's all over and done with, some 40 years ago."

"I love you so much I could still be a bit jealous," she said with unconscious irony. "You gave me to understand I was the first girl you ever fell in love with."

"And so you were. And that's the truth."

"How annoying you are this evening! Perhaps you'd like us to return and spend a few days fishing in Toome?"

"No, I wouldn't want that. I have never been back there since I left."

"Is she still alive, this person?"

"No, she died shortly after I left. She died in a boating accident. I read an account of it in the papers. May God have mercy on her."

He glanced away from the interrogating eyes of his wife and looked at the window, at the blurred reflection of his hands, his white hair, and his face.

"She was married to a man years older than herself. When he had drink taken he was rough with her. For some reason she used to confide in me. She felt, I suppose, that I would understand and wouldn't gossip."

He raised a hand and it fell back limply on his knee. "Ah, Margaret, we'll let the long past lie in peace," and he shook his head with a sad gesture.

"So she confided in you because she trusted you. And here we are at this distance on in our lives and you've no wish to confide in me."

"After 40 years I'm not absolved from the promises she made me give her. Time should not erode one's faith and trust. She asked me never to repeat what she had confided in me, and I have never done that."

"I'm not asking you to. But surely you could tell me what she looked like and how she dressed."

He paused and gave a resigned smile.

"She had black hair. It was very black and her eyes were a kind of gray or green. She usually wore a blouse and skirt. Sometimes a yellow blouse or a white or green one and a rose pinned to it."

"For a young lad just fresh from the training college you took good stock of her."

"I see her in memory only. It's your questions that bring it all back."

"But what reason had she to confide in you?"

"I don't know. There were only the two of us all day long in the school. I suppose the poor girl was lonely and had no one else to talk to. It was her confidence in me that made me leave and look out for another school. At lunch-hour when the children were out in the playground and the two of us were drinking tea she used to roll up her sleeve and show me the dark bruises on her arm and the marks of a man's fingers. I had pity for her. I often yearned to put my arm round her to console her."

He shook his head: "There are times, Margaret, when sympathy and pity can be dangerous."

"You'd think, John, you had never heard of the ninth commandment."

"Yes, it was that that made me leave so suddenly. I knew it couldn't go on. . . . When I saw the tears in her eyes it took my whole strength to hold back from lifting her hand and kissing it. . . . And the way she could sing. I used to pause in my work to listen as she led the children through *The Last Rose of Summer*. That song, God knows, is sad enough. But the way she sang it made it the saddest of all songs."

The train whistled and the wheels rocking unevenly over a roadcrossing drowned his voice, and he clasped his hands and drooped them between his knees and fell silent.

"Go on, John, let me know more about this woman. Did you ever kiss her?"

"Never!"

"On your oath?"

"Why do you pester me, Margaret, over an incident that happened 40 years ago? I didn't kiss her, I tell you!"

"But you would have liked to!"

"She was another man's wife. But I was horrified one day on our way home from school to see chalked up on a

stone by the roadside our initials: J.T. loves M.D. Mary
Doyle, you see, was her name. I rubbed the initials off
with a sod I pulled out from the ditch. She laughed and
said: "Aren't they the little divils!" I was more distressed
than she was. But she really loved the children – you could
sense that by the way she spoke to them. Even when she
was angry they sensed her love for them. "How would
you like to see your own mothers' names chalked up on
gateposts?" she said to them. And do you know, Margaret,
they loved and respected her so much it never recurred
again. I was glad of that. If her husband had heard of it or
seen it God knows what he would have thought."

A sudden squall struck the windows, and the rain rattled
against them as hard as pebbles. He sighed, stared at the
swaying leather strap of the window, and went on.

"And yet there was nothing wrong in this friendship of
ours. She it was who opened the school early in the morning, and in the afternoon, because my road led past her
house, she used to ask me to wait for her while she tidied
up the rooms. And the silence then, with the children
gone, was like no other silence I can remember ever since.
The clock, which we couldn't hear all day, tocked on the
wall like the blows of a mallet. And around us were the
empty desks, a boy's torn cap on a peg, and on one wall
the large map of Ireland patched with sticking-plaster. I
can see it all as if it were yesterday. She seemed reluctant to
leave it. It was like home for her, I suppose. And after she
had powdered her face at a little mirror no bigger than a
postcard I held her coat for her as she struggled into it. She
used to smile at that and say in her musical voice: "Oh,
how kind you are." And then on our way home we talked
about books. She liked reading but her husband didn't. I
used to lend her books, but her husband burnt one in one
of his rages and she refused after that to accept another.
That was the kind of her – always thoughtful of others. I
remember one day on going home like this she saw a
child's ribbon in the dust of the road, and, instead of kicking it with her toe, she lifted it. And put it in her handbag,

and in the morning she had it washed and ironed and sought out its owner. Isn't it sad, Margaret, a young wife like that to be drowned in a boating accident?"

"From what you say I gather you were in love with this Doyle woman. Were you?"

"No, I don't think I was. Ah, how could I be and she with a wedding ring on her finger."

"And was she in love with you, do you think?"

"I don't know that either. She never did anything or said anything to express it as far as I know."

"Would you have been shocked if she had done something?"

"I intended for my own soul's sake to leave. She was already married. I used to find myself thinking of her — thinking of her coarse husband and how cruel he was to her, and she so gentle. In the mornings her eyes were often red from crying. But I never let on I noticed it, and then as the day progressed she became happier, younger looking. The presence of the children she loved had that effect on her. She was happiest when she was teaching or when she was drying the children's wet coats by the fire in the school. And how brisk and graceful she was in all her movements."

"Did you ever meet that husband of hers?"

"I did, but I never exchanged many words with him. He had plenty of money but he squandered it foolishly. And to see her coming from Mass on a Sunday, so light on her feet, and he with his coarse laugh, his heaviness, and his bulging waistcoat, I always wondered why she had married him."

"And not you — is that what you thought?"

"Even if she had been single I couldn't have married her. I had nothing to marry on. It took all I earned to pay for my lodgings. But, anyway, the thought of marrying never entered my head. It wasn't that, Margaret: it was just that she was miserable and I wished, in what way I don't know, that she could be happy."

"What did she say when you told her you were

leaving?"

"She was sorry I was going. She pleaded with me to change my mind. And on my last day she gave me a fountain pen and asked me to write to her."

"And you wrote, of course?"

"No, Margaret, She asked me to address the letter to the school."

"A woman can speak for a woman, John. This Doyle one was in love with you! God only knows what would have been the end of the story if you had remained on."

"I may not have met you."

"And would you have regretted that after what you have told me?"

"Margaret, what are you saying? After 40 years you don't doubt my love for you. I never used the pen she gave me. It's the one that's lying in its case in a drawer at home."

"You never used it! I always wondered why you never gave that pen away – you that's so generous, generous to a fault. It was a keepsake, I suppose. That's why you never parted with it. It reminds you of her."

"I once offered it to you. But you wouldn't use it. Its nib was too broad, you said."

"But you could have given it away."

"That never occurred to me. But I'll give it away when we get home. I could give it to some jumble sale or other."

"You're saying that now, because I have caught you out. You may hold on to it for another 40 years for all I care."

He shook his head, leaned forward, and patted the back of her hand. She shrugged away from him and took up her knitting.

"The poor girl hadn't much of a life," he went on. "She died, you might say, before she had begun to live. And her death. . ."

"I don't want to hear another word about her!" and plucking at her needles she upset the ball of wool and it rolled off the seat on to the floor. He retrieved it and left it

100

on her lap.

"Their boat was found capsized. A sudden squall must have struck it. The mainsail, you see, had been tied – it said so in the papers. . . . Her husband's body was washed ashore on one of the islands, but hers was never found . . . never found. . . . It was probably carried down the river in flood and into the sea . . . To think she died like that, and she so young, so light on her feet, and so thoughtful of others. . . . God have mercy on her."

He leant back against the headrest and closed his eyes. His wife continued her knitting with grim speed, the train rattling loosely on its journey through the night.

The White Mare

"WHAT ABOUT Paddy, Kate? He'll be raging if we let him lie any longer and it such a brave morning."

"Och, let him rage away, Martha. He'll know his driver before night if he ploughs the field."

"'Deed that's the truth, and with an old mare that's done and dropping off her feet."

"He'll get sense when it's too late. And to hear him gabbling you'd think he was a young man and not the spent old thorn that he is. But what's the use of talking! Give him a call."

Kate, seated on a stool, blew at the fire with the bellows, blew until the flames were spurting madly in and out between the brown sods. Martha waited until the noise of the blazing fire had ceased, and then rapped loudly at the room door off the kitchen. The knocking was answered by a husky voice.

Paddy was awake, sitting up in the bed, scratching his head with his two hands and blinking at the bare window in the room. His face was bony and unshaven, his moustache grey and straggly. Presently he threw aside the blankets and crawled out backwards on to the cold cement floor. He stood at the window. In the early hours of the morning it had rained, but now it was clear. A high wind had combed the white hair of the sky, and on the bare thorn at the side of the byre shivered swollen buds of rain. Across the cobbled street was his stubble field, bounded on one side by a hedge and a hill, and on the other sides by loose stones. Two newly-ploughed furrows ran down the centre and at the top of them lay his plough with a crow swaying nervously on one of the handles. Last evening when the notion took him he had commenced the ploughing, and today, with the help of God, he'd finish it. He thought of the rough feel of the handles, the throb of the coulter cutting the clay, and the warm sweaty smell from his labouring mare.

With difficulty he stretched himself to his full height, his bony joints creaking, and his lungs filling with the rain-washed air that came through the open window; he drew in great breaths of it, savouring it as he would savour the water from a spring well. As he was about to turn away, the crow rose up suddenly and flew off. At that moment Kate was crossing to the byre, one hand holding a can, and the other a stick. Paddy watched, trying to guess from her movements the kind of temper she was in this morning. But he noted nothing unusual about her. There was the same active walk, the black triangle of shawl dipping down her back, and the grey head with the man's cap on it. To look at her you wouldn't think she was drawing the pension for over six years. No, there wasn't another house in the whole island with three drawing the pension – not another house! We're a great stock and no mistake; a great pity none of us married!

Kate's voice pierced the air as she shouted at a contrary cow. Oh, a good kind woman, but a tartar when you stirred her. He'd hold his tongue this morning till he had the mare tackled and then they could barge away. Anyway what do women know about a man's job, with their milking cows, and feeding hens, and washing clothes? H'm! a field has to be ploughed and it takes a man to plough it.

When he came from the room Kate was just in from milking and Martha moved slowly about the table arranging the mugs and the farls of bread. Paddy stooped and took his clay-caked boots from below the table. He knew by the look of his sisters that he'd have to lace them himself this morning. It always caused him pain to stoop, but what matter, he'd soon be out in the quiet of the fields where no one would say a word to him.

They all sat at the table together, eating silently and with the slow deliberation that comes with the passing years. Now and again as Paddy softened his bread in the tea, Kate would give him a hard little look. It was coming, he knew it. If only they'd keep silent until he had finished. But it was coming; the air was heavy with stifled talk.

"I suppose you'll do half the field today," began Kate.

"'Deed and I'll do it all," he replied with a touch of hardness in his voice knowing he must be firm.

"Now, Paddy, you should get Jamesy's boys over to help you," said Martha pleadingly.

"Them wee buttons of men! I'd have it done while they'd be thinkin' about it. I wouldn't have them about the place again, with their ordering this and ordering that, and their tea after their dinner, and wanting their pipes filled every minute with good tobacco. I can do it all myself with the help of God. All myself!" and with this be brought his mug down sharply on the table.

"If you get another attack of the pains it's us'll have to suffer," put in Kate, "attending you morning, noon and night. Have you lost your wits, man! It's too old you're getting and it'd be better if we sold the mare and let the two bits of fields."

Paddy kept silent; it was better to let them fire away.

"The mare's past her day," Kate continued. "It's rest the poor thing wants an' not pulling a plough with a done man behind it."

"Done, is it? There's work in me yet, and I can turn a furrow as straight as anyone in the island. Done! H'm, I've my work to be doing."

He got up, threw his coat across his shoulder, and strode towards the door. His two sisters watched him go out, nodding their heads. "Ah, but that's a foolish, hard-headed man. There's no fool like an old fool!"

Paddy crossed to the stable and the mare nickered when she heard his foot on the cobbled street. Warm, hay-scented air met him as he opened the door. Against the wall stood the white mare. She cocked her ears and turned her head towards the light. She was big and fat with veins criss-crossing on her legs like dead ivy roots on the limbs of a tree. Her eyes were wet-shining and black, their upper lids fringed with long grey lashes. Paddy stroked her neck and ran his fingers through her yellow-grey mane.

A collar with the straw sticking out of it was soon buckled on, and with chains rattling from her sides he led her through the stone-slap into the field. He looked at the sky, at the sea with its patches of mist, and then smilingly went to this plough. Last evening the coulter was cutting too deep and he now adjusted it, giving it a final smack with the spanner that rang out clear in the morning air. The mare was sniffing the rain-wet grass under the hedge and she raised her head jerkily as he approached, sending a shower of cold drops from the bushes down his neck. He shivered, but spoke kindly to the beast as he led her to be tackled. In a few minutes all was ready, and gripping the handles in God's name, he ordered the horse forward, and his day's work began.

The two sisters eyed him from the window. His back was towards them. Above the small stone fence they could see his bent figure, his navy-blue trousers with a brown patch on the seat of them, his grey shirt sleeves, the tattered back of his waistcoat, and above his shabby hat the sway-ing quarters of the mare.

"Did you ever see such a man since God made you! I declare to goodness he'll kill that mare," said Martha.

"It's himself he'll kill if he's not careful. Let me bold Paddy be laid up after this and 'tis the last field he'll plough, for I'll sell the mare, done beast and all as she is!" replied Kate, pressing her face closer to the window.

Paddy was unaware of their talk. His eyes were on the sock as it slid slowly through the soft earth and pushed the gleaming furrows to the side. He was living his life. What call had he for help! Was it sit by and look at Jamesy's boys ploughing the field, and the plough wobbling to and fro like you'd think they were learning to ride a bicycle.

"Way up, girl," he shouted to the mare, "'way up,

Maggie!" and his veins swelled on his arms as he leant on the handles. The breeze blowing up from the sea, the cold smell of the broken clay, and the soft hizzing noise of the plough, all soothed his mind and stirred him to new life.

As the day advanced the sun rose higher, but there was little heat from it, and frosty vapours still lingered about the rockheads and about the sparse hills. But slowly over the little field horse and plough still moved, moved like timeless creatures of the earth, while alongside, their shadows followed on the clay. Overhead and behind swarmed the gulls, screeching and darting for the worms, their flitting shadows falling coolly on Paddy's neck and on the back of the mare. At the end of the ridge he stopped to take a rest, surveying with pleasure the number of turned furrows, and wondering if his sisters were proud of him now. He looked up at the house: it was low and whitewashed, one end thatched and the other corrugated. There seemed to be no life about it except the smoke from the chimney and a crow plucking at the thatch. Soon it flew off with a few straws hanging from its bill. It's a pity he hadn't the gun now, he'd soon stop that thief; at nesting-time they wouldn't leave a roof above your head. But tomorrow he'd fix them. He spat on his hands and gripped the handles.

At two o'clock he saw Kate making down at the top of the field and he moved to the hedge. She brought him a few empty sacks to sit on; a good kind girl when you took her the right way. She had the real stuff in the eggpunch, too, nothing like it for a working man.

When he had taken his first swig of tea she said quietly, "It's time you were quitting, Paddy."

He must be careful. "Did you see that devil of a crow on the thatch?"

"I didn't, thank God. But I've heard it said that it's the sure sign of a death."

"Did you now?" he replied with a smile. "Isn't that queer, and me always thinking that it was the sign of new life and them nesting?"

106

It's no use trying to frighten him, she thought, no use talking to him; he'll learn his own lesson before morning. Up she got and went off.

"Give the mare a handful of hay and a bucket of water," he called after her.

He lay back, smoking his pipe at his ease, enjoying the look of the ribbed field and the familiar scene. To his right over the stone fence lay the bony rocks stretching their lanky legs into the sea; and now and again he could hear the hard rattle of the pebbles being sucked into the gullet of the waves. Opposite on a jutting headland rose the white column of the East Lighthouse, as lonely-looking as ever. There never was much stir on this side of the island anyway. It was a mile or more from the quay where the little sailing boats went twice a week to Ballycastle. But what little there was of land was good. As he looked down at the moist clay, pressing nail-marks in it with his toe, he pitied the people in the Lower End with their shingly fields and stunted crops. How the news would travel to them tonight about his ploughing! Every mouthful of talk would be about him and the old white mare. He puffed at his pipe vigorously and a sweet smile came over his wrinkled face. Then the shouts of the children coming from school made him aware of the passing time.

He must get up now for the sun would set early. He knocked out his pipe on the heel of his boot. When he made to rise he felt stiff in the shoulders, and a needle of pain jagged one of his legs making him give a silly little laugh. It's a bad thing to sit too long and the day flying. He walked awkwardly over to Maggie, and presently they were going slowly over the field again. The yellow-green bands at each side of the dark clay grew narrower and narrower as each new furrow was turned. Soon they would disappear. The sky was clear and the sun falling; the daylight might hold till he had finished.

The coulter crunched on a piece of delph and its white chips were mosaiced on the clay. "Man alive, but them's the careless women," he said aloud. "If the mare cut her

107

feet there'd be a quare how-d'ye-do!" At that moment Kate came out to the stone fence and gathered clothes that had been drying. She stood with one hand on her cheek, looking at the slow, almost imperceptible, movement of the plough. She turned, shooshed the hens from her feet, and went in slamming the door behind her.

Over the rock heads the sun was setting, flushing the clay with gold, and burnishing the mould-board and the buckles on the horse. Two more furrows and the work was done. He paused for a rest, and straightened himself with difficulty. His back ached and his head throbbed, but what he saw was soothing. On the side of a hill his three sheep were haloed in gold and their long shadows sloped away from them. It was a grand sight, praise be to God, a grand sight! He bent to the plough again, his legs feeling thick and heavy. "Go on, Maggie!" he ordered. "Two more furrows and we're done."

The words whipped him to a new effort and he became light with excitement. One by one the gulls flew off and the western sky burned red. A cold breeze sharp with the smell of salt breathed in the furrows. And then he was finished; the furrows as straight as loom-threads and not a bit of ground missed. A great piece of work, thanks be to God; a great bit of work for an old man and an old mare. He put on his coat and unyoked her. She felt light and airy as he led her by the head across the cobbles. Gently he took the collar from her, the hot vapour rising into the chilled air, and with a dry sack wiped her sides and legs and neck. A great worker; none better in the whole island. He stroked her between the ears and smiled at the way she coaxingly tossed her head. He put her in the stable; later on he'd be back with a bucket of warm mash.

It was semi-dark when he turned his back on the stable and saw the orange rectangle of light in the kitchen window. It was cold, and he shivered and shrugged his shoulders as he stood listening at the door.

In the kitchen it was warm and bright. The turf was piled high, and Martha and Kate sat on opposite sides of

108

the hearth, Kate knitting and Martha peeling potatoes. He drew a chair to the fire and sat down between them in silence. The needles clicked rapidly, and now and then a potato plopped into the bucket. He must get out his pipe; a nice way to receive a man after a day's ploughing. The needles stopped clicking and Kate put her hands on her lap and stared at him from behind her silver-rimmed spectacles. Paddy took no notice as he went slowly on cutting his plug and grinding it between his palms. Then he spat in the fire, and Kate retorted by prodding the sods with her toe, sending sparks up the chimney. The spit hissed in the strained silence. The kettle sang and he rose to feed the mare.

"Just leave that kettle alone, Mister MacNeil," said Martha.

"The mare has to be fed!"

"It's little you care about the poor dumb beast, and you out killing yourself and her, when it would suit you better to be in peeling these spuds."

"It's little you do in the house but make the few bits of meals, and it's time you were stirring yourself and getting a hard-worked man a good supper."

"If you're hard-worked, who's to blame, I ask you?" flared Kate.

He was done for now. He could always manage Martha; if he raised his voice it was the end of her. But Kate – he feared her though he wouldn't admit it to himself.

"Do you hear me, Paddy MacNeil? Who's to blame? Time and again we have told you to let the fields and have sense. But no; me bold boy must be up and leppin' about like a wild thing. And what'll the women in island be talking about, I ask you? Ah! well we know what they'll be saying. "It's a shame that Paddy MacNeil's mean old sisters wouldn't hire a man to work the land. There they have poor Paddy and his seventy years, out in the cold of March ploughing with the old white mare. And the three of them getting the pension. I always knew there was a mean streak in them MacNeils." That's what they'll be saying, well we know it!"

"Talk sense, Kate, talk sense. Don't I know what they'll be saying. They'll be putting me up as an example to all and sundry. And ..."

"But mark my words," interrupted Kate, shaking a needle at him, "if you're laid up after this you can attend to your pains yourself. I'm sick, sore and tired plastering and rubbing your shoulder and dancing attendance on you, and God knows I'm not able. I'm a done old woman myself, slaving from morning to night and little thanks I get for it." Her voice quavered; crying she'll be next. It was best to keep silent.

"Get him his supper, Martha, till we get to bed — another day like this and I'm fit for nothing." She lifted her hands from her lap and the needles clicked slowly, listlessly.

In silence he took his supper. He was getting tired of these rows. When he had finished he went out with a bucket of warm mash for the mare. He felt very weary and sleepy, but the cold night braced him a little. The moon was up and the cobbles shone blue-white like the scales of a salmon. Maggie stirred when she heard the rasping handle of the bucket.

He closed the half-door of the stable, lit the candle, and sat on an upturned tub to watch the mare feeding. It was very still and she fed noisily, lifting her head now and again, the bran dripping from her mouth. Above the top of the door he could see the night-sky, the corrugated roof of the house, and the ash tree with its bare twigs shining in the moon. A little breeze blew its wavering pattern on the roof, and looking at it he thought of the gulls on the clay and the cool rush of their wings above his head. He shivered, and got up and closed the top half of the door. It was very still now; the mare had stopped feeding, her tail swished gently, and the warm hay glowed in the candlelight. There was great peace and comfort here. Under the closed door stole the night-wind, the bits of straw around the threshold rising gently and falling back again. A mouse came out from under the manger, rustled towards the bucket blinking its little eyes at the creature on the tub. Paddy squirted a spit at it and smiled at the way it raced off. He looked at the mare, watching slight tremors passing down her limbs. He got up, stroked her silky neck and scratched her between the ears. Then he gave her fresh hay and went out.

It was very peaceful with the moon shining on the fields and the sea. He wondered if his sisters were in bed. He hesitated at the stone fence looking at the cold darkness of the field and the bits of broken crockery catching the moonlight. Through the night there came to him clear and distinct the throb, throb of a ship's engine far out at sea. He held his breath to listen to it and then he saw its two un-steady mastlights, rounding the headland and moving like stars through the darkness. It made him sad to look at it and he sighed as he turned towards the house. He sniffed the air like a spaniel; there'd be rain before long; it would do a world of good now that the field was ploughed.

His sisters were in bed; the lamp was lowered and the ashes stirred. He quenched the lamp and went up to his room. The moonlight shone in the window so he needn't bother with a candle. He knelt on a chair to say his prayers; he'd make them short tonight, for he was tired, very tired. But his people couldn't be left out. The prayers came slowly. His mind wandered. The golden shaft of the lighthouse swept into the room, mysteriously and quietly — light — dark — light — dark. For years he had watched that light, and years after when he'd be dead and gone it would still flash, and there'd be no son or daughter to say a prayer for him. It's a stupid thing for a man not to get married and have children to pray for him; a stupid thing indeed! It was strange to be associating death with a lighthouse in the night, but in some way that thought had come to him now that he was old, and he knew that it would always come. He didn't stop to examine it. He got up and sat on the chair, fumbling at his coat.

He climbed into bed, the straw mattress rustling with his

weight. He lay thinking of his day's work, waiting for sleep to fall upon him. He closed his eyes, but somehow sleep wouldn't come. The tiredness was wearing off him. He'd smoke for awhile, that would ease his mind. He was thinking too much; thinking kills sleep. The moonlight left the room and it became coldly dark. He stretched out his hand, groping for his pipe and matches. The effort shot a pain through his legs and he stifled a groan. At the other side of the wooden partition Kate and Martha heard him, but didn't speak. They lay listening to his movements. Then they heard the rasp of the match on the emery, heard him puffing at the pipe, and saw in their minds its warm glow in the cold darkness. There would be a long interval of silence, then the creak of his bed, and another muffled groan.

"Do you hear him?" whispered Kate. "We're going to have another time of it with him. He has himself killed. But this is the last of it!"

"He'll be harrowing the field next," said Martha.

"Harrow he will not. Tomorrow, send a note to the horse-dealer in Ballycastle."

"Are you going to sell the mare, Kate?" Martha asked incredulously.

"Indeed I am. There's no sense left in that man's head while she's about."

"Will you tell Paddy?"

"I'll tell him when she's sold, and that's time enough. So off with the note first thing in the morning."

A handful of rain scattered itself on the tin roof above their heads. For awhile there was silence – deep and dark and listening. Then with a tree-like swish the rain fell, fell without ceasing, filling the room with cold streaks of noise.

Paddy lay listening to its hard pattering. He thought of the broken field soaking in the rain, and the disturbed creatures seeking shelter under the sod, rushing about with weakly legs clambering for a new home, while down in the sea the fish would be hiding in its brown tangled lair disturbed by no plough. It's strange the difference between the creatures; all the strange work of God, the God that knows all. Louder and louder fell the rain. "It's well the mare's in that night," he said to himself, "and it's well the field's ploughed." He pictured the sheep pressing into the wet rocks for shelter, and the rabbits scuttling to their holes. Then he wondered if he had closed the stable door; it was foolish to think that way; he closed it, of course he closed it. His thoughts wouldn't lie still. The crow on the thatch flew into his mind. He'd see to that villain in the morning and put a few pickles in her tail. Some day he'd have the whole house corrugated. Maybe now the kitchen'd be flooded. He was about to get up, when the rain suddenly ceased. It eased his mind, and listening now to the drip-drop of water from the eaves, he slipped into sleep.

But in the morning he didn't get up. His shoulders, arms and legs were stiff and painful. Martha brought him his breakfast, and it was a very subdued man that she saw.

"Give me a lift up, Martha, on the pillows. That's a good girl. Aisy now, aisy!" he said in a slow, pained voice.

"Do you feel bad, Paddy?"

"Bravely, Martha, bravely. There's a wee pain across me shoulder, maybe you'd give it a rub. I'll be all right now when I get a rest."

"You took too much out of yourself for one day."

"I know, I know! But it'd take any other man three days to do the same field. Listen, Martha, put the mare out on the side of the hill; a canter round will do her a world of good."

And so the first day wore on with his limbs aching, Martha coming to attend him, or Kate coming to counsel him. But from his bed he could see the mare clear as a white rock on the face of the hill, and it heartened him to watch her long tail busily swishing. On the bed beside him was his stick and on the floor a battered biscuit tin. Hour after hour he struck the tin with his stick when he wanted something – matches, tobacco, a drink, or his shoulder rubbed. And glad he was if Martha answered his knocking.

Two days passed in this way, and on the morning of the third the boat with the dealer was due. Time and again Martha went out on a hill at the back of the house, scanning the sea for the boat. At last she saw it and hurried to Kate with the news. Kate made a big bowl of warm punch and brought it to Paddy.

"How do you feel this morning?" she said when she entered the room.

"A lot aisier, thank God, a lot aisier."

"Take this now and turn in and sleep. It'll do you good."

Paddy took the warm bowl in his two hands, sipping slowly, and giving an odd cough as the strong whisky caught his breath. Whenever he paused his eyes were on the window watching the mare on the hillside, and when he had finished, he sighed and lay back happily. His body felt deliciously warm and he smiled sweetly. Poor Kate; he misjudged her; she has a heart of corn and means well. Warm eddies of air flowed slowly through his head, stealing into every corner, filling him with a thoughtless ecstasy, and closing his eyes in sleep.

As he slept the dealer came, and the mare was sold. When he awakened he felt a queer emptiness in the room, as if something had been taken from it. Instinctively he turned to the window and looked out. The mare was nowhere to be seen and the stone-slap had been tumbled. He seized his stick and battered impatiently on the biscuit tin. He was about to get out of bed when Kate came into the room.

"The mare has got out of the field!"

"She has that and what's more she'll never set foot in it again."

He waited, waited to hear the worst, that she was sick or had broken a leg.

"The dealer was her an hour ago and I sold her, and, let me tell you, I got a good penny for her," she added a little proudly.

His anger roused him, and he stared at his sister, his eyes fiercely bright and his mouth open. Catching the rail of the bed he raised himself up and glared at her again.

"Lie down, Paddy, like a good man and quieten yourself. Sure we did it for your own good," she said, trying to make light of it, and fixing the clothes up around his chest. "What was she but a poor bit of a beast dying with age? And a good bargain we made."

"Bargain, is it? And me after rearing her since she was a wee foal . . . No; he'll not get her, I tell you! He'll not get her!"

"For the love of God, man, have sense, have reason!"

But he wasn't listening, he threw back the clothes and reached for his trousers. He brushed her aside with his arm, and his hands trembled as he put on his boots. He seized his stick and made for the door. They tried to stop him and he raised his stick to them. "Don't meddle with me or I'll give you a belt with this!"

He was out, taking the short-cut down by the back of the house, across the hills that led to the quay. He might be in time; they'd hardly have her in the boat yet. Stones in the gaps fell with a crash behind him and he didn't stop to build them up, not caring where sheep strayed or cattle either. His eyes were fixed on the sea, on the mainland where Maggie was going. His heart hammered wildly, hammered with sharp stinging pains, and he had to halt to ease himself.

He thought of his beast, the poor beast that hated noise and fuss, standing nervous on the pier with a rope tied round her four legs. Gradually the rope would tighten, and she would topple with a thud on the uneven stones while the boys around would cheer. It was always a sight for the young, this shipping of beasts in the little sailing boats. The thought maddened him. His breath wheezed and he licked his dry, salty lips.

And soon he came on to the road that swept in a half circle to the quay. He saw the boat and an oar sticking over the side. He wouldn't have time to go round. Below him jutted a neck of rock near which the boat would pass on her journey out. He might be able to hail them.

He splashed his way through shallow sea-pools on to the rock, scrambled over its mane of wet seaweed, until he reached the furthest point. Sweat was streaming below his hat and he trembled weakly as he saw the black nose of the boat coming towards him. He saw the curling froth below her bow, the bending backs of the men, and heard the wooden thump of the oars. Nearer it came, gathering speed. A large wave tilted the boat and he saw the white side of his mare, lying motionless between the beams. They were opposite him now, a hundred yards from him. He raised his stick and called, but he seemed to have lost his voice. He waved and called again, his voice sounding strange and weak. The man in the stern waved back as he would to a child. The boat passed the rock, leaving a wedge of calm water in her wake. The noise of the oars stopped and the sail filled in the breeze. For a long time he looked at the receding boat, his spirit draining from him. A wave washed up the rock, frothing at his feet, and he turned wearily away, going slowly back the road that led home.

A Half-Crown

BEFORE DUSK, nine or ten over-excited boys were going round the houses in the street begging stuff for their annual Fifteenth-of-August bonfire. Anything at all would do they boldly announced to the neighbours: old boxes, oilcloth, newspapers, broken chairs, and thrown-out mattresses – and they would point to the middle of the street where a miscellaneous heap of these articles was stacked as high as the arms of the lamp-post. In two hours time when the blue darkness of summer would slowly descend upon the street they would blacken or paint their faces, wear bowler hats and old garments, and sprinkling the heap with paraffin they would accompany the first bursts of flame by singing *The Soldiers' Song*: then they would dance round the ring of flame, shouting and laughing, letting off fireworks, while their mothers and fathers, gathered in an outer circle, would encourage their wild Indian antics.

Now as they pressed round the doors they cheered when anything was handed out to them, and as they carried these objects shoulder-high or dragged them to the spreading pile they would cheer again and dash off once more, promising themselves that this would be the greatest bonfire that was ever seen in their district. Presently they reached the end-house of the street where an old woman lived alone; here they halted in a compact group, whispering and debating among themselves whether to rap the door or turn back. They feared this woman, for she was always muttering mysteriously to herself and seldom opened her door except to threaten them with the police or with a stick whenever they came to play handball against the gable of her house. But tonight their tense feelings had numbed their fear of her, and the biggest boy among them struck his chest stoutly and volunteered to knock the door even if no one else would venture with him. He stepped out from the group and rapped the door with flourishing importance. There was no answer to his knock though a few of the smaller boys standing safely out from the door began to whisper: "She's staring out at us. . . . She's upstairs. . . . I seen the curtains moving. . . . She's in. . . . I seen her with my own two eyes."

The door was rapped again, and this time the biggest boy hearing the shuffle of feet in the hallway, edged away from the door. The door was slowly opened, and before they could see her they chorused out: "Could you please give us something for the bonfire?" She smiled at them and the smile drew their confidence, and they all crowded closer, each pleading with her to give them something.

"All right," she said. "Go round to the back-door and I'll give you something."

They moved round dubiously. "Maybe it's a bucket of water she'll throw round us!" the biggest said; and they all laughed – a laugh that was strange and low-pitched.

They heard the stiff bolt of the back-door scringing as she levered it back.

"There – would that be of any use for your bonfire?" she said, pointing to a black sofa that was mottled with mildew and propped up with bricks to support a missing leg. They buzzed round it where it lay under a sideless shelter, and in a few minutes had it hauled through the door and out to the gable-end where they turned it over and examined it. Two coils of spring were bursting through the rust-stained sacking and a boy ripped them out, tied them to his feet with string and began to walk round, shouting: "The latest in stilts, boys! A walking jack-in-the-box!"

"Aw, give us a pair," the young ones whined as the stuffing and springs were torn out of the sofa by the bigger boys. It was then that a half-crown jingled on the ground and one boy pounced on it.

"Finder is keeper!" he said and tried to put it in his pocket.

"No, you won't!"

"It's mine. I found it. I seen it first."

"It's the oul' woman's," they shouted, balked into honesty.

"Come on and we'll give it back to her," the leader said.

"That's right! That's fair! Give it back to her!" they all chanted except the one who held the coin in his fist.

"All right," he agreed dolefully, and they threw their caps in the air and went back with him to the old woman. They told her they found a half-crown in the lining of the sofa.

"Are you sure it's not your own?" she said.

"Naw, where'd we get a half-crown?"

She took the silver coin in her hand, turned it over, and stared at a small hole near the rim. She went out with them to the old sofa and they pointed to the exact place where the coin had fallen. For a moment she stood without speaking and the boy who had the springs tied to his feet, disengaged them shyly, fearful that he had done something that had annoyed her.

"Keep the half-crown and buy sweets for yourselves," she said quietly. They gave a cheer of delight, hoisted the sofa on their shoulders like a coffin and marched off singing *The Boys of Wexford*.

As she stared after them a long sigh broke from her. She was trembling and she went into the house and sat near the fire in the kitchen. She gripped the arms of the rocking-chair to steady herself, and over and over again she said aloud: "Calm yourself! Calm yourself!" for her mind was leaping back to a night, fifteen years ago, when her only son went to that door, never to come back. Where he went to she didn't know, and whether he was alive or dead she might never know. She had grown tired watching for the postman, and though letters came regularly from her two married daughters the letter she prayed for, never came.

Her tears flowed freely – tears of remorse and of baffled pity. One thing she now knew; she knew it now – her son had not lied to her when he swore he didn't steal his sister's half-crown. It was good to know that, though her home was broken on account of it and she was alone and had nobody to tell it to.

She shrugged her shoulders and poked up the fire. She could believe him now: believe him with all her heart and without forcing herself to believe. And if only he'd step into the kitchen this very moment, she'd go down on her knees and ask his forgiveness.

She sighed, put a hand to her forehead, and spoke aloud to herself: "Ah, son, wherever you are this day, be you alive or dead, I believe you. You didn't steal the half-crown. It was lying hid in the sofa all these years. That's where it was – in the old sofa!" She swayed to and fro, and the rocking-chair creaked under her weight.

God in Heaven, she never could forget that night he quarrelled with her and left the house. More than anything else she thought about it. And not a morning passed and not an evening passed but she prayed with all her might that he'd come back.

But why hadn't she believed him when he swore he didn't touch the half-crown? Oh, maybe she'd have done it if only her daughters hadn't screeched and cried out against him. And the language they used that night – it was scandalous! Language they picked up in the factory and the mills – they didn't hear it from her: at least she could say that for herself.

"But wait a minute, wait a minute," she said aloud to her own memory. "Wait a minute till I get it all clear again."

It was in the evening it all happened. And the first in from work that evening was Mary and Anne. And what did they do first: they tidied themselves at the jar-tub in the scullery while I got their tea ready. They were in good form the pair of them. They were singing and they were laughing, and each was urging the other to hurry for they were going to see a picture in the First House of "The Clonard".

"And where are you getting the money from?" I asked them.

"We have it ourselves. We've a half-crown. There it is and there's a hole in it for luck."

It was Mary who took the half-crown from her apron pocket: the black shiny apron she used at work — and she laid the half-crown on the mantelpiece beside the clock. It was beside the clock she left it, for I remember when they discovered it was gone they lifted up the clock and shook it, and they lifted up the two brass candlesticks and the tea-canister and the two delph dogs. But it wasn't there; it wasn't anywhere about the kitchen.

But wait now, wait now, I'm going too quick. What happened after they left the half-crown on the mantelpiece? Let me see: I made their tea and I poured it out for them and sat on the sofa watching them. I didn't lift the half-crown; I didn't touch it; I didn't look at it to see the wee hole that was in it for luck. I am sure of that. I knew it was there on the mantelpiece for I heard it click the time Mary planted it down beside the clock. And as I sat on the sofa I heard Jimmy's rat-tat at the door. He came in and he, too, was in the best of form. I remember he was in no hurry out. He was a good boy, Jimmy; he loved a book and he wasn't using the house as a lodging-house like them two straps of girls. They were always on the go — two runners if ever there were ones: two clips of daughters that didn't give a straw whether I was left alone one night or two nights or every night. No, they didn't give a rap about me, but poor Jimmy did.

But I'm wandering again. Where was I? I was where Jimmy came in. He took off his oily linens and poured hot water into a basin in the scullery for him to wash himself with. Nothing could take the oily grease off him like hot water and washing-soda. The oily smell of his clothes was like the oil I used in the sewing-machine that made me sick. I remember he was singing. He used to sing one thing and another that he picked up at his work. But he always sang: *My feet are here on Broadway this blessed harvest morn* — he knew I liked that, for he knew that I was reared in a country parish that seen many a decent girl and boy set off for America.

My mind's wandering on me again. Where was I? Yes, Jimmy washed himself in the scullery and I boiled a fresh egg for his tea. He didn't want any hot water for shaving for he said he wasn't going out. Merciful God, he wasn't going out! He said he was in no hurry for his tea and he'd wait till Mary and Anne had got theirs. He lay on the sofa — his shirt was open at the neck and his face was red and fresh after the good washing he gave himself. I handed him his slippers that I had warming at the side of the hob and I lifted his working shoes to give them a brush or two for the morning. And then when the girls had finished their tea I cleared away the soiled dishes and asked Jimmy to sit over to the table. The girls were brushing their hair at that looking-glass on the wall.

"Where are you set for, the night? You're in a hell of a hurry," Jimmy said.

"The pictures."

"Who's taking you?"

"We're taking ourselves."

"You must have plenty of spondulics when you can go every night in the week to the damned pictures."

"It's our own money. We never see much of yours. You'd never ask us to the pictures — not if you got in for nothing."

"I'd like my job taking you two anywhere."

I disremember rightly what happened after that but I think Mary sat on the sofa and Anne went upstairs for her good coat from the back of the door and I went out to the yard for a shovel of coal. That coal was always damp and I mind the way it hissed on the fire and Jimmy saying he must put sides on that shelter in the yard. It was then that I seen Mary standing on the fender and looking on the mantelpiece and asking if I saw her half-crown.

"It's there beside the clock where you left it," I said.

"It's not."

She stood on a chair and lifted up the clock and looked under it and behind it.

"Did you take it, Mother?"

"I didn't lay a finger on it."

Anne came into the kitchen with her good coat on, ready for the road. I don't know what happened next for my mind is all in a tangle. But I remember the both of them talking at once and asking Jimmy to fork up the half-crown and not be codding any more and keeping them late. Jimmy laughed and I thought by the way he laughed he was fooling them and hiding the money on them. They eyed the time by the clock and they shouted at him to stop the bloody nonsense and give them the half-crown and not keep them late.

"I didn't touch it I tell you," he said.

"You're a liar!" they shouted back at him, and I told them to hush and not let the next-door neighbour hear them fighting.

"You're a liar!" Mary shouted again, for she had a she-devil's temper when you roused her. She tapped her foot on the floor and glared at him.

"You put your collar-stud on the mantelpiece when you were going to wash," she said. "The stud's there for all to see but the half-crown's not!"

Jimmy put down his cup and smiled at her.

"Give it to them, son, if you have it, and don't keep them late," I said.

"Didn't I tell you I never seen it!"

"You're a thief!" Mary screeched. "That's what you are – a bloody thief!"

Jimmy jumped up from the table then and struck her, for I remember Mary crying and expressions flying from her mouth that'd have shamed any decent-minded girl. Oh, them factories and warerooms is no place, let me tell you, to rear your children in: they hear every filth and it sticks in their minds like grease in an old pot. I done my best to quieten them and I told Jimmy he done wrong to hit her.

"I'll do it again if she calls me a thief!"

"You're a coward," Anne said. "Only a coward would strike a girl."

Jimmy sat down again and I knew by the way his cup rattled on the saucer that he was sorry for what he'd done. I looked under the square of linoleum near the fender for the half-crown, and I looked under the sofa, and I took the tongs and searched in the ashes in the grate but I couldn't find it.

"It's no use looking for it," Anne said. "That playboy has it well hid. Make him give it up to us."

"Jimmy, son," I said, "give them the half-crown. It didn't fly off the mantelpiece by itself."

He stared at me and I'll remember that look to my dying day.

"So you don't believe me either. As sure as there's a God above me I didn't take it."

"You needn't bring God into it," I said, for I was annoyed at hearing him swear like that.

"He'd damn his soul over the head of it," Mary shouted.

I don't know what made me do it, but I remember asking Jimmy to turn out his pockets. Ah, God forgive me for asking him to do the like of that! Sure I should have known he hadn't it after he swore he hadn't.

He got up from that side of the table near the looking-glass and he pushed in his chair slowly – I'll never forget that! He went upstairs to his room and after five or six minutes of rummaging and rumbling he came down the stairs and banged the front door on his way out.

"Under God where is he away to?" I said.

"He's away to spend it," Mary jeered.

I went upstairs to his room and I saw nothing behind the back of the door only a bare coat-hanger, and on my way downstairs I noticed his heavy overcoat was gone from the rack in the hall.

"He's left us," I said.

"He'd be good riddance if he did," Mary said.

"He'll come back," I said, "Jimmy's not the kind of boy that'd run away from home."

Little did I know then, and it fifteen years ago, that he wouldn't come back. Yes, indeed, fifteen long and lonesome years.

She rocked herself gently on the chair and began to cry. Then she dried her eyes in her apron and looked slowly round the cheerless kitchen. There was no light in it except the dull glow of the fire, and in the window space a blue sky was sprinkled with stars.

She shuddered and as she leaned forward to lever up the coal in the grate there was a loud knock at the door that startled her. She rested the poker on the hob and waited. The knock came again. She hoisted herself from the chair, and as she walked down the hallway she heard the impatient shuffle of feet outside. She opened the door slowly and a few boys shouted breathlessly at her: "Hurry up, Missus, we're going to light the bonfire now."

She hesitated for a moment in the hallway, and then pulling a shawl over her shoulders she made her way down to the middle of the street. The street lamps were in darkness and there was nothing but the tapping of feet, the mumble of unseen crowds, and a warm smell of paraffin. Boys, strangely dressed and their faces painted, were screaming like Indians and applying torches of paper to the heap of stuff they had collected. Then in a few minutes there came a hurl and burl of flame, a crackling of sticks, and a cheer from the crowd that drowned the noises of the fire. The flames lit up the faces and hands of the crowd and tilted their shadows on the red-brick houses. Flames like flowing water sped over the old sofa, a bicycle tyre was a ring of flame, leafy branches of trees hissed in the heat, and a rubber boot entangled among the twigs was furred with flame and dripped drops of fire from its writhing toe.

The old woman moved out from the heat with its sickening smell of paraffin, and stood in the cooler shadows cast by the outer ring of swaying onlookers. No one noticed her. They began to sing *Kevin Barry*, and when the singing came to an end a loud cheer volleyed above the houses, squibs banged in the fire, and a rocket gushed into the sky trailing behind it an arc of bright blue stars. The noise frightened the old woman and she hurried away from it. Near her home she looked back and saw the smoke lighted up by the fire and heard an accordion playing an Irish reel. She didn't stop to listen to it. She went into the house and halting in the hallway she clasped her hands and cried: "Mother of God, are you listening to me? Wherever Jimmy is this night tell him that I believe him — tell him that from me!"

Evening in Winter

CHARLEY WAS six at the time, or maybe seven. His Mammie was beside him in a white apron, her hands on her lap doing nothing. His Daddy lay stretched in sleep on the sofa. Sunday evening was always quiet. The fire-glow filled the room. It glowed redly on Charley's knees and face, glinted on the fender, and threw shadows on the ceiling and the red-tiled floor. It was nice to be sitting alone with your Daddy and Mammie, feeling the heat on your knees, and listening to the kettle singing, and ashes falling in the grate. In the fire you could see animals and sometimes men and sometimes ships, and when your eyes got sticky you could just sit and look at nothing.

Suddenly the milkman knocked and Charley jumped. His Mammie went into the scullery for the white jug. His Daddy wakened and took out his big watch in the fire-glow.

"Boys-o-boys!" he said. "Is it that time?"

He got up and was on his feet when Mammie came back and placed the jug on the clean table. Daddy was very tall standing on the floor, with the fire winking on his watch-chain and his face all red and rosy.

"Do you think you'll go this evening?" Mammie said.

"Indeed I will," said Daddy.

"Maybe you'd take Charley with you, he never gets anywhere."

So Charley was going out with his Daddy, out at night when the lamps would be lit and all other wee boys in bed.

His mother put on his little round hat with the elastic that nipped him under the chin, and when he was going out the front door she stopped and kissed him.

"Say a prayer for your Mammie who has to stay at home," she said.

And now they were walking down the street. He felt big to be out so late with the sky dark and the lamps lit. The snow had fallen. It wasn't deep snow, but it covered the ground, and lines of it lay on the black garden railings, and on the arms of the lamp-posts. The milkman's cart was near a lamp and its brass fittings shone and steam came from the horse's nose. The milkman said to his Daddy, "A cold evening that," and steam came from his mouth, too. Then his cans rattled. The cart moved on in front and the wheels began to unwind black ribbons on the snow.

They walked out of the street on to the road, on to the road where the trams ran. Charley put his hand in his Daddy's pocket and it was lovely and warm. Up in the sky it was black, as black as ink, and far away was the moon which Mammie called God's lamp, and stars were round it like little candle lights.

A tram passed, groaning up the hill where they were walking. Sparks, green ones and red ones and blue ones, crackled from the trolley, but the tram went on and slithered out of sight. And now there was nothing on the road only the snow and the black lines where the trams ran. Up above were the telephone wires covered with crumbs of snow, but the trolley wires were all dark. Presently they lit up with gold light and soon a black motor-car came slushing down the hill, covered with snow. Then it was very quiet.

Other people, big people all in black, were out and most of them were walking in the same direction as Charley and his Daddy. They passed shops, the sweetshop with Mrs. Dempsey standing at the door.

"Good-night, Mister Conor," she said. His Daddy raised his hat, the hard hat that he wore on Sundays.

"Do you know Missus Dempsey, Daddy?"

"I do, son."

"I know her; that's where I buy when I've pennies." But

his Daddy looked in front with the steam coming out of his mouth.

They passed policemen standing in doorways, stamping their feet, the policemen who chased you for playing football in the streets. But Charley wasn't afraid now, he was walking with his hand clutched tightly in his Daddy's – inside the big warm pocket.

After a while they came to the chapel. All the people seemed to be going to the chapel. It was dark outside, but a man stood in a lighted porch holding a wooden plate, and on the plate Charley's father put pennies.

Inside it was warm and bright. You could smell the heat as you walked up the aisle. His Daddy's boots squeaked and that was a sign they weren't paid for. They went into a seat up near the altar and his father knelt down with a white handkerchief spread under his knees. Charley sat with his legs swinging to and fro. At the sides were windows, and when tram-cars passed you could see lightning and blue diamonds and red diamonds.

Someone came in at the end of their seat and Charley and his Daddy had to move up. It wasn't nice for people to move you into a cold place, when you had the seat warmed.

A priest came out. Charley could answer the prayers like the rest and he felt very big. After a long time they stood up to sing and Charley turned round to look at the organ-man away high up at the back of the Church. The organ looked like big, hot-pipes. At the end of the hymn he said:

"Are we going home now, Daddy?"

"S-s-sh," his Daddy said softly.

"Well, when are we going home?"

His Daddy didn't answer. Charley lifted the little round hat and began crackling the elastic and putting it in his mouth. His Daddy told him to sit at peace.

A priest came into the pulpit. He talked about lightning, and he said that the sun would be dark, and that the stars would fall from Heaven. He talked for a long, long time, but Charley fell asleep. After a while his father caught him

by the arm and with difficulty he opened his eyes. A big
boy with a long taper was lighting rows of candles and
Charley began to count them. One candle didn't light at
first, and he had to come back and touch it a few times.
Soon the altar was all lit up and here and there were
bunches of flowers. Dim lights shone from the brass bell
that stood on the altar steps like a big gold mushroom.

The organ began playing softly, very softly, and
Charley turned to see what was wrong. A woman in the
seat behind him was praying, her lips moving in a low
whistle. He watched the moving lips and then they stopped suddenly. The woman was making a face at him and
he turned and sat closer to his Daddy.

He filled his mind with everything, everything to tell his
big brothers and sisters. There were boys with fat brass
candlesticks and a priest with a golden cloak that sparkled
with lights. God was on the altar, too, behind a little glass
window with gold spikes all around it. A boy was shaking
a silver thing like a lamp and smoke came out of it, nice-
smelling smoke, and if you shut your eyes it made a noise
like nails in a tin.

The organ began to growl and people to sing. Charley
put his fingers to the flaps of his ears. You could hear the
noise very small, then it would get big like thunder, and if
you moved your fingers in and out the noise would go ziz-
zaz and a ah-aha-aaah! But it soon stopped. People bowed
their heads and Daddy bowed his head too. Charley
covered his eyes with his hands, but looked through his
fingers to see what was going on. Someone coughed far,
far away. Someone else coughed. Then it became so still
you could hear your heart thumping.

The bell on the altar rang once. His Daddy whispered
something to himself, and when the bell rang again
Charley heard him say, "My Lord and my God!" He
thought of his Mammie and he told God to love his Mammie who had to stay at home. He closed his eyes and he
saw her in a snowy apron, the white jug on the table and
he wondered if she would have cake for his tea, cake with

currants in it.

And now they were going home, out into the cold air, and on to the road where the trams ran.

His big brothers and sisters were in when he got home. They were taking tea and there was cake with currants in it on the table. They asked him questions, but laughed at his answers, so he just sat and ate his cake. But his Mammie was good and he told her that when the bell rang Daddy said, "My Lord and my God!" But his Daddy didn't laugh at this. He just said, "That child is dying with sleep, he should be in bed."

So his Mammie brought him to bed, up to the bedroom where the red-lamp was, the red-lamp that burned like a tulip's head before a picture of Holy God. He knelt and said his prayers on the cold, oilcloth floor. In bed it was cold, too, colder that the seat in the chapel. But it soon got warm; and he thought of the organ in his ears . . . the candle that wouldn't light . . . the tram that went up the hill with lights crackling from the trolley . . . and stars falling . . . falling. . . .

The Mother

SHE WAS seated at the parlour window in a blue frock, a gilt bangle on her wrist, and a copy of *Woman's Notes* open on her lap. Her attention was not given to the book, for she was watching the people passing in the street and the last of the autumn sun mellowing the small red-bricked houses opposite. Behind her in the hall her two little boys were playing and to their play she was giving no ear. Everyone that passed the window would glance at the fire blazing in the grate and then abruptly look away when they caught sight of the blue frock. She knew well what they'd be thinking. There she is, they would say, on the look-out for another husband and her other man not two years in his grave. And little cause she has to be marrying again, they'd add, and she with two nice little boys to keep her company and her widow's pension to keep her comfortable; and hadn't she her own father a while back with her, drawing his old-age pension and helping to keep the house respectable. But would they add that he smoked all his pension-money in his pipe? They would not. After all what did they really know about the inside of any house — nothing; nothing, except what their own evil natures would tell them.

Since she first came into the street she had made sure the neighbours wouldn't know much of her business. She had kept herself to herself, gave harm or hindrance to no one, and didn't join in the general borrowings of tea and sugar, and the running in and out of one another's houses. She had looked after her husband when he was alive, dressed her two boys neatly for school, saw them off in the morning, and instead of having a gossip with her next-door neighbour she would close the door, attend to her house and keep it clean in spite of the smuts from the factory chimneys that whorled down upon the street both day and night. But keeping herself to herself didn't please the neighbours. Too high in her ways she was. And hadn't they often shouted things at her little boys: "Run home now and tell that to your ladylike mother – her that was never seen with a thumb-mark of black-lead at the side of her nose. Her with her grand airs and graces and her face powdered and painted like a clown's in a circus – trying to look like twenty and she on the wrong side of forty." It wasn't once or twice they shouted that at her two innocent children. But did they ever remember the priest at the mission who began his sermon: "Is it wrong for a woman to paint her face?" and then took a handkerchief leisurely from his sleeve, blew his nose, and put the handkerchief back again. "No," he answered, "No, it is not wrong as long as she does it to attract a husband or to keep the one she has got," Very few of them, she was sure, remembered that. And this evening if Frank asked her would she marry again she would say yes – that'd let the neighbours see what she thought of them! She gave a laugh, half of joy and half of scorn, and *Woman's Notes* fell onto the oilclothed floor.

As she stooped to pick it up, she paused, listening to her two boys at play. She gripped the book and drew near to the open parlour door that led into the hall.

"You be granda now for awhile," John was saying to Tom.

"Lend me the stick then," Tom answered.

"No, no. Pretend you're him up in the workhouse – you're best at that. Lie down on the mat like you done before."

Tom stretched out on the mat and pillowed his head on his arms and began to imitate his granda: "'Tis terrible to be shut up within four black walls and you without a friend in the world. 'Tis terrible that you work hard all your life and this is the end of it. Me that once wrought in the country and knew the name of every bush and every tree. 'Tis terrible to be old and be ordered away from your bit of fire, and now I am without spoon or cup to call my own. And I have to smoke at set hours and have no little boys to chat with me of an evening."

"O, Tom, if granda heard you he'd laugh his eyes out, so he would. Go on and give us more, Tom. Pretend you're talking to the man in the next bed. Begin: 'Are you asleep there, Billdoe?' "

But Tom at that moment saw his mother standing her full height in the doorway, and he sat up on the mat and stared at her with a guilty, frightened look.

"Tom! John!" she said, the words husky in her throat. Her breast heaved and she turned the bangle on her wrist. "Go inside to the kitchen and I'll speak to you in a minute." There was the sound of a lagging step in the street outside, and her heart pounded in her ears, but the step passed on. She turned into the parlour, and in the mirror above the mantlepiece looked at her face and dabbed away the tears that had risen to her eyes. She powdered her face, and rolling the magazine in her hand went into the boys, now sitting in the dusk of the kitchen.

Her voice was cold: "Where did I tell you your granda was. Where?" she said to Tom. For a moment he didn't answer. She caught him by the arm: "Where have you to say your granda is? Do you hear me, Tom? Answer me — I'm not going to beat you."

"He's away to the country for the good of his health," Tom said.

"Say it again so that you'll not forget it. And you say it with him John."

"He's away to the country for the good of his health," they said together.

"Don't let me ever hear you say anything else about him. If your granda was back at this fireside it wouldn't answer the two of you. It's not boots you'd have on your feet — you'd be running about barefoot like some of the other good-for-nothings in this locality." She rolled and unrolled the magazine as she spoke, and then some look in the younger's face reproached her and she put her arm round his shoulder and stroked his head: "Go on to bed now like good little boys. You've got your tea," and she stood and watched them climb the stairs.

"Shout down when you're in," she said. "And don't forget to say your prayers."

She went into the parlour again and took her seat at the window. The sun had set, and above the roof-tops a greenish light was tightly stretched across the sky. The lamplighter was passing up the street with his yellow pole over his shoulder, and a crowd of little girls scampered in front of him and held out their pinafores as they stood under a lamp awaiting the first pale blossom of light. Then as the pole was manoeuvred into the lamphead, the mantle lit with a plop, and they all shouted: "Silver and gold I hold in my lap," and ran ahead to the next lamp.

They should all be in bed, she thought, running mad about the streets to this time of night, and nobody to care about them whether they're hungry or whether they're dirty. She saw faces in the kitchen-windows opposite and the curtains pulled to the side to let in the last light of the day. She saw her own firelight reflected in the cold window-pane and the first stars appearing in the sky. The street was quiet now, and then a woman appeared in a doorway and called harshly: "Cissie, Jackie, where the hell are ye to this time o' night. Wait'll I lay my hands on ye!" There was a scurry of feet and a clash of doors. Darkness fell, and through the silence there was the rumble of machinery from the factory at the head of the street, a rumble that nobody noticed for it had become part and parcel of their lives as much as the ticking of a clock. But someday, please God, she'd get away from all this roughness, away to the fringes of the city where she'd have a house with an extra room, and, maybe, take her father out of the workhouse and bring him home again where he could sun himself in a patch of garden at the back and maybe see the whins in bloom on the mountain and hear the larks singing. "O God," she said aloud, "if one had to live one's life again!" Wasn't she always at Peter, when he was alive, to move away from this street and go to a place where the boys could get a corner of a field to kick football. But you couldn't move him! "The rent is cheap here," he always said. "The rent is cheap and what we save we'll put past for their education." It wasn't as if she hadn't thought about their education herself and how it would break her heart to see them astride a bicycle when they leave school and the name of some grocer painted in white on a big plate between the bars.

She sighed, rolled and unrolled the magazine on her lap, and glanced at the table set for two and the firelight glinting on the cups.

"We're in bed now, mother," Tom shouted from the room above the parlour.

She went up to them and sat on the bed and ran her fingers through their hair. "I'll tell you a secret and you mustn't breathe it to anyone," she whispered. "It's a secret, mind you, and you mustn't mention it to a living soul. Some day you'll have your granda back. And you'll have fields to play in and a real ball to kick on the grass, and never again will you be kicking a rag-ball between the lampposts in the street and have the neighbours complaining about you breaking their windows and tormenting their babies out of their sleep. It'll be a great day for us the day we bring your granda back."

"And will it come soon," they asked and laughed with nervous expectancy.

"It'll come soon, please God, and you'll see the fine house we'll have with three bedrooms. Not like this one with only two, and maybe we'll afford one with a bath in it. But, whatever comes, there'll be a bit of grass at the back where you can play ball."

"Can we get a dog?" John asked.

"I'll get you a dog. And maybe you'll have a new father that will make things for you and make a box for your

136

dog."

"Where'll the house be?"

"It'll not be far away."

"How far?"

"It's a secret. Go asleep now, and when I bring you to see your granda tomorrow you mustn't tell him about it. It's to be a surprise for him."

"Is the man coming tonight again," Tom asked excitedly.

"Sh, sh," she said.

She pushed the clothes around them and stood at the window looking down at the lamplighted street and its sweepings lying in little heaps awaiting the Corporation men to shovel them into their shambling cart. Her hand toyed with the tassel of the blind and it tocked against the pane.

"Don't pull down the blind, mother," Tom said.

"Close your eyes. If I hear another word out of you I'll come up and pull it down." Her hand rested on her cheek. The lamplight shone through the window and stretched a shadow of the sash on the ceiling. There was a shuffling step at the front door and presently a knock. It'll be Frank, she thought. She'd let him knock again so that a neighbour or two might get a look at him – it'd give them something more to talk about.

She went down and opened the door, helped him off with his overcoat and hung it on the rack in the hall. He smoothed his thick grey hair with his hand and took the newspaper out of his pocket.

"How are you this evening, Mary?" he said, putting his arm round her waist as they stepped into the parlour.

She threw back her head and smiled up at him: "The same as usual, Frank. The woman at the window they'll be calling me."

"Who'll be calling you the woman at the window?" he asked.

"The neighbours," she said, lighting the gas with a piece of twisted paper.

"The neighbours be damned. They'd find worse fault if you sat outside on the window-sill."

"I'm glad you think of them that way," she said. "Poor Peter, God rest him, always told me it was my imagination when I used to tell him how the neighbours were spying at me. He had always excuses for them because he was foreman in their factory, and was, in many ways, like one of themselves."

"You wouldn't like to spend all your days here?" he put in.

"I would not indeed. It'd be lovely to be in a place where you'd get fresh air and see flowers and trees growing," and she laughed. "That reminds me of a story Peter used to tell of a poor woman used to live next door to the factory and the only smell she got every day and every night was the oily smell from the wired factory-windows. And then one day that poor woman went to the country to spend a week and when she wakened in the morning she used to sniff and sniff and wonder what the smell was until some one told her it was fresh air."

"God above — that's a good one. Fresh air, she smelt. That poor woman wasn't about much in her life, I'd say," and he sat down in an arm-chair at the fire. "The old man will be fairly filling his lungs with fresh air these fine days, I'm thinking. Any word from him?"

"He's doing bravely," she said.

"He's a lucky man to have a place to go to in the country."

"All the same I miss him out of the house, Frank."

"The only thing I missed was the smell of his oul' pipe as I came in the door. He was too quiet — he hadn't a word to throw to a dog."

"Ah, Frank, if you knew him better you'd get on well together. He's an interesting man, and I often heard people say he knew more about country customs than you'd get in any book."

On the floor above them there was the pound of running feet and she stood, listening.

"One of them out of bed," she smiled, and when she went up the stairs he could hear her scolding and hooshing them.

"It was Tom," she said when she came into the parlour again. "He was looking out of the window."

"They have you tormented, Mary," he said, opening out his newspaper. "Why don't you pack them off to the country to their granda. The old man was fond of them and it'd do them a world of good to get to the country for awhile. There's nothing to beat the country for growing lads."

"I'd be lonely without them," she said, standing with one hand resting on the table and looking at him holding wide the wings of the paper.

"Lonely! Sure you'll have me."

She smiled and waited for him to add something more but he only turned back the wings of the paper, the stir of air shaking the flames in the fire.

"I'll wet the tea," she said, "I'll not be a tick."

When they were seated at the table and she was helping him to some salad there was the rumble of a cart outside, and then another pad of feet overhead and a laugh from the two boys.

"Aren't they the divils," she said.

"Wait and I'll go up to them, Mary."

"No, no, Frank, you might frighten them."

"Frighten them!"

"Well, I didn't mean frighten – I meant – how will I explain it."

"Aye, just how will you explain it! Look, " and he shook his knife in the air, "them two boyos is playing on you. I know what I'm talking about and if you'd take my advice you'd pack them off to the country."

"Och, after all, Frank, they're only children and I often think if I could get one of the new houses at the outskirts of the city they'd get as much of the country that'd do them," and looking up at the ceiling she shouted: "Get into bed there, and go asleep or I'll go up with the strap."

In the street there was the scrape of a shovel on stone and then a cart knocking its way past the window. She smiled: "They were watching the council men lifting the sweepings off the street."

Frank said nothing. He drank what was left of his tea and rattled the cup down on the saucer with an air of finality. She stretched out her hand: "Another cup, Frank?"

"I've had enough," he said. She tried to coax him, and as she held out the teapot towards him he covered the mouth of his cup with his hand. "If I wanted it I'd take it," he tried to say casually.

She smiled at him: "You're an awful man!"

He lit a cigarette and turned round in his chair toward the fire. She, herself, stopped eating, and with her little finger toyed with the crumbs on the plate. A heavy constraint pressed upon her. She sighed.

"Do you know what I was thinking?" he said, flicking the ash of his cigarette into his cup. "What about coming for a walk on Sunday night now that the moon is full. A walk these nights would do you good and there'd be nobody to bother us."

She sat irresolute for awhile, manoeuvring the crumbs into a tiny heap and disarranging them again.

"Well, what to you say?" he pressed.

"I'd love to go Frank, but it's impossible," and she motioned with her hand to the ceiling. "I've never left them in the house by themselves."

"So you care more about them than you do for the man that loves you!"

"Frank!" and she leaned over and touched his hand. "God knows what mischief they'd be up to."

"They're big enough and old enough to look after themselves for one night," he said, withdrawing his hand from hers.

"But look, Frank, if I met you outside the house it would be wrong and when I meet you inside the house it's wrong."

140

"How?"

"The neighbours!"

"So that's it! The neighbours!" he sneered. "You've the damned neighbours on the brain. . . . I'll see you at the tram-depot at eight on Sunday night and we'll go up the Glen Road together." He turned completely round to the fire, took the tongs and lifted pieces of unlit coal and piled them on the handful of glow in the centre of the fire. There was a knock on the ceiling.

"At it again," he said, and opened his newspaper.

Another knock followed and Tom's voice rhyming: "Mother, John wants a drink of water. . . . John wants a drink of water. . . . John wants a drink . . ."

Without a word she got up, went into the scullery for a cup of cold water, and while John was drinking it she stood silently by the bare window gazing down at the clean, moonlit street.

"If there's another word out of you I'll not bring you to see your granda tomorrow!" she said with sudden anger.

Frank was on his feet when she came back to the parlour.

"You're not going so soon?" she said.

"I promised my sisters I'd be home early tonight," and he looked into the mirror and combed back his hair.

"Stay for awhile," and she placed a hand on his shoulder.

"I can't," he said, and he stooped and kissed her, "Sure it won't be long till Sunday."

When he was at the door he looked at the moon skimming through the shreds of cloud: "Look at that for a night! And there we were stuck in the house."

"It's lovely," and she gave a half smile.

"Sunday at eight," he said. "Don't forget."

She nodded, and when he was gone she sat for awhile staring into the fire and twisting the wedding ring on her finger. Then realising that she was crying, she shrugged her shoulders, and lifting the cups and saucers on to a tray she carried them into the scullery to wash.

The following morning, Saturday, she was on her knees scrubbing the front doorstep before the smoke was rising from the chimney-pots in the neighbouring houses. She hummed to herself as she rubbed the soap on the scrubber and swept it in a half-circle in front of the door. Blinds were drawn in all the houses and a cat on a windowsill lay asleep beside two empty milk bottles. Nothing ruffled the chilly stillness of the morning except the streaky noise of the scrubber, the sharp rattle of her bucket, and the unchanging hum-hum of the factory at the top of the street. Steam rose from her fingers as she wrung out the cloth and got to her feet to wipe a few scribbles of chalk from the wall of the house. "It's always my house, they use as a blackboard," she said to herself, as she rubbed off a child's handwriting from the bricks. "Please God, it'll not be long till I leave this place for good." She came inside, put the boys' clean shirts to warm at the fire, and when she had made the breakfast she awakened them to pay their weekly visit to the workhouse.

As she walked down the street, John at one side of her and Tom at the other, she held her head high for she noticed the kitchen blinds being raised and a man in his shirt and trousers lifting a milk-bottle from a windowsill. Where is she off to at this time of the morning, they'd be saying — and God knows what answers they'd make for themselves. If they knew where the old man was they'd soon raise the colour to her cheeks and maybe get one of the children to chalk it up on the flagstones of the street or even on the wall of the house. Little they knew about where he was and she'd make sure they'd never know it. She always arrived early at the workhouse to have her visit over before the crowd of visitors thronged the main entrance gates.

This morning she was very silent as she got off the tram and made her way through the workhouse grounds with the autumn leaves hopping on the wind at her feet and her two boys tugging at her coat and asking to be allowed to

142

run on in front. She spoke to them in a hushed voice and they, themselves, spoke back in the same way, quelled by the mysterious quiet of her manner. But when at last they came to the long flight of stairs that led to the ward they broke away from her, and when they entered the ward with its twelve aluminium-painted beds their granda saw them and he sat up in his red-flannel jacket and held out his hands to them as they ran to each side of his bed. "You're the early fellas," he said. "First in and first to go. . . . And how are ye at all, at all," and he ruffled Tom's hair and then John's. Tom noticed an egg-stain on the red-jacket: "I see they've been stuffing eggs into you."

"Aw, aw, is that you, Tommy, my oul' codger!" said the granda.

"Don't be telling me you don't know me."

"I know you all right, my oul' jack-in-the-box. Come closer till I feel your muscles." And when he got Tom near him he rubbed his bristly chin against the boy's. "Do you feel the jag of that! Will you tell Smith, the barber, to come up and give me a decent shave. The fella, they've here, is no good and he charges me a sixpence that I can ill afford."

The mother came into the ward, walking down between the beds, looking neither to right nor left, and sat down on a chair at the bedside, her handbag on her lap, a small brown parcel dangling from her finger.

"My mother is going to get us a dog, granda," John was saying.

The mother leaned across the bed and handed the parcel to the old man: "There's a little tobacco and some tea," she put in.

"Thank you kindly, girl," he said, and his hands fumbled to open the knot of the parcel.

"You needn't open it – there's only an ounce of plug and a quarter of tea in it."

"You're a good girl," he said, leaving the parcel on the table at the head of the bed. "And how are you keeping since?"

"The same as usual," she said, keeping very erect on her chair, her eyes now on the ivory buttons of his red jacket, and now on his metal watch tied with a shoe-lace to the rail of his bed.

"We're getting a dog soon," John said again.

"Stop chattering and let me talk to your granda," she said, and she glanced to the foot of the ward and saw an old man beckoning to them. "There's your old friend with the ear-phones calling you. Away the both of you and hear the music." And when they were gone, her father looked at her eyes without flinching: "Anything strange?" he said.

"Nothing," she said, avoiding his eyes. "Are you keeping well, yourself?"

"Too well, daughter, too well. If I'd pain or ache I might sleep for awhile and not feel the long days passing. But I'm too well, and there's nobody to talk to. Old Billdoe in the next bed is as deaf as a stone and the only comfort left me is to say my beads. . . . Aw, girl, the doctor'll be sending me back to the body of the house – amongst the derelict, the nameless and the shameless. Would you not take me out, girl, till after Christmas and maybe in the spring of the year I might take a run down to the country and get a corner in some old neighbour's house."

She bent her head and smoothed out a crease in her skirt. A woman with a black shawl on her head shuffled in to visit Billdoe and she looked at Mary before sitting down. "That's a coul' mornin', Missus, the climb up them stairs hasn't left a grain of breath in me – not a damned happorth has it left." She let the shawl fall slack from her head and shouted into Billdoe's ear: "I've brought you some of Quinn's best sausages," and her voice rang through the ward. She tore the paper off the parcel and held out a clump of pork sausages: "They cost a bob a pound – they're the very best."

Billdoe took them in his hand and began eating a raw sausage.

"Give them to the nurse and she'll cook them for you," she shouted, trying to take them from him.

He stared at her with a stupid, affronted look: "I wouldn't give them God's daylight if I could keep it from them."

She arranged the shawl about her head and looked across at Mary: "There's the cross-grained article I've to deal with, Missus. But I fair miss him out of the house all the same — I do indeed."

Mary smiled thinly and patted the white quilt on the bed. Tom came running back: "Granda, I heard a drum and a fiddle on the ear-phones and the man said it came through the air from Paris."

"We'll be going soon," Mary said; and Tom ran back to get John.

"What's troubling you, girl?" and he leant close to her.

"Nothing," and she shook her head.

"There's something, girl, and if it's that Frank fella that's running after you, in God's name put him out of your head. He's no good, I tell you. He's no good," and he raised his voice.

"Hoosh, hoosh," she said. "The people will hear you."

He took her hand and she noticed how cold and thin it was. He lowered his voice: "I'm not thinking of myself, girl, God knows I'm not. I'm thinking of what's best for you and the two boys. But Frank — ah, God in heaven — he's not worth that!" and he snapped his fingers in the air. "He's not worth a dead match, so he's not. He's too settled in his ways and he'll not fit in with your ways and there'll be nothing but trouble."

"It's cold," she said, rubbing the backs of her hands and trying to ward off his talk.

"I never heard him speak a kind word to the children since the first day he darkened the door. I never seen him bring them a little toy or a wee bit of a sweet like many another. He has no nature in him, Mary. Ah, if you were thirty I'd tell you to marry again, but not to the likes of him. You're forty-three come next 12th December."

She flushed on hearing her age breathed so loudly, and she glanced at the shawled woman to see if she had heard.

"Who said I was going to marry again," she whispered and tried to smile.

"It'd be better for us all to get away to a place in the country where'd we live out our simple bit of life," he said.

"The country! I couldn't bury myself in the country – not after all I came through. And the boys' education?"

"They'll get education enough that'll do them. Look at me since I left the country fifty years ago. Look at me – ruined and flung to the side and not a place of my own to lay my head. And didn't I see the schoolmaster's son in the country and the policeman's son and the priest's nephew all going to big colleges and not one of them ever earned his bit of bread in his own country – out to foreign lands they went every man jack of them, and God knows if they're alive now or dead. Education! Is there one of them that wouldn't envy a man ploughing his own bit of land or talking about his own beasts in the fields? There is not! I had a good life at my own doorstep in the country and I didn't know I had it. I left it fifty years ago and now I know it! Blessed God in Heaven, I know it – and me shut between the black walls of a workhouse and my end coming."

"Shoosh, shoosh," Mary said.

Tom and John came running back and stared at Billdoe picking up the crumbs of raw sausage from the bed-clothes.

"You're back again," the granda sighed to them.

"We'll have to go now," Mary said, for she saw another visitor enter the ward – some day someone would be sure to see her if she wasn't careful!

"Well, John," said the granda, "what about that big dog you were telling me about."

"He's getting no dog," the mother said. "Come now till we get home." And she stood up to take her leave.

"Wait now," said the granda, and he put his hand under the pillow and produced his purse tied with string. He gave them a penny each. "And, Tommy, don't forget to tell Smith to come up and give me a decent shave."

Mary shook her father's hand and he held on to it and looked up at her: "Night and day I'll pray you'll do the right thing." She smiled wanly down at him.

"Hurry up and get better," Tom said as they walked away.

At the door the boys turned round and waved to him and he waved back, and farther at the foot of the ward the man with the earphones was sitting up and waving too.

The mother walked quickly, and passing visitors with baskets she kept a handkerchief to her face, and held her head down in case some of them might know her. But once outside the main gates she cut down a nearby street and only then did she speak, scolding John for mentioning the dog.

"Will granda be home soon?" Tom said.

"I don't know," she said with obvious impatience.

"Will he be home for Christmas?" he persisted.

"I don't know. And what's more don't be giving granda's message to Smith. He's well enough shaved without sending a special man up for him."

Entering her own street she saw a few neighbours gossiping as usual at their doors. "Where's your granda if anybody asks you?" she warned the boys.

"He's away to the country for the good of his health," they answered.

"Quick now," she said, as she hurried up the street past the neighbours. At her own door she halted and though she held the key in her hand she pretended to search for it in her handbag. She'd just show the neighbours she wasn't a bit flustered about them. But out of the corner of her eye she saw that they had turned their backs to her. "Hm," she said aloud, and thought how they'd be gossiping about her now. Tomorrow night she'd give them something else to talk about when she'd go for her walk with Frank and leave the boys for the first time in her life to mind the house. She opened the door and let the lads enter in front of her. After all they were big enough and old enough to stay alone in their bed for a few hours of a Sunday evening. She had them spoiled – there was no mistake about that. If they were anybody else's children in the street their mothers wouldn't give it a second thought.

She hung up her hat and coat in the hall and finding a smell of stale cigarette smoke coming from the parlour she went in and opened the window. On a chair she found a folded newspaper and her rolled-up *Woman's Notes*. She lifted the paper, and suddenly there came to her a sharp resentment against Frank: the way he refused the second cup of tea and the way he spread himself out before the fire. She paused; and then she saw herself mending and cooking for him, her boys with no education, and maybe her father dying a lonely death in the workhouse. "No," she said and she squeezed up the newspaper in a ball and flung it on the cold grate. "No, I'll not go to meet him tomorrow night! I'll not stir hand or foot out of the house. I'll see what he'll do then!"

When Sunday morning came her determination not to meet Frank had wavered, and throughout the day she was afraid to face the question whether or not she should go for the walk with him. If she stopped for a minute and put the question to herself she felt she'd give in to his arrangement, but rather than come to a decision she plunged herself into her work and tried to put him from her mind. She let the boys go up to the Park to gather chestnuts. After all if the worst came to the worst and she did go it'd be better if her boys were tired so that they'd settle down to sleep before she went out.

In the early evening when they had come back from their walk, hungry and tired, each had three glossy chestnuts which they held out to show her, and as she prepared their tea she watched them boring a hole in the chestnuts with a nail and threading a string through the hole. They began to play: Tom held his chestnut dangling from the end of a string and John whacked at it with his chestnut, and time and again they had to call to her to settle a dispute. But when they had taken their tea and were ready for bed she took the chestnuts from them and put them on the mantelpiece where they would take no harm until morning. Then she dressed and got ready to go out to meet Frank.

She went up to their room and was pleased to see the moon shining through the bare window: "Go asleep," she said, "I'll not be long till I'm back."

"Tell us a story," John pleaded, "and it will make us sleepy."

"I'll tell you one tomorrow night if you're good. If there's any knocks at the door don't open it, do you hear?"

"Are we going to get the dog?" John said.

"Yes."

"When's granda coming home?" Tom added.

"I don't know."

"Will he be home for Christmas?"

"We'll see. . . . Go asleep now." And as she bent over to kiss them they smelt the warm thick perfume from her clothes.

They heard the front door close and her quick footsteps down the street. No neighbour had seen her, but once out of the street her steps lagged and she stopped under the light from a streetlamp and looked in her handbag to see if the key was safe. "I'm not doing right," she said to herself. "It's not right to leave them by themselves." She hesitated for a minute and then walked ahead. Frank shouldn't have asked her to do the like of this. Wasn't the comfort of the house and a fire better at this time of the year than rambling about the cold country roads. And what with his talk about the moon you'd think he was just a lad into long trousers. She should have laughed him out of that notion. Why must she be always playing a part and giving ear to his silly talk. Her father had said he's too settled in his ways – God knows he may be right, for there's something in what he said, now that she came to think about it.

She reached the road and just missed a tram, and while waiting for another a massive cloud trailed across the moon and scooped the light from the street. And then there came into her mind the sight of the boys' room, the moonlight slipping from it, leaving nothing only the slanting light from the street lamp and the shadow of the window-sash on the ceiling. A tram passed in the opposite direction and she saw the people within, warm and bright. The sky was black now, the moon entirely hidden. The night would be dark – what'd be the use of going, and it might rain and they'd have to turn back in any case. No, she needn't go. A tram came forward and she stepped away from the tram-stop and into the darkness. The car sped on. She crossed the road and hurried towards home. Up the street she went, her heels hard and clicking on the pavement. She put the key in the latch, and as she did so she heard the boys pounding up the stairs.

"Come back here!" she said. "Come back here!" Her voice was edged with anger. "Didn't you promise me not to get out of bed!" And she turned up the gaslight in the kitchen.

"We came down for a drink."

"What's that in your hand?"

"Chestnuts."

"I'll chestnut ye!" and in her anger she took the chestnuts and flung them into the fire.

They began to cry.

"That's for crying for nothing!" she said as she slapped each of them on the back of the hand. "Now go back and not another word out of you this night. You've my heart broken."

They ran from her, and she heard John sobbing as she hung up her hat and coat. She looked into the fire and tried to retrieve the chestnuts with the poker but the more she levered at them the more they disappeared into the red heart of the fire. She went to the foot of the stairs and called up to them: "Go asleep. I'll get you some chestnuts tomorrow."

She went into the parlour and put a match to the already prepared fire. She sat on a chair. It was a quarter past eight.

He'd be sure to come when she didn't turn up. She went to the door. The darkness in the sky was loosening; she held out her hands, palms upward, in the hope of feeling spits of rain. But as she stood there the moon slid out and swung its shadows on roof and window.

She came into the parlour again, lifted her *Woman's Notes* but couldn't read it. Her head throbbed. She did the right thing in turning back – after all you'd never know what tricks Tom and John would be up to. A knock came to the door, and as she was tidying her hair before opening it the knock came again.

"I'm glad you came," she said, when Frank stepped in the hall. "Take off your coat."

"I'm not for staying. I'm foundered standing at the depot and searching every damned tram that came and turned."

She explained to him how she had gone out and turned home as she thought it would rain.

"Rain!" he said. "Rain – and the sky as smooth as silk. And why the blazes didn't you come up and tell me what you thought. Couldn't we've come back here if it had rained," and he sat on the edge of the table, swinging his hat in his hand.

"I never thought of that, Frank."

"No, you think of nothing only yourself and them two clips upstairs."

"Don't bring poor Tom and John into it."

"What about poor Frank," he said, and he got down from the table and buttoned his coat. "Well," he said, "are you going to come for the walk or are you not?"

She sat on the arm-chair, rolling and unrolling her magazine. "Is it not too late?" she said meekly.

"Are you coming? – Yes or no?" he said, and the sharpness of his voice frightened her.

She turned a page in the magazine and then another. "Do you hear me – are you coming now or are you not?" Upstairs the boys startled by his voice began to cry and call to her. She drew herself erect from the chair: "No,

Frank," she said slowly, "I'm not going tonight."

"All right," he said, and he put on his hat, and opened the front door to let himself out. In the stillness she heard her children crying, and she went up and lay down on top of the bed, her arms across them.

"What are you crying for? Go asleep."

"Is the man gone?" Tom said.

"He is and he'll never be back," and she combed her fingers through his hair.

There was a great stillness in the room and outside in the street where the moon was shining. She clenched and unclenched her hands to stifle the sob in her throat.

"When are you getting us the dog?" John asked her eagerly.

"Soon," she said.

"And will granda be home for Christmas?" Tom asked.

"He'll be out before it, before it," she said. "Not another word. . . . Go asleep," and in the darkness as the tears flowed from her eyes she made no effort to stop them.

The Poteen Maker

WHEN HE taught me some years ago he was an old man near his retirement, and when he would pass through the streets of the little town on his way from school you would hear the women talking about him as they stood at their doors knitting or nursing their babies: "Poor man, he's done . . . Killing himself . . . Digging his own grave!" With my bag of books under my arm I could hear them, but I could never understand why they said he was digging his own grave, and when I would ask my mother she would scold me: "Take your dinner, like a good boy, and don't be listening to the hard backbiters of this town. Your father has always a good word for Master Craig — so that should be enough for you!"

"But why do they say he's killing himself?"

"Why do who say? Didn't I tell you to take your dinner and not be repeating what the idle gossips of this town are saying? Listen to me, son! Master Craig is a decent, good-living man — a kindly man that would go out of his way to do you a good turn. If Master Craig was in any other town he'd have got a place in the new school at the Square instead of being stuck for ever in that wee poky bit of a school at the edge of the town!"

It was true that the school was small — a two-roomed ramshackle of a place that lay at the edge of the town beyond the last street lamp. We all loved it. Around it grew a few trees, their trunks hacked with boy's names and pierced with nibs and rusty drawing-pins. In summer when the windows were open we could hear the leaves rubbing together and in winter see the raindrops hanging

153

on the bare twigs.

It was a draughty place and the master was always complaining of the cold, and even in the early autumn he would wear his overcoat in the classroom and rub his hands together: "Boys, it's very cold today. Do you feel it cold?" And to please him we would answer: "Yes, sir, 'tis very cold." He would continue to rub his hands and he would look out at the old trees casting their leaves or at the broken spout that flung its tail of rain against the window. He always kept his hands clean and three times a day he would wash them in a basin and wipe them on a roller towel affixed to the inside of his press. He had a hanger for his coat and a brush to brush away the chalk that accumulated on the collar in the course of the day.

In the wet windy monttth of November three buckets were placed on the top of the desks to catch the drips that plopped here and there from the ceiling, and those drops made different music according to the direction of the wind. When the buckets were filled the master always called me to empty them, and I would take them one at a time and swirl them into the drain at the street and stand for a minute gazing down at the wet roofs of the town or listen to the rain pecking at the lunch-papers scattered about on the cinders.

"What's it like outside?" he always asked when I came in with the empty buckets.

"Sir, 'tis very bad."

He would write sums on the board and tell me to keep an eye on the class and out to the porch he would go and stand in grim silence watching the rain nibbling at the puddles. Sometimes he would come in and I would see him sneak his hat from the press and disappear for five or ten minutes. We would fight then with rulers or paper-darts till our noise would disturb the mistress next door and in she would come and stand with her lips compressed, her fingers in her book. There was silence as she upbraided us: "Mean, low, good-for-nothing corner boys. Wait'll Mister Craig comes back and I'll let him know the angels he has. And I'll give him special news about *you*!" – and she shakes her book at me: "An altar boy on Sunday and a corner boy for the rest of the week!" We would let her barge away, the buckets plink-plonking as they filled up with rain and her own class beginning to hum, now that she was away from them.

When Mr. Craig came back he would look at us and ask if we disturbed Miss Lagan. Our silence or our tossed hair always gave him the answer. He would correct the sums on the board, flivell the pages of a book with his thumb, and listen to us reading; and occasionally he would glance out of the side window at the river that flowed through the town and, above it, the bedraggled row of houses whose tumbling yard-walls sheered to the water's edge. "The loveliest county in Ireland is County Down!" he used to say, with a sweep of his arm to the river and the tin cans and the chalked walls of the houses.

During that December he was ill for two weeks and when he came back amongst us he was greatly failed. To keep out the draughts he nailed perforated plywood over the ventilators and stuffed blotting paper between the wide crevices at the jambs of the door. There were muddy marks of a ball on one of the windows and on one pane a long crack with fangs at the end of it: "So someone has drawn the River Ganges while I was away," he said; and whenever he came to the geography of India he would refer to the Ganges delta by pointing to the cracks on the pane.

When our ration of coal for the fire was used up he would send me into the town with a bucket, a coat over my head to keep off the rain, and the money in my fist to buy a stone of coal. He always gave me a penny to buy sweets for myself, and I can always remember that he kept his money in a waistcoat pocket. Back again I would come with the coal and he would give me disused exercise books to light the fire. "Chief stoker!" he called me, and the name has stuck to me to this day.

It was at this time that the first snow had fallen, and

someone by using empty potato bags had climbed over the glass-topped wall and stolen the school coal, and for some reason Mr. Craig did not send me with the bucket to buy more. The floor was continually wet from our boots, and our breath frosted the windows. Whenever the door opened a cold draught would rush in and gulp down the breath-warmed air in the room. We would jig our feet and sit on our hands to warm them. Every half-hour Mr. Craig would make us stand and while he lilted O'Donnell Abu we did a series of physical exercises which he had taught us, and in the excitement and the exaltation we forgot about our sponging boots and the snow that pelted against the windows. It was then that he did his lessons on Science; and we were delighted to see the bunsen burner attached to the gas bracket which hung like an inverted T from the middle of the ceiling. The snoring bunsen seemed to heat up the room and we all gathered round it, pressing in on top of it till he scattered us back to our places with the cane: "Sit down!" he would shout. "There's no call to stand. Everybody will be able to see!"

The cold spell remained, and over and over again he repeated one lesson in Science, which he called: *Evaporation and Condensation.*

"I'll show you how to purify the dirtiest of water," he had told us. "Even the filthiest water from the old river could be made fit for drinking purposes." In a glass trough he had a dark brown liquid and when I got his back turned I dipped my finger in it and it tasted like treacle or burnt candy, and then I remembered about packets of brown sugar and tins of treacle I had seen in his press.

He placed some of the brown liquid in a glass retort and held it aloft to the class: "In the retort I have water which I have discoloured and made impure. In a few minutes I'll produce from it the clearest of spring water." And his weary eyes twinkled and although we could see nothing funny in that, we smiled because he smiled.

The glass retort was set up with the flaming bunsen underneath, and as the liquid was boiling, the steam was trapped in a long-necked flask on which I sponged cold water. With our eyes we followed the bubbling mixture and the steam turning into drops and dripping rapidly into the flask. The air was filled with a biscuity smell, and the only sound was the snore of the bunsen. Outside was the cold air and the falling snow. Presently the master turned out the gas and held up the flask containing the clear water.

"As pure as crystal!" he said, and we watched him pour some of it into a tumbler, hold it in his delicate fingers, and put it to his lips. With wonder we watched him drink it and then ours eyes travelled to the dirty, cakey scum that had congealed on the glass sides of the retort. He pointed at this with his ruler: "The impurities are sifted out and the purest of pure water remains." And for some reason he gave his roguish smile. He filled up the retort again with the dirty brown liquid and repeated the experiment until he had a large bottle filled with the purest of pure water.

The following day it was still snowing and very cold. The master filled up the retort with the clear liquid which he had stored in the bottle: "I'll boil this again to show you that there are no impurities left." So once again we watched the water bubbling, turning to steam, and then to shining drops. Mr. Craig filled up his tumbler: "As pure as crystal," he said, and then the door opened and in walked the Inspector. He was muffled to the ears and snow covered his hat and his attaché case. We all stared at him — he was the old, kind man whom we had seen before. He glanced at the bare firegrate and at the closed windows with their sashes edged with snow. The water continued to bubble in the retort, giving out its pleasant smell.

The Inspector shook hands with Mr. Craig and they talked and smiled together, the Inspector now and again looking towards the empty grate and shaking his head. He unrolled his scarf and flicked the snow from off his shoulders and from his attaché case. He sniffed the air, rubbed his frozen hands together, and took a black notebook from his case. The snow ploofed against the windows, the wind hummed under the door.

"Now, boys," Mr. Craig continued, holding up the tumbler of water from which a thread of steam wriggled in the air. He talked to us in a strange voice and told us about the experiment as if we were seeing it for the first time. Then the Inspector took the warm tumbler and questioned us on our lesson. "It should be perfectly pure water," he said, and he sipped at it. He tasted its flavour. He sipped at it again. He turned to Mr. Craig. They whispered together, the Inspector looking towards the retort which was still bubbling and sending out its twirls of steam to be condensed to water of purest crystal. He laughed loudly, and we smiled when he again put the tumbler to his lips and this time drank it all. Then he asked us more questions and told us how, if we were ship-wrecked, we could make pure water from the salt sea water.

Mr. Craig turned off the bunsen and the Inspector spoke to him. The master filled up the Inspector's tumbler and poured out some for himself in a cup. Then the Inspector made jokes with us, listening to us singing and told us we were the best class in Ireland. Then he gave us a few sums to do in our books. He put his hands in his pockets and jingled his money, rubbed a little peep-hole in the breath-covered window and peered out at the loveliest sight in Ireland. He spoke to Mr. Craig again and Mr. Craig shook hands with him and they both laughed. The Inspector looked at his watch. Our class was let out early, and while I remained behind to tidy up the Science apparatus the master gave me an empty treacle tin to throw in the bin and told me to carry the Inspector's case up to the station. I remember that day well as I walked behind them through the snow, carrying the attaché case, and how loudly they talked and laughed as the snow whirled cold from the river. I remember how they crouched together to light their cigarettes, how match after match was thrown on the road, and how they walked off with the unlighted cigarettes still in their mouths. At the station Mr. Craig took a penny from his waistcoat pocket and as he handed it to me it dropped on the snow. I lifted it and he told me I was the best boy in Ireland . . . .

When I was coming from his funeral last week – God have mercy on him – I recalled that wintry day and the feel of the cold penny and how much more I know now about Mr. Craig than I did then. On my way out of the town – I don't live there now – I passed the school and saw a patch of new slates on the roof and an ugly iron barrier near the door to keep the home-going children from rushing headlong on to the road. I knew if I had looked at the trees I'd have seen rusty drawing-pins stuck into their rough flesh. But I passed by. I heard there was a young teacher in the school now, with an array of coloured pencils in his breast pocket.

The Road to the Shore

"'TIS GOING to be a lovely day, thanks be to God," sighed Sister Paul to herself, as she rubbed her wrinkled hands together and looked out at the thrushes hopping across the lawn. "And it was a lovely day last year and the year before," she mused, and in her mind saw the fresh face of the sea where, in an hour or two, she and the rest of the community would be enjoying their annual trip to the shore. "And God knows it may be my last trip," she said resignedly, and gazed abstractedly at a butterfly that was purring its wings against the sunny pane. She opened the window and watched the butterfly swing out into the sweet air, zigzagging down to a cushion of flowers that bordered the lawn. "Isn't it well Sister Clare wasn't here," she said to herself, "for she'd be pestering the very soul out of me with her questions about butterflies and birds and flowers and the fall of dew?" She gave her girdle of beads a slight rattle. Wasn't it lovely to think of the pleasure that little butterfly would have when it found the free air under its wings again and its little feet pressing on the soft petals of the flowers and not on the hard pane? She always maintained it was better to enjoy Nature without searching and probing and chattering about the what and the where and the wherefore. But Sister Clare! – what she got out of it all, goodness only knew, for she'd give nobody a minute's peace – not a moment's peace would she give to a saint, living or dead. "How long would that butterfly live in the air of a classroom?" she'd be asking. "Do you think it would use up much of the active part of the air – the oxygen part, I mean? ... What family would that butterfly belong to? . . . You know it's wrong to say that a butterfly lives only a day. . . . When I am teaching my little pupils I always try to be accurate. I don't believe in stuffing their heads with fantastical nonsense however pleasurable it may be. . . ." Sister Paul turned round as if someone had suddenly walked into the room, and she was relieved when she saw nothing only the quiet vacancy of the room, the varnished desks with the sun on them and their reflections on the parquet floor.

She hoped she wouldn't be sitting beside Clare in the car today! She'd have no peace with her – not a bit of peace to look out at the countryside and see what changes had taken place inside twelve months. But Reverend Mother, she knew, would arrange all that – and if it'd be her misfortune to be parked beside Clare she'd have to accept it with resignation; yes, with resignation, and in that case her journey to the sea would be like a pilgrimage.

At that moment a large limousine drove up the gravel path, and as it swung round to the convent door she saw the flowers flow across its polished sides in a blur of colour. She hurried out of the room and down the stairs. In the hall Sister Clare and Sister Benignus were standing beside two baskets and Reverend Mother was staring at the stairs. "Where were you, Sister Paul?" she said with mild reproof. "We searched the whole building for you. . . . We're all ready this ages. . . . And Sister Francis has gone to put out the cat. Do you remember last year it had been in all the time we were at the shore and it ate the bacon?" As she spoke a door closed at the end of the corridor and Sister Francis came along, polishing her specs with the corner of her veil. Reverend Mother glanced away from her, that continual polishing of the spectacles irritated her; and then that empty expression on Sister Francis's face when the spectacles were off – vacuous, that's what it was!

"All ready now," Reverend Mother tried to say without any trace of perturbation. Sister Clare and Sister Benignus lifted two baskets at their feet, Reverend Mother opened the hall-door, and they all glided out into the flat sunlight.

161

The doors of the car were wide open, the engine purring gently, and a perfume of new leather fingering the air. The chauffeur, a young man, touched his cap and stood deferentially to the side. Reverend Mother surveyed him quickly, noting his clean-bright face and white collar. "I think there'll be room for us all in the back," she said.

"There's a seat in the front, Sister," the young man said, touching his cap again.

"Just put the baskets on it, if you please," said Reverend Mother. And Sister Clare who, at that moment, was smiling at her own grotesque reflection in the back of the car came forward with her basket, Sister Benignus following. Sister Paul sighed audibly and fingered her girdle of beads.

"Now, Sister Paul, you take one of the corner seats, Sister Clare you sit beside her, and Sister Benignus and Sister Francis on the spring-up seats facing them – they were just made for you, the tiny tots!" And they all laughed, a brittle laugh that emphasised the loveliness of the day.

When they were all seated, Reverend Mother made sure that the hall-door was locked, glanced at the fastened windows, and then stood for a minute watching the gardener who was pushing his lawn-mower with unusual vigour and concentration. He stopped abruptly when her shadow fell across his path. "And, Jack," she said, as if continuing a conversation that had been interrupted, "you'll have that lawn finished today?"

"Yes, Mother," and he took off his hat and held it in front of his breast. "To be sure I'll have it finished today. Sure what'd prevent me to finish it, and this the grandest day God sent this many a long month – a wholesome day!"

"And Jack, I noticed some pebbles on the lawn yesterday – white ones."

"I remarked them myself, Mother. A strange terrier disporting himself in the garden done it."

"Did it!"

"Yes, Mother, he did it with his two front paws,

scratching at the edge of the lawn like it was a rabbit burrow. He done it yesterday, and when I clodded him off the grounds he'd the impertinence to go out a different way than he came in. But I've now his entrances and exits all blocked and barricaded and I'm afraid he'll have to find some other constituency to disport himself. Dogs is a holy terror for bad habits."

"Be sure and finish it all today," she said with some impatience. She turned to go away, hesitated, and turned back. "By the way, Jack, if there are any drips of oil made by the car on the gravel you'll scuffle fresh pebbles over them."

"I'll do that. But you need have no fear of oil from her engine," and he glanced over at the limousine. "She'll be as clean as a Swiss clock. 'Tis them grocery vans that leak — top, tail and middle."

Crossing to the car, she heard with a feeling of pleasure the surge of the lawn-mower over the grass. Presently the car swung out of the gate on to a tree-lined road at the edge of the town. The nuns relaxed, settled themselves more comfortably in their seats and chatted about the groups on bicycles that were all heading for the shore.

"We will go to the same quiet strip as last year," said Reverend Mother, and then as she glanced out of the window a villa on top of a hill drew her attention. "There's a house that has been built since last year," she said.

"No, no," said Sister Francis. "It's more than a year old for I remember seeing it last year," and she peered at it through her spectacles.

Reverend Mother spoke through the speaking-tube to the driver: "Is that villa on the hill newly built?" she asked.

He stopped the car. "A doctor by the name of McGrath built it two years ago," he said. "He's married to a daughter of Solicitor O'Kane."

"Oh, thank you," said Reverend Mother; and the car proceeded slowly up the long hill above the town.

Sister Francis took off her spectacles, blew her breath on

163

them, and rubbed them with her handkerchief. She took another look at the villa and said with obvious pride: "A fine site, indeed, I remember last year that they had that little gadget over the door."

"The architrave," said Sister Clare importantly.

"Aye," said Sister Paul, and she looked out at the trees and below them the black river with its strings of froth moving through the valley. How lovely it would be, she thought, to sit on the edge of that river, dabble her parched feet in it and send bubbles out into the race of the current. She had often done that when she was a child, and now that river and its trees, which she only saw once a year, brought her childhood back to her. She sighed and opened the window so as to hear the mumble of the river far below them. The breeze whorled in, and as it lifted their veils they all smiled, invigorated by the fresh loveliness of the air. A bumble bee flew in and crawled up the pane at Reverend Mother's side of the car. She opened the window and assisted the bee towards the opening with the top of her fountain-pen, but the bee clung to the pen and as she tried to shake it free the wind carried it in again. "Like everything else it hates to leave you," said Sister Benignus. Reverend Mother smiled and the bee flew up to the roof of the car and then alighted on the window beside Sister Paul. Sister Paul swept the bee to safety with the back of her hand.

"You weren't one bit afraid of it," said Sister Clare. "And if it had stung you, you would in a way have been responsible for its death. If it had been a Queen bee – though Queens wouldn't be flying at this time of the year – you would have been responsible for the deaths of potential thousands. A Queen bumble bee lays over two thousand eggs in one season!"

"'Tis a great pity we haven't a hen like that," put in Sister Francis, and they all laughed except Sister Clare. Sister Francis laughed till her eyes watered and, once more, she took off her spectacles. Reverend Mother fidgeted slightly and, in order to control her annoyance, she fixed her gaze on Sister Clare and asked her to continue her interesting account of the life of bumble bees. Sister Paul put her hands in her sleeves and sought distraction in the combings of cloud that streaked the sky.

Reverend Mother pressed her toe on the floor of the car and, instead of listening to Sister Clare, she was glaring unconsciously at Sister Francis who was tapping her spectacles on the palm of her hand and giving an odd laugh.

"Your spectacles are giving you much trouble today," she broke in, unable any longer to restrain herself. "Perhaps you would like to sit in the middle. It may provide your poor eyes with some rest."

"No, thank you," said Sister Francis, "I like watching the crowds of cyclists passing on the road. But sometimes the sun glints on their handlebars and blinds me for a moment and makes me feel that a tiny thread or two has congregated on my lenses. It's my imagination of course."

"Maybe you would care to have a look at *St. Anthony's Annals*," and Reverend Mother handed her the magazine.

"Thank you, Mother. I'll keep it until we reach the shore, for the doctor told me not to read in moving vehicles."

The car rolled on slowly and when it reached the top of a hill, where there was a long descent of five miles to the sea, a strange silence came over the nuns, and each became absorbed in her own premeditation on the advancing day. "Go slowly down the hill," Reverend Mother ordered the driver.

Boys sailed past them on bicycles, and when some did so with their hands off the handlebars a little cry of amazement would break from Sister Francis and she would discuss with Sister Clare the reckless irresponsibility of boys and the worry they must bring to their parents.

Suddenly at a bend on the hill they all looked at Sister Paul for she was excitedly drawing their attention to a line of young poplars. "Look, look!" she was saying. "Look at the way their leaves are dancing and not a flicker out of the other trees. And to think I never noticed them before!"

"I think they are aspens," said Sister Clare, "and anyway they are not indigenous to this country."

"We had four poplars in our garden when I was growing up — black poplars, my father called them," said Sister Paul, lost in her own memory.

"What family did they belong to? There's *angustifolia, laurifolia,* and *balsamifera* and others among the poplar family."

"I don't know what family they belonged to," Sister Paul went on quietly. "I only know they were beautiful — beautiful in very early spring when every tree and twig around them would still be bleak — and there they were bursting into leaf, a brilliant yellow leaf like a flake of sunshine. My father, God be good to his kindly soul, planted four of them when I was young, for there were four in our family, all girls, and one of the trees my father called Kathleen, another Teresa, another Eileen, and lastly my own, Maura. And I remember how he used to stand at the dining-room window gazing out at the young poplars with the frost white and hard around them. "I see a leaf or two coming on Maura," he used to say, and we would all rush to the window and gaze into the garden, each of us fastening her eye on her own tree and then measuring its growth of leaf with the others. And to the one whose tree was first in leaf he used to give a book or a pair of rosary beads. ... Poor Father," she sighed, and fumbled in her sleeve for her handkerchief.

"Can you not think of what special name those trees had?" pressed Clare. "Did their leaves tremble furiously — *tremula, tremuloides?*"

"They didn't quiver very much," said Sister Paul, her head bowed. "My father didn't plant aspens, I remember. He told us it was from an aspen that Our Saviour's rood was made, and because their leaves remember the Crucifixion they are always trembling. ... But our poplars had a lovely warm perfume when they were leafing and that perfume always reminded my father of autumn. Wasn't that strange?" she addressed the whole car, "a tree coming into leaf and it reminding my poor father of autumn."

"I know its family now," said Clare, clapping her hands together. "*Balsamifera* – that's the family it belonged to – it's a native of Northern Italy."

"And I remember," said Paul, folding and unfolding her handkerchief on her lap, "how my poor father had no gum once to wrap up a newspaper that he was posting. It was in winter and he went out to the poplars and dabbed his finger here and there on the sticky buds and smeared it on the edge of the wrapping paper."

"That was enough to kill the buds," said Clare. "The gum, as you call it, is their only protective against frost."

"It was himself he killed," said Paul. "He had gone out from a warm fire in his slippers, out into the bleak air and got his death."

"And what happened to the poplars?" said Clare. But Sister Paul had turned her head to the window again and was trying to stifle the tears that were rising to her eyes.

"What other trees grew in your neighbourhood?" continued Clare. Sister Paul didn't seem to hear her, but when the question was repeated she turned and said slowly: "I'm sorry that I don't know their names. But my father, Lord have mercy on him, used to say that a bird could leap from branch to branch for ten miles around without using its wings."

Sister Clare smiled and Reverend Mother nudged her with her elbow, signing to her to keep quiet; and when she, herself, glanced at Paul she saw the sun shining through the fabric of her veil and a handkerchief held furtively to her eyes.

There was silence now in the sun-filled car while outside cyclists continued to pass them, free-wheeling down the long hill. Presently there was a rustle of paper in the car as Sister Francis drew forth from her deep pocket a bag of soft peppermints, stuck together by the heat. Carefully she peeled the bits of paper off the sweets, and as she held out the bag to Reverend Mother she said: "Excuse my fingers." But Reverend Mother shook her head, and Clare and Benignus, seeing that she had refused, felt it would be improper for them to accept. Francis shook the bag towards Paul but since she had her eyes closed, as if in prayer, she neither saw nor heard what was being offered to her. *"In somno pacis,"* said Francis, popping two peppermints into her own mouth and hiding the bag in her wide sleeve. "A peppermint is soothing and cool on a hot day like this," she added with apologetic good nature.

A hot smell of peppermint drifted around the car. Reverend Mother lowered her window to its full length, and though the air rushed in in soft folds around her face it was unable to quench the flaming odour. Somehow, for Reverend Mother, the day, that had hardly begun yet, was spoiled by an old nun with foolish habits and by a young nun unwise enough not to know when to stop questioning. Everything was going wrong, and it would not surprise her that before evening clouds of rain would blow in from the sea and blot out completely the soft loveliness of the sunny day. Once more she looked at Paul, and, seeing her head bowed in thought, she knew that there was some aspect of the countryside, some shape in cloud or bush, that brought back to Paul a sweet but sombre childhood. For herself she had no such memories – there was nothing in her own life, she thought, only a mechanical ordering, a following of routine, that may have brought some pleasure into other people's lives but none to her own. However, she'd do her best to make the day pleasant for them; after all, it was only one day in the year and if the eating of peppermints gave Sister Francis some satisfaction it was not right to thwart her.

She smiled sweetly then at Francis, and as Francis offered the sweets once more, and she was stretching forward to take one there was a sudden dunt to the back of the car and a crash of something falling on the road. The car stopped and the nuns looked at one another, their heads bobbing in consternation. They saw the driver raise himself slowly from his seat, walk back the road, and return again with a touch of his cap at the window.

"A slight accident, Sister," he said, addressing Reverend Mother. "A cyclist crashed into our back wheel. But it's nothing serious, I think."

Reverend Mother went out leaving the door open, and through it there came the free sunlight, the cool air, and the hum of people talking. She was back again in a few minutes with her handkerchief dabbed with blood, and collected other handkerchiefs from the nuns, who followed her out on to the road. Sister Paul stood back and saw amongst the bunch of people a young man reclining on the bank of the road, a hand to his head. "I can't stand the sight of blood," she said to herself, her fingers clutching her rosary beads. She beckoned to a lad who was resting on his bicycle: "Is he badly hurt, lad? He'll not die, will he?"

"Not a bit of him, Sister. He had his coat folded over the handlebars and the sleeve of it caught in the wheel and flung him against the car."

"Go up, like a decent boy, and have a good look at him again."

But before the lad had reached the group the chauffeur had assisted the injured man to his feet and was leading him to the car. The handkerchiefs were tied like a turban about his head, his trousers were torn at the knee, and a holy medal was pinned to his braces.

"Put his coat on or he'll catch cold," Reverend Mother was saying.

"Och, Sister, don't worry about me," the man was saying. "Sure it was my own fault. Ye weren't to blame at all. I'll go back again on my own bicycle – I'm fit enough."

Reverend Mother consulted the chauffeur and whatever advice he gave her the injured man was put into the back of the car. Sister Francis was ordered into the vacant seat beside the driver, the baskets were handed to Paul and Clare, and when the man's bicycle was tied to the carrier they drove off for the hospital in the town.

The young man, sitting between Reverend Mother and

Sister Paul, shut his eyes in embarrassment, and when the blood oozed through the pile of handkerchiefs Reverend Mother took the serviettes from the baskets and tied them round his head and under his chin, and all the time the man kept repeating: "I'm a sore trouble to you, indeed. And sure it was my own fault." She told him to button his coat or he would catch cold, and when he had done so she noticed a Total Abstinence badge in the lapel.

"A good clean-living man," she thought, and to think that he was the one to meet with an injury while many an old drunkard could travel the roads of Ireland on a bicycle and arrive home without pain or scratch or cough.

"'Tis a blessing of God you weren't killed," she said, with a rush of protectiveness, and she reached for the thermos flask from the basket and handed the man a cup of tea.

Now and again Sister Paul would steal a glance at him, but the sight of his pale face and the cup trembling in his hand and rattling on the saucer made her turn to the window where she tried to lose herself in contemplation. But all her previous mood was now scattered from her mind, and she could think of nothing only the greatness of Reverend Mother and the cool way she took command of an incident that would have left the rest of them weak and confused.

"How are you feeling now?" she could hear Reverend Mother asking. "Would you like another sandwich?"

"No, thank you, Sister; sure I had my good breakfast in me before I left the house. I'm a labouring man and since I'm out of work this past three months my wife told me to go off on the bike and have a swim with myself. I was going to take one of the youngsters on the bar of the bike but my wife wouldn't let me."

"She had God's grace about her," said Reverend Mother. "That should be a lesson to you," and as she refilled his cup from the thermos flask she thought that if the young man had been killed they, in a way, would have had to provide his widow and children with some help.

"And we were only travelling slowly," she found herself saying aloud.

"Sure, Sister, no one knows that better than myself. You were keeping well into your own side of the road and when I was ready to sail past you on the hill my coat caught in the front wheel and my head hit the back of your car."

"S-s-s," and the nuns drew in their breath with shrinking solicitude.

They drove up to the hospital, and after Reverend Mother had consulted the doctor and was told that the wound was only a slight abrasion and contusion she returned light-heartedly to the car. Sister Clare made no remark when she heard the news but as the wheels of the car rose and fell on the road they seemed to echo what was in her mind: *abrasion and contusion, abrasion and contusion.* "Abrasion and contusion of what?" she asked herself. "Surely the doctor wouldn't say 'head' – abrasion and contusion of the head?" No, there must be some medical term that Reverend Mother had withheld from them, and as she was about to probe Reverend Mother for the answer the car swung unexpectedly into the convent avenue. "Oh," she said with disappointment, and when alighting from the car and seeing Sister Francis give the remains of her sweets to the chauffeur she knew that for her, too, the day was at an end.

They all passed inside except Reverend Mother who stood on the steps at the door noting the quiet silence of the grounds and the heat-shadows flickering above the flower-beds. With a mocking smile she saw the lawnmower at rest on the uncut lawn and found herself mimicking the gardener: "I'll have it all finished today, Sister, I'll have it all finished today." She put a hand to her throbbing head and crossed the gravel path to look for him, and there in the clump of laurel bushes she found him fast asleep, his hat over his face to keep off the flies, and three empty porter bottles beside him. She tiptoed away from him. "He has had a better day than we have had," she said to herself, "so let him sleep it out, for it's the last he'll have at my expense. . . . Oh, drink is a curse," and she thought of the injury that had befallen the young man with the Abstinence Badge and he as sober as any judge. Then she drew up suddenly as something quick and urgent came into her mind: "Of course! — he would take the job as gardener, and he unemployed this past three months!" With head erect she sped quickly across the grass and into the convent. Sister Paul was still in the corridor when she saw Reverend Mother lift the phone and ring up the hospital: "Is he still there? . . . He's all right? . . . That's good. . . . Would you tell him to call to see me sometime this afternoon?" There was a transfigured look on her face as she put down the receiver and strode across to Sister Paul. "Sister Paul," she said, "you may tell the other Sisters that on tomorrow we will set out again for the shore." Sister Paul smiled and whisked away down the corridor: "Isn't Reverend Mother great the way she can handle things?" she said to herself. "And to think that on tomorrow I'll be able to see the poplars again."

A Schoolmaster

BELIEVE ME the queerest man I ever met was a schoolmaster, a distant relation of my own, a man by the name of Neeson. He was unmarried, and like most of my relations he was bald, but that had nothing to do with his queerness. He was the principal of a two-teacher school in the townland of Killymatoskerty about five miles from Ballymena, and in that draughty cage of a school I taught under him for one long, miserable year. Of course if I had known the manner of man he was I wouldn't have gone near him.

I was young and had little knowledge of the world when he first put his paws on me. I was just out from the Training College when a letter, without a stamp, came to me from Master Neeson saying he required an assistant and that he could get me appointed. I paid the surcharge on the letter and wrote accepting the job. A week later another stampless letter arrived telling me that he would meet my train on Saturday at Ballymena and escort me to my digs at Killymatoskerty. The letters without stamps puzzled me and, being suspicious by nature I came to the conclusion that Master Neeson had innocently given the letters to a schoolboy to post and that the lad had pocketed the stamp-money.

"About your letters," I probed cautiously when I was walking with him from Ballymena station.

"Yes, yes, of course," he answered, taking my arm confidentially. "Now you're going to tell me about the stamps. Sure I knew you wouldn't mind paying a penny or two for a letter. You know, Michael, it's very difficult to get stamps where I teach, and I just toss the letters — the ones to my special friends of course — into the roadside post-box. Soon enough, Michael, you'll learn that teaching in Killmatoskerty has its little drawbacks, its little in-conveniences — miles away from civilisation." And then he told me how he had tried every garage in Ballymena to hire a car to drive us out to Killymatoskerty and divil the one was to be had for love nor money: "McCambridge's is the only garage I didn't try," and he took my arm and whispered to my ear: "Maybe, Michael, you'd have better luck than I." It was very warm as we walked along the sun-scorched street, and Master Neeson took off his hat and fanned his shiny head. He pointed out McCambridge's to me and while he held my suitcase I went up and stood waiting in the thick greasy heat of the garage. In a few minutes I was waving and smiling to him: "Come on — we're in luck!"

When we were seated in the motor he rubbed his thin little hands together: "It's grand, Michael, we were lucky enough to get a car. A five-mile-walk in that heat would suffocate you." And as the car raced into open country I looked out at the fields and saw men stripped to the waist sweeping scythes through the ripe corn. "Grand harvest weather, Michael," and he put down the window and felt the cooling breeze on his bald head. Hens slept in holes un-der the shade of the hedges and a dog licked the drops that dripped from a pump. At a wayside pub I stood the Master a bottle of stout and while he was drinking it he told me that on account of his weak digestive system only one bottle agreed with him.

Into the car we got again and I lay back and lit my pipe. He asked me what kind of brand I smoked and I asked him to try a fill. He borrowed my matches, lit his pipe, and put the matchbox in his pocket.

"Nice cool tobacco," he said. "You'd get nothing like that around these parts. . . . My God, that's a grand blend! A lovely blend!" — his admiration mounting with each puff. "Leave it to you to pick out the good stuff!" and he

174

joined his hands across his stomach, closed his narrow little eyes, and blew out the smoke with whistling satisfaction. Then he pointed the shank of his pipe at Slemish where cloud-shadows were moving to pilfer the sun from the fields. "Climb up there some day and you'll see the grandest sight in Ireland. . . . All County Antrim spread at your feet and a breeze that you could drink coming up from the sea! I could be happy there myself herding pigs!" and he opened his mouth in a gale of laughter.

At his house he ordered the driver to stop, and he got out for a few minutes telling me to stay where I was as I had still another two miles to go. From where I sat I could see the grey school; its three windows with empty flower-pots, a few discarded lunch-papers lying at the porch, and the red post-box built into the pillar of the gate.

"I was just telling the housekeeper I'd not be back for tea," he said, sinking down on the seat again. He clapped and rubbed his hands: "We can have tea together in your digs and celebrate the evening. You'll be at the very pinnacle of comfort where I'm bringing you." He put his pipe in his pocket and leaned forward with a hand on my knee: "You'll get plenty of fresh eggs and fresh butter and bacon and chickens." And he said this with such keen delight that even the very words seemed to contain the flavour of the food. The car stopped at a slated farmhouse, and while Master Neeson carried in my suit-case I paid the driver.

In the low sitting-room – two steps down off the kitchen – we dined off cold chicken, beetroot and fresh lettuce. Master Neeson, with his head down near the plate, simply tore at the food and at the end wiped his mouth with the palm of his hand and winked an eye: "If you don't mind, Michael, I'll wrap up this leg of a chicken for my housekeeper just to show her how a chicken should be cooked." He wrapped it carefully in a piece of newspaper, put in his pocket, and sat down in the arm-chair. Though the air was warm there was a fire of turf in the grate and he stretched out his short legs in front of it and joined his hands across his stomach. His boots were thickly soled, and though he was a thin man he wore a celluloid collar with a black bow, a Donegal tweed suit and a silver chain with a heavy watch. "If you don't mind, Michael," he said, blinking his eyes, "I'll have forty winks. That glass of stout has overpowered me and the long walk in to meet the train was very exhausting. You know, Michael, I didn't want you to be straying round Ballymena like a lost pup."

I slipped out to have a look at the countryside and when I came back the Master was snoring, the tea dishes cleared away. I sat down quietly and while I was looking for something to light my pipe I noticed a piece of greasy newspaper lying in the fender and in the red heart of the fire the dark outline of a chicken bone. The smell of my tobacco wakened him and he took out his pipe and asked me to oblige him with another fill. Shortly afterwards he left for home.

For the first few weeks it never occurred to me to criticise Master Neeson, but I couldn't close my ears to the gossip of the country people, for whenever his name was mentioned there were surreptitious giggles and furtive winkings of the eye: "You haven't a spare match on you," someone would say, imitating Master Neeson's voice. The group would give an inward chuckle until someone else would drawl: "Now you wouldn't happen to have a wee tiny bit of solution to mend a puncture," or "I hear Master Neeson needs a new housekeeper – don't all rush!" I learned from them that he cut his own turf in the moss, wheeled it out himself, and instead of employing a man to cart it home he very ingeniously made a one-wheeled trailer, affixed it to the back fork of his bicycle and in this way was able to bring home six or seven basketfuls of turf after school-hours. When he cycled past the houses someone was sure to say: "There's Master Neeson away by" and someone ask: "Has he the baby with him?" – meaning the basket on the trailer.

In school he was like a machine, now and again glancing out of the window in dread of an inspector's visit. He tried very indulgently to fashion my life in accordance with his

176

own: "Always be early, Michael! Never miss a day! Keep your books corrected; and above all – oh, above all – keep to the time-table!" He was a slave to that time-table and even in the coldest days of winter he would be out in the yard, his hat on his head, putting his shivering class through their physical jerks. One morning I was late; I came in at 9-30 and inserted 9-15 in the teachers' roll; he told me that it was dishonest and that I had committed a serious breach of the regulations. He lectured me on punctuality; then he lectured me on thrift, producing from his desk a little black notebook which he assured me was twenty years old. He licked his thumb and turned the pages: in it he had tabulated the names of past pupils who had owed him pennies or halfpennies for books. Then he whispered into my ear: "When you know the country people as well as I do you'll find they're all out to fleece you!"

At lunch-time I didn't go home, but made tea on a primus stove. And one day he joined me and gave as much praise to the tea as he had done to the blend of my tobacco, rubbing his hands and saying: "Michael, that housekeeper I have can't make tea. I think I'll get rid of her." He could form habits quickly and every day now he sat down with me at lunch-hour and gave out his unctuous litany. But the gossips had affected me; I was ashamed of him and never revealed to anyone that he was a distant relation of my own. Then after Christmas I bought a second-hand bicycle and cycled to my digs at lunch-hour, leaving him to tinker, if he liked, with my primus stove.

Cold frosty weather set in and I took a day off. He was up to see me after school-hours and sat on the edge of the bed, talking incessantly: "The average is going down. . . . When a teacher stays away it's a bad example for the children. . . . There'll be forty per cent. absent tomorrow." He ran his forefinger round the circumference of his celluloid collar and stretched out his empty palm over the bed-clothes: "What capitation-grant will I lift at the end of the year? Nothing! Not a solitary penny!"

"But I've a temperature!" I almost shouted.

"A temperature! A young man like you to have a temperature! My God you talk like a medical student! Do you know how many days I've missed within the last twenty years?" I had heard it all before so I turned my head to the wall. He leaned over the bed-clothes: "Not one day have I missed! There's a record for you. . . . And here you are – a young man with rich, luscious blood to be talking about a temperature!" Then he whispered close to my ear: "You'll be in tomorrow, Michael? Don't let me down." To get rid of him I said "Yes!" and though the next morning I arrived after ten I was confronted with his ponderous watch which lay ticking beside the teachers' roll. He rubbed his hands, and while I signed my time on the roll-book I was conscious of his scrutinising eyes.

I was tired of him and looked out for a change. Easter approached, and he described with great volubility how he was yearning for the week's holidays. "Where do you intend going?" I asked him.

"To the old home. . . . To my mother's across the Bann. . . . I never go anywhere else on my holidays. I've been doing that for the past thirty years – there's a record for you!" And that Easter when I was going to Ballymena to catch the train I saw him perched on his bicycle ready to set off for his mother's. He had on his only suit – the heavy Donegal tweed; a spring clip was fixed to the rim of his hat and attached to it was a piece of cord which in turn was swivelled to a button on his coat. On the trailer was a crate of hens, poking out their heads, and chuckling hysterically when a dog came over and sniffed at them. "Have a good time," he said to me and then got down from the saddle and whispered: "I'm taking some of the hens with me for the week. That housekeeper, I have, would starve them." But later when I came back after the week's holidays it was rumoured throughout the country that he had taken the laying hens with him for the week and left the others with the housekeeper.

I avoided him now as much as possible and saw little of

him except during school-hours or when he rode past the house on a sunny afternoon on his way to the moss. But towards the end of June he asked me to his house to help him with the rolls and averages for the school-year.

It was late in the evening when I arrived, and his housekeeper brought me into his bare little sitting-room. The turf was set in the grate, the white papers sticking out ready to be lit. She told me that Master Neeson had to go out as the parish priest had sent for him, and she handed me a note which the Master had left. In it he advised me how to proceed with the calculations and admonished me – underlining the words heavily – to be sure and do the calculations in pencil and he would check them.

"Would you put a match to the fire?" I asked the housekeeper.

"Oh, sir," she said, twisting her apron, "I think you shouldn't light it till the Master comes back. There's a way in lighting it or it'll smoke the place."

I bent down and lit the fire and she stood with a hand to her cheek, watching me. I smiled to her: "I'll take the blame." She stared at me with wide knowing eyes and then went out quickly.

On a round table near the window was a corkless bottle of ink with a jagged top, a pen, four roll-books backed with brown paper and on the ledge of the window a few dead flies, a *Superseded Spelling Book* and a Nesfield's *English Grammar*. In that atmosphere I worked steadily for two hours, looking through the window now and again to see if the Master were coming. I lit the lamp, but there was little oil in it and after half an hour it went dead. I hammered on the table for the housekeeper, but she didn't hear me, and getting up I struck matches and went to look for her. She was sitting in the kitchen, a kettle simmering on a sunken fire, a skimpy light stretching from the lamp on the wall which was bare except for a grocer's calendar.

I turned the lamp up full. "Oh, sir!" she started. I told her about the lamp in the room. She shook her head and told me that the Master had the key of the outhouse where the oil was stored. I sat on the table and chatted to her and because I had a splitting headache I asked her to make me a cup of tea.

"Sir, sir, I couldn't!" and she looked up at me with frightened eyes. "Not till Master Neeson arrives." I understood everything, and I stretched up my hand to the mantelpiece and lifted down the tea-canister. "I'll make it!" I said. "Many's the cup I made in school for the Master."

"Please, sir," she pleaded, "don't meddle with it! He has it marked!"

"How – marked?"

"He has a livin' fly in the inside of the canister, sir, and if she gets out he'll know somebody was at the tea."

I took the lid off the canister and a fly rose out, circled round the lamp, and then flew up to the white ceiling to join her companions. Under my breath I damned the Master and wished that he had come in while I was making the tea. I sat on the table, drank the tea, and gorged myself with four thick slices of his loaf. The housekeeper joined and unjoined her hands, refused to take the tea I had poured out for her telling me that tea would put her off her sleep. Near midnight I left for home.

In the morning he was waiting for me in the school-porch. I smiled to him and he blazed at me with his narrow little eyes: "What right have you to interfere in my domestic affairs! Are you going to teach me how to manage my own house – a young pup from the city that knows nothing of country life or country people!" The sweat gleamed on his bald head; his celluloid collar was clammy on his neck and he wiped it with his handkerchief. He asked me to apologise and I walked in past him and signed my time heavily on the teachers' roll.

For a whole week we did not speak to one another and a week later I sent in my resignation and shortly afterwards returned home.

Yesterday the postman brought me a letter without a stamp. I looked at the familiar handwriting on the envelope and handed it back to the postman. But, being suspicious by nature, I've been wondering ever since what it was he had to say to me and why he still considers me as one of his "special friends".

Six Weeks On And Two Ashore

IN the early hours of the night it had rained and the iron gate that led to the lightkeepers' houses had rattled loose in the wind, and as it cringed and banged it disturbed Mrs. O'Brien's spaniel where he lay on a mat in the dark draughty hallway. Time and time again he gave a muffled growl, padded about the hall, and scratched at the door. His uneasiness and the noise of the wind had wakened Mrs. O'Brien in the room above him, and she lay in bed wondering if she should go down and let him into the warm comfort of the kitchen. Beside her her husband was asleep, snoring loudly, unaware of her wakefulness or of the windows shaking in their heavy frames. The rain rattled like hailstones against the panes and raced in a flood into the zinc tank at the side of the house. God in Heaven, how anybody could sleep through that, she said—it was enough to waken the dead and there he was deep asleep as if it were a calm summer night. What kind of a man was he at all! You'd think he'd be worrying about his journey to the Rock in the morning and his long six weeks away from her. He was getting old—there was no mistake about that. She touched his feet—they were cold, as cold as a stone you'd find on a wintry beach.

The dog growled again, and throwing back the bedclothes she got up and groped on the table for the matchbox. She struck one match but it was a dead one, and she clicked her tongue in disapproval. She was never done telling Tom not to be putting his spent matches back into the box but he never heeded her. It was tidy he told her; it was exasperating if she knew anything. She struck three before coming upon a good one, and in the spurt of flame she glanced at the alarm-clock and saw that it was two hours after midnight. She slipped downstairs, lit the lamp, and let the dog into the kitchen. She patted his head and he jumped on the sofa, thumped it loudly with his tail and curled up on a cushion. On the floor Tom's hampers lay ready for the morning when the boatmen would come to row him out to 'the lighthouse to relieve young Frank Coady. She looked at the hampers with sharp calculation, wondering if she had packed everything he needed. She was always sure to forget something – boot polish or a pullover or a corkscrew or soap – and he was always sure to cast it up to her as soon as he stepped ashore for his two weeks leave. She could never remember a time when he arrived back without some complaint or other. But this time she was sure she had forgotten nothing for she had made a list and ticked each item off as she packed them into the cases. Yes, he wouldn't be able to launch any of his ill-humour on her this time!

She quenched the lamp, and returning to her room she stood at the window for a moment and saw the lighthouse beam shine on the clouds and sweep through the fine wire of falling rain. Tom was still asleep, heedless of his coming sojourn on that windy stub of rock. But maybe if the wind would hold during the night the boatmen would be unable to row him out in the morning. But even that would be no comfort – waiting, and waiting, and watching the boatmen sheltering all day in the lee of the boathouse expecting the sea to settle. It'd be better, after all, that they'd be able to take him. She got into bed and turned her back to him, and as she listened to the rain she thought of how it would wash the muddy paw-marks from the cement paths and save her the trouble of getting down on her hands and knees in the morning.

She awoke without aid of the alarm-clock, and from her bed she saw the washed blue of the sky, and in the stillness heard the hollow tumult of the distracted sea. He'd have to go out this morning – there was no doubt about that! But

183

God grant he'd return to her in better form! She got up quietly, and buttoning her frock at the window she gazed down at the Coadys' house. The door was open to the cold sun and Delia Coady was on her knees freshly whitening the doorstep that had been streaked in the night's rain. All her windows were open, the curtains bulging in the uneasy draught. Delia raised her head and looked round but Mrs. O'Brien withdrew to the edge of the window and continued to watch her. Delia was singing now and going to the zinc tank at the side of the house for a bucket of water.

Tom stirred in his bed and threw one arm across the pillow.

"Do you hear her?" his wife said.

"Hear who?" he mumbled crossly and pulled the clothes up round his chest.

"Delia Coady is singing like a lark."

"Well, let her sing. Isn't it a free country?"

The alarm clock buzzed on the table and she let it whirl out to the end of its spring.

Tom raised his head from the pillow and stared at her. "Isn't it a great wonder you didn't switch that damned thing off and you up before it?"

"You better get up, Tom. Delia will think you're in no hurry to take her Frank off the rock."

"I'll go when it suits me – not a second faster. When young Coady's as long on the lights as I am he'll not hurry much. The way to get on in my job is to go slow, slow, slow – dead slow, snail slow, and always slow. Do you remember what one of the Commissioners said to me on the East Light in Rathlin? 'Mister O'Brien,' he said, "there's not as much dust in the whole place as would fill a matchbox.' And the secret is – slow."

"No Commissioner would use such a word as 'matchbox'."

"And do you think, woman, that I'm making up that story? What would you have him say?" and he affected a mincing feminine accent: " 'Lightkeeper O'Brien, there is not as much elemental dust in the hallowed precincts of

184

this Lighthouse as would fill a silver snuff-box.' Is that what you would have him say?" he added crossly.

"I don't think he'd pass any remark about dust or dirt."

"You don't think! You don't think! It's a wonder you didn't think of switching off the damned alarm-clock and you knowing I hate the sound of it."

She said nothing. All their quarrels seemed to arise out of the simplest remarks – one remark following another, spreading out and involving them, before they were aware, in a quarrel of cold cruelty. She, herself, was to blame for many of them. She should have let him have his little story of "the matchbox". What on earth possessed her to turn a word on him and this the last day she'd be speaking to him for six long weeks? She checked a long sigh, tidied the things in the room quietly, and all the time tried to find something to say that would soften her last words to him. She crossed to the window and put her hand to the snib to lower it. Delia was still singing and standing out from the door the better to see the freshly whitened window-sills and doorstep.

"She has a lovely frock on," she said over her shoulder. "I never saw her in that before; it fairly becomes her."

"Didn't I tell you she was married in blue! It'll be the same frock."

"She has a nice voice."

"I think you're jealous of her."

"Hm, I used to be able to sing very well myself."

"I must say I heard precious little of it."

"Maybe you didn't! Maybe you'd be interested to know I gave that up shortly after we were married – some twelve years ago."

"And whose fault was that?"

"Oh, I don't know," she said, controlling herself.

He pulled the clothes over his shoulder and she pleaded with him to get up and not be the sort that'd deprive another man of even one hour of his leave on shore.

"Is it Frank Coady I'd hurry for! Not me! I'll take my time. I'm over thirty years on the lights and he's a bare half-dozen. He doesn't rush much if he's coming out to relieve me."

"You can't blame him and he not long married," she said, scarcely knowing what she was saying as she spoke into the mirror and brushed her hair.

"Last time he came out to relieve me I was waiting for the boat all morning and it didn't come to the afternoon. And what did he say as he stepped ashore? 'God, Tom, I'm sorry the boat's late. I took a hellish pain in my stomach and had to lie down for a couple of hours.' That's what the scamp said to me instead of offering to give me an extra day on account of his hellish pains. Well, I feel tired this morning and I'm not stirring hand or foot for another hour at least!"

She turned round in her chair from the mirror: "I'm beginning to get tired of that word 'tired' of yours. You were tired last night, tired the night before – always tired. You've said nothing else since you stepped ashore two weeks ago. Tired! – it's not out of any consideration you show me. Going off to the pub of an evening and waiting there till somebody gives you a lift home."

"And what do you want me to do? What do you want off me?"

"Oh, nothing," she almost cried, "nothing! I'm used to loneliness now! I'm used to my married widowhood! In my marriage! You won't come for a game of Bridge of an evening. You're tired – you always say. And if I go you won't wait up till I come back. You lower the lamp and go to your bed. Oh, it's no wonder my hair is beginning to turn grey at the temples."

"My own is white!"

"What do you expect and you nearing sixty?"

"You're lovely company!"

"Company! Only for the companionship of the old dog I'd go out of my mind."

"If you'd go out of this room I might think of getting up."

"Oh, if I'd thought I was keeping you back I'd have

186

gone long ago," and she lifted the alarm-clock, the box of matches, and hastened from the room.

He stretched his arms and looked at the glass of water on the table. He'd not drink that! The stale taste of it would upset him – and what with his stomach upset and his mind upset he'd be in a nice fix for a journey on the sea. He'd smoke a cigarette – and stretching out to the chair for his coat, he lit one, and lay back on the pillows, frowning now and then at the cold air that blew through the open window. He could hear Delia singing and he wondered if Mag sang when she was expecting him home. He doubted it! She was more attached to that damned old dog, and she thought nothing of walking five miles of an evening for a game of cards and bringing the old dog with her. If she were on the rock for awhile it'd soon tether her, soon take the skip out of her step. Ah, he should have married somebody less flighty, somebody a bit older and settled, somebody that'd enjoy a glass of stout with you of an evening and not be wanting to drag you over the whole blasted country in search of a game of Bridge.

Downstairs he heard Mag opening the front door and letting out the dog for a run, and he heard her speak across to Delia and say how glad she was that it had cleared up in time for Frank's homecoming. Hm, he thought, she's greatly concerned about the neighbours. He looked at the cigarette in his hand, and from the bed he tried to throw it through the open window but it struck the pane and fell on the floor, and he had to get up and stamp on the lighted end.

His clothes were folded neatly for him on the edge of the table: a clean white shirt, his trousers creased and the brass buttons on his jacket brightly polished. He pulled on the cold starched shirt and gave a snort of contempt. He wished she'd be less particular – ye'd think he was expecting a visit from the Commissioners on the Rock. Damn the thing you ever saw out there except an exhausted pigeon or a dead cormorant that you'd have to kick into the sea to keep the blowfly from stalking around it. It's remarkable the nose a blowfly has for decaying flesh – flying two or three miles out to sea to lay its eggs on a dead sea bird. Nature's remarkable when you come to think about it – very remarkable!

Mag tapped the stairs with her knuckles and called out that his breakfast was ready, and when he came down, she glanced at him furtively, trying to read from his face the effect of her remark to him about his white hair. If only she could tell him that she was sorry. But it was better not to – it was better to let it pass and speak to him as if nothing had happened.

"Oh, Tom," she said brightly, "Delia was over to see what time you expected to go."

"And how the hell do I know at what time I'm expected to go? I'll wait till the boatmen call – and to my own slow and unhurried time."

"She has plenty of paint on, this morning," she added to restore ease.

"Who has?"

"The old boat, I mean," she flashed back.

There it was again: they were back to where they started from – chilling one another with silent hostility or with words that would spurt in bitter fury. Oh, she thought, if only he had shown some of his old love for her during the past two weeks they would not now be snapping at one another and there would be ease and satisfaction and longing in this leave-taking.

She brought a hot plate of rashers and eggs from the range and poured out tea for him.

"Maybe, Tom, I should run over and tell Delia you'll be ready as soon as the boatmen arrive. I'd like to take the full of my eyes of her place as she does of ours. I always think there's a heavy smell of paraffin in her kitchen. Do you ever find it, Tom?"

"That smell's been in my nose ever since I joined the Lights. Do you know what I'm going to tell you?" and he raised the fork in his hand as she sat down opposite him. "There's nothing as penetrating and as permanent as the

188

smell of paraffin. It's remarkable. It seeps into the walls and it would ooze out again through two coats of new paint. It's in my nose and I wouldn't know the differs between it and the smell of a flower."

She smiled for she at that moment caught sight of two cases of Guinness's stout on the floor and she yearned to tell him jokingly that he had a fine perfume for something else. But she repressed that desire and turned to the dog as he laid his nose on her lap. She threw him a few scraps from the table and he snapped at them greedily. She fondled his head and toyed with one of his ears, turning it inside out.

"It's a great wonder you wouldn't put out that dog and let me get my breakfast in some sort of Christian decency. There's a bad smell from him."

"And you said a moment ago that you could smell nothing only paraffin."

"Well, I get the smell of him — and that's saying something."

At that moment the dog walked under the table to his side and he made a kick at it and it yelped and ran under the sofa.

"Come here, Brian," she called coaxingly, and the dog came out and walked timorously towards her.

"Either he goes out of this or I don't finish my breakfast!"

Without a word she got up and let the dog out.

"Maybe that'll please you," she said, coming back to the table. "Anything I love, you despise."

"That's a damned lie!"

"It's true — and because you thought I was jealous of Delia you praised her."

"That's another infernal lie!"

"It's too true, Tom. Nothing pleases you — you used to be so different. You used to be so jolly — one could joke and laugh with you. But of late you've changed."

"It's you that's changed!"

She took her handkerchief and blew her nose. She felt the tears rising to her eyes and she held her head, trying to

189

regain her self-control.

A shadow passed the window. There was a knock at the door and she opened it to admit three of the boatmen.

"We'd like to catch the tide, Mister O'Brien," they said, and lifting the hampers they shuffled out of the house.

Tom finished his breakfast slowly and went upstairs. He came down after a short time, dressed and ready for the road. In a glance she saw that he hadn't a breast-pocket handkerchief, and telling him to wait for a minute she ran upstairs to get one, and coming down again she found he was gone. She hurried after him and overtook him at the iron gate.

"Don't keep me back," he said, "didn't you hear as well as I did that we've to catch the tide!" But she held him, and as he tried to wrench himself free she folded the handkerchief into his pocket.

"Tom, don't go away from me like that!" and she looked up at him with an anxious pleading face.

"You're making a fine laughing-stock of me!" he said, and pushing the handkerchief out of sight into his pocket he walked off.

She stood at the gate waiting for him to turn and wave his hand to her but he went on stolidly, erect, along the loose sandy road to the shore. He smoked his pipe, the road sloping before him, its sand white in places from the feet of the boatmen and dark with rain where it was untrodden.

The men were already in the boat, baling out the night's rainwater, and as Tom picked his steps over the piles of slabby wrack on the shore they kept calling out to him to be careful. They assisted him into the boat and he sat in the stern, his legs apart, and his arms dangling between his knees. The boatmen spat on their hands, gripped the oars, and in a few minutes were out from the shelter of the cove and saw ahead of them the black rock with its stub of a lighthouse like a brooding sea-bird. The men rowed with quick, confident strokes, and the boat rose and fell, cutting white swathes on the green sward of the sea.

"Take your time," Tom said, "take your time. You're

not paid for sweating yourselves. We'll be there soon enough."

They said nothing, and as they came nearer to the rock they saw the white path curving from the top to the water's edge and saw the waves jabbing and shouldering one another in mad comfusiom. They dipped their oars now in short, snappy strokes, their eyes on the three lightkeepers who awaited them.

"Ye'll have to jump for it, Mister O'Brien, when we give the word. We'll get the cases landed first," and while one held off the boat with a boat hook, two stood at the stern with a case waiting their chance to hoist it on to the outstretched hands of those on shore. When the cases were roped and landed Frank Coady jumped and alighting on the gunwale he balanced himself on one leg as lightly as a ballet dancer. "The fairy godmother!" he said, and folding his arms he spun round on his toe with emphatic daintiness, and then bowing he kissed his fingers to those on shore.

Tom O'Brien lumbered up to him putting his pipe in his pocket.

"Now, Tom, my lad, let me give you a hand," said Coady, stretching out his hand to him.

"Get away from me, you bloody fool!" said O'Brien, steadying one foot on the gunwhale.

"Be careful now, Mister O'Brien, be careful!" the boatman shouted. "Wait till that big fellow passes. Take him on the rise!"

But O'Brien wasn't listening to them. He took his leap on the descent of the wave, missed the path, and was all but disappearing into the sea when the lightkeepers gripped him and hauled him ashore.

"I'm all right! I'm all right!" he said, as they laughed at his soaked trousers, the knee-cap cut and the blood oozing out of it.

"Are you O.K., Tom?" shouted Coady from the boat.

"Ah, go to hell, you!" said O'Brien.

"He's a cranky oul divil," Coady said to the boatmen as he took off his coat and lifted an oar. "Now, my hearties, let us see how you can make her leap!" He pulled on his oar with all his strength: "Up, my hearty fellows! Up she jumps! That's the way to make her skip! I'll leave a pint for all hands in the pub! A pint from Frank Coady!"

Near the shore he turned his head and saw his wife awaiting him.

"There she is, my hearty men! Knitting and waiting for her darling Frank!" He threw down his oar and perched himself on the bow ready to jump ashore.

"Take care you don't go like O'Brien," they laughed.

"O'Brien's as stiff as a man on stilts! Here she goes!" and he jumped lightly on to the rock and spinning round he warded off the boat with his foot.

In a minute he was in his wife's arms, and linked together they went off slowly along the sandy road, and for a long time the boatmen could hear him laughing and they knew he was laughing at O'Brien.

Through the iron gate they went arm in arm. Mag O'Brien was outside her house with the dog and as Frank drew near he told her with much joyous relish how Tom had cut the knee of his trousers.

"He wasn't hurt?" she said.

"Hurt – not a bit! He strode up the path after it like a man in training for the half-mile. The only thing you need to worry about is to get a nice patch." And taking Delia by the hand they swung across to their house, stood for a minute admiring the whitened doorstep, and going inside they closed the door.

Mag withdrew and sat for a minute at her own window that overlooked their house. Her head ached, and she thought how careless she was in forgetting to pack a bandage or a taste of iodine that he could daub on his bruised knee. One can't think of everything, she said, and she laid her hands on her lap and gazed across at Coady's house that was now silent and still. With an effort she got to her feet and withdrew from the window, and taking a stick she called her dog and set off through the iron gate and away to the shore that was nearest to the rock.

She scanned the rock and the white path down to the sea. If only he saw her and came out on the parapet as he used to do and signal to her she'd be content – her mind would be eased. She sat down on a green slope and waited. There was no stir about the rock, only a gull or two tilting and gliding above the sea. She got up and waved her hand. The dog scratched at the ground, leapt sideways, impatient to be off. She waved again – still there was no sign that she was being seen. She turned and felt the soft wind – it was light and tired: exhausted after its rampage. She stretched herself and stood facing it but it was too weak even to shake her hair. If only it were strong, blowing against her with force she would delight in it. But there was no strength in it – it was indolent and inert, as tired as an old man. She looked once more at the Rock, and seeing a black whorl of smoke rising from it she knew that it was Tom putting on a good fire. He would take a book now, or a bottle of Guinness and his pipe and after that he would close his eyes and sleep.

The dog barked and ran up the slope after a rabbit. She followed after him and looking to the right she saw the iron gate and the clump of houses she had just left. There was nothing there but silence and sunlight, and behind her the stir of the cold sea.

The Wild Duck's Nest

THE SUN was setting, spilling gold light on the low western hills of Rathlin Island. A small boy walked jauntily along a hoof-printed path that wriggled between the folds of these hills and opened out into a crater-like valley on the cliff-top. Presently he stopped as if remembering something, then suddenly he left the path, and began running up one of the hills. When he reached the top he was out of breath and stood watching streaks of light radiating from golden-edged clouds, the scene reminding him of a picture he had seen of the Transfiguration. A short distance below him was the cow standing at the edge of a reedy lake. Colm ran down to meet her waving his stick in the air, and the wind rumbling in his ears made him give an exultant whoop which splashed upon the hills in a shower of echoed sound. A flock of gulls lying on the short grass near the lake rose up languidly, drifting like blown snowflakes over the rim of the cliff.

The lake faced west and was fed by a stream, the drainings of the semi-circling hills. One side was open to the winds from the sea and in winter a little outlet trickled over the cliffs making a black vein in their grey sides. The boy lifted stones and began throwing them into the lake, weaving web after web on its calm surface. Then he skimmed the water with flat stones, some of them jumping the surface and coming to rest on the other side. He was delighted with himself and after listening to his echoing shouts of delight he ran to fetch his cow. Gently he tapped her on the side and reluctantly she went towards the brown-mudded path that led out of the valley. The boy was about to throw a final stone into the lake when a bird flew low over his head, its neck a-strain, and its orange-coloured legs clear in the soft light. It was a wild duck. It circled the lake twice, thrice, coming lower each time and then with a nervous flapping of wings it skidded along the surface, its legs breaking the water into a series of silvery arcs. Its wings closed, it lit silently, gave a slight shiver, and began pecking indifferently at the water.

Colm with dilated eyes eagerly watched it making for the further end of the lake. It meandered between tall bulrushes, its body black and solid as stone against the greying water. Then as if it had sunk it was gone. The boy ran stealthily along the bank looking away from the lake, pretending indifference. When he came opposite to where he had last seen the bird he stopped and peered through the sighing reeds whose shadows streaked the water in a maze of black strokes. In front of him was a soddy islet guarded by the spears of sedge and separated from the bank by a narrow channel of water. The water wasn't too deep – he could wade across with care.

Rolling up his short trousers he began to wade, his arms outstretched, and his legs brown and stunted in the mountain water. As he drew near the islet, his feet sank in the cold mud and bubbles winked up at him. He went more carefully and nervously. Then one trouser fell and dipped into the water; the boy dropped his hands to roll it up, he unbalanced, made a splashing sound, and the bird arose with a squawk and whirred away over the cliffs. For a moment the boy stood frightened. Then he clambered on to the wet-soaked sod of land, which was spattered with sea gulls' feathers and bits of wind-blown rushes.

Into each hummock he looked, pulling back the long grass. At last he came on the nest, facing seawards. Two flat rocks dimpled the face of the water and between them was a neck of land matted with coarse grass containing the nest. It was untidily built of dried rushes, straw and feathers, and in it lay one solitary egg. Colm was delighted. He looked around and saw no one. The nest was

195

his. He lifted the egg, smooth and green as the sky, with a faint tinge of yellow like the reflected light from a buttercup; and then he felt he had done wrong. He put it back. He knew he shouldn't have touched it and he wondered would the bird forsake the nest. A vague sadness stole over him and he felt in his heart he had sinned. Carefully smoothing out his footprints he hurriedly left the islet and ran after his cow. The sun had now set and the cold shiver of evening enveloped him, chilling his body and saddening his mind.

In the morning he was up and away to school. He took the grass rut that edged the road for it was softer on the bare feet. His house was the last on the western headland and after a mile or so he was joined by Paddy McFall; both boys dressed in similar hand-knitted blue jerseys and grey trousers carried home-made school bags. Colm was full of the nest and as soon as he joined his companion he said eagerly: "Paddy, I've a nest – a wild duck's with one egg."

"And how do you know it's a wild duck's?" asked Paddy slightly jealous.

"Sure I saw her with my own two eyes, her brown speckled back with a crow's patch on it, and her yellow legs. . . ."

"Where is it?" interrupted Paddy in a challenging tone.

"I'm not going to tell you, for you'd rob it!"

"Ach! I suppose it's a tame duck's you have or maybe an old gull's."

Colm put out his tongue at him. "A lot you know!" he said, "for a gull's egg has spots and this one is greenish-white, for I had it in my hand."

And then the words he didn't want to hear rushed from Paddy in a mocking chant, "You had it in your hand! . . . She'll forsake it! She'll forsake it! She'll forsake it!" he said, skipping along the road before him.

Colm felt as if he would choke or cry with vexation.

His mind told him that Paddy was right, but somehow he couldn't give in to it and he replied: "She'll not forsake it! She'll not! I know she'll not!"

But in school his faith wavered. Through the windows he could see moving sheets of rain – rain that dribbled down the panes filling his mind with thoughts of the lake creased and chilled by wind; the nest sodden and black with wetness; and the egg cold as a cave stone. He shivered from the thoughts and fidgeted with the inkwell cover, sliding it backwards and forwards mechanically. The mischievous look had gone from his eyes and the school day dragged on interminably. But at last they were out in the rain, Colm rushing home as fast as he could.

He was no time at all at his dinner of potatoes and salted fish until he was out in the valley now smoky with drifts of slanting rain. Opposite the islet he entered the water. The wind was blowing into his face, rustling noisily the rushes heavy with the dust of rain. A moss-cheeper, swaying on a reed like a mouse, filled the air with light cries of loneliness.

The boy reached the islet, his heart thumping with excitement, wondering did the bird forsake. He went slowly, quietly, on to the strip of land that led to the nest. He rose on his toes, looking over the ledge to see if he could see her. And then every muscle tautened. She was on, her shoulders hunched up, and her bill lying on her breast as if she were asleep. Colm's heart hammered wildly in his ears. She hadn't forsaken. He was about to turn stealthily away. Something happened. The bird moved, her neck straightened, twitching nervously from side to side. The boy's head swam with lightness. He stood transfixed. The wild duck with a panicky flapping, rose heavily, and flew off towards the sea. . . . A guilty silence chilled the boy. . . . He turned to go away, hesitated, and glanced back at the dark nest; it'd be no harm to have a look. Timidly he approached it, standing straight, and gazing over the edge. There in the nest lay two eggs. He drew in his breath with delight, splashed quickly from the island, and ran off whistling in the rain.

Look at the Boats

"OH, SISTER, look at the boats!" The boy pointed at the docks where red funnels of ships rose in the air, the wintry sun shining on their varnished masts.

"You'll see plenty of boats, Peter, where you are going. Come quickly now or you'll miss the train," said the nun, walking along with her head down and her hands in her sleeves.

Around them was the pulse and traffic of the city, but Peter paid no heed as he began to spell aloud the enormous black letters printed on the shipping sheds: G-L-A-S-G-O-W, L-I-V-E-R-P-O-O-L, H-E-Y-S-H-A-M.

They came on to the iron-latticed bridge and in sight of the station. The nun walked slowly, allowing Peter to enjoy the grand view of the boats from the bridge. The harbour was blue and sparkled with cold sunlight, but under the bridge the water was brown and carried on its back whirls of soot and orange peel. Peter leaned over the parapet, fascinated by the long line of ships and the gulls that flew around them.

Over the bridge they went. A one-legged man sat beside his charcoal drawings and a few coppers lay in his cap, but Peter had no eyes for him; he kept craning his head towards the ships, and when he came into the chilly station he could see them no more.

"Don't you worry, madam," said the railway guard to the nun. "I'll see him right to Downpatrick."

The nun placed a hand on Peter's shoulder: "Be a good boy now and work hard for your new master." And as she passed out of the station she sighed: "They're getting a

198

manly little fellow anyway."

Peter, carrying his belongings in a brown parcel, walked along the platform, and the guard opened a carriage door for him: "Sit in there, and don't be sticking yer head out of the window. She'll be going out in a minute or two."

The carriage was heated, the windows closed, and a stale tobacco smell lingering in the air. He sat down on the seat with the parcel on his lap, and waited for the train to start.

He was a sturdy lad of fifteen, black haired, dressed in a grey suit and grey stockings; and swivelled to a button on his coat was a label with his new address printed in ink:

PETER McCLOSKEY,
   c/o. MR. & MRS. ROBERT GILL,
      KILLARD,
         STRANGFORD, CO. DOWN.

He was fingering the label when the guard came in and told him about the people he was going to: "Aw, Robert Gill is as dacent a man as you'll find in the whole countryside. He'll be at Downpatrick to meet you . . . . . . Aw, you'll have a nice place with Robert."

Slowly the train moved out, and sunlight crossed and recrossed the carriage like pages turning in a book. Out past the backs of grey houses it rumbled and he saw chalk-markings on the doors, pigeon-sheds on the yard walls, a clothes-line with two pegs, and in one place the paper tails of a kite entangled in the telegraph wires. Stations with tin advertisements rattled past, and then came a great brightness in the carriage as the train raced into the open country.

The hedges were black and ragged, and deserted nests stuck out as clear as thrown sods. The fields were newly ploughed, and around the farm houses were hay stacks and bare trees. Sheep rushed madly from the thundering train; the long twisted roll of smoke shook itself over the fields, tore through the hedges, and trailed away in tattered rags.

Here and there at a station groups of shawled women with baskets waited for the train, and sometimes the guard opened Peter's door: "Everything all right, lad? It won't be long now till we're there." He would wave his green flag and the train, with many a protesting grunt, would chug away from the silent box of a station.

The country became more hummocky, and from the window he saw the lovely triangular mountains of Mourne. Presently the train curved and rumbled between rushy lakes that were littered with wild ducks and suddenly the ducks arose and circled in great scattered flocks until the noise of the train was swallowed up in Downpatrick station.

Peter sat patiently in the carriage; doors opened and slammed; and then the guard appeared, accompanied by a small man smoking a pipe.

"This is your lad, Robert. A fine lump of a fella he looks!"

Robert nodded his head and shook Peter's hand. They passed out of the station, Robert a little in front, the tail of his green-black overcoat spattered with mud, and a tweed cap on the back of his head. They went over to a cart where a woman stood at the horse's head.

"Alice!" Robert said to her. "This is our boy . . . . . What's this now yer name is?" . . . . . Peter! A good solid name! 'Thou art Peter and upon this Rock' . . . . . Man, I knew my catechism when I was at school. And do ye know, the schoolmaster wanted me to go on for the Church . . . . ."

"Here quit the swaggering till we get on the road," interrupted Alice. "The boy's perished with the cold. I'm sure you're hungry, son . . . . . Come on, Robert, and we'll go over to Fitzsimon's atin'-house for a mouthful of tay."

They crossed to a shop that displayed in the window dishes of soda farls and four bottles of lemonade, a flowerpot with no flowers, and a card announcing in scraggy letters: TEA, BREAD, and BUTTER – 6d.

When they came out again, the faint sun was low in the sky, a frosty wind was skimming over the road, and the horse was stamping impatiently. They moved slowly out of the hilly town, Robert and Alice walking alongside the cart, and Peter sitting in it with a black shawl pinned around his shoulders. Up and up they climbed, with Downpatrick, a grey town of hills and hollows, clumped behind them. The sun had now exhausted itself, and its light shone on the ploughed land and the gables of white cottages.

They topped the braes and descended towards flat-spreading land with the long arm of Strangford Lough stretching into it. Robert motioned with his pipe to a white column that marked the mouth of the lough and the open sea. "Fornenst that is the house, Peter. We're down at the very jaws of the sea!" And he shook the rope-reins of the horse and she moved quickly down the hill. He looked at his big watch and then turned his head towards the lowering sun: "It'll be dark afore we're home." And he handed the reins to Alice and pared a stump of a candle for the lamp. His hands were red with the cold and when he shut his fists white marks appeared on his knuckles.

The cart bumped and jolted on the road. A cold wind swept over the land and the candle brightened in the increasing darkness. The horse began to pull harder and a brisker sound rattled from her hooves as she came into the full blast of the sea. The land was now dark and lights from the scattered homes glimmered like little sparks; Peter could see them through the bare hedges and sometimes his eyes shut as he gazed at the shadows of the wheel revolving in the light of the lamp. But when he heard the waves break on the stones he sat up alert and occupied, gazing across the black land to the steely sea.

The horse stopped and Robert stretched himself and groaned: "Thank God, we're landed!"

The key was turned in the door, and Alice, without taking off her hat and coat, went cautiously over to the oil-lamp on the wall, and when it was lit Peter saw the interior of his new home. The fire was out, the floor was stone flagged, a towel hung from a nail on the back door, and above it was a horseshoe covered with silver paper.

Robert stamped about and rubbed his hands: "That

night's as dark as a grave. Hurry up, Alice, and get a blink in the fire."

Then he began to spar playfully with Peter. "Man, boy, when I was at sea I was a great fighter. I mind once when we landed at Bombay and one of them Indian coolies – aw, a towering giant of a fella – he starts to give up ould guff."

"Here!" ordered Alice. "Will you stop your ould guff and hack a bit of stick for the fire . . . . . Here, child! He wouldn't think of offering you a seat itself with his ould blether. Sit over at the hearth, though there's no fire in it 'tis warmer than around the door."

Peter sat on the stool. Above him were black rafters with rows of salted fish and coils of rope, and in one corner an old checked school-bag which caught his eye every time he raised his head.

Soon the sticks were crackling and Robert, with his overcoat around him and his cap pushed back from his bald head, took a chair by the fire. He began to light his pipe and Peter watched the glow on his brown face and his eyes shining as dark as sloes. He pulled deeply at the pipe and pressed the lighted paper down into the bowl.

"Do ye know," says he, without taking his eyes off the bowl of the pipe, "what is the nearest thing to death about a house?"

Nobody answered him and he made another spill to light his pipe. "Well, I'll tell ye. . . . . A hearth without a fire and a house without a woman!"

He spat into the fire with great satisfaction and swayed back on the chair till its front legs rode off the floor.

Alice listened to him and her mind stumbled back through the years, and from the tangles of her memory she sought for the things that had been her life: marrying Robert when he came from sea; buying the house and the land; black winters and poor harvests that they had lived through; and now when old age had crept upon them they had brought in a boy to help with the land and the fishing. She turned and saw him with his hands on his knees, her shawl around his shoulders and the pin of it catching the firelight. She sighed to herself: "The years are flying." And as if to hold them back and get something done she bustled so quickly about the table that Robert looked at her with pride. "Man, Alice, you're the girl can hustle herself when hunger's in the air."

Peter sat quite still. Outside was the noising sea, and he thought of the boats that he had seen in the morning, leaving the orphanage with the nun, the train and the guard, and then the tiresome journey on the cart. It seemed such a long, long time for one day.

"Now, Peter, eat yer fill. Butter his bread for him, Alice . . . . . Them newspapers tell ye not to eat goin' to bed. But don't heed them. Always take plenty of ballast aboard for a night's journey."

Alice smiled and he noticed that she was eating nothing. "Are yer pains back again, Alice?"

"No, no, the journey's upset me," and she split a farl in two and forced herself to eat.

After the tea Peter drowsed by the fire, listening to the slow contented pulls of Robert's pipe and Alice making a yellow mash for the hens. Then the sounds became blurred, his eyes closed, and his head jerked towards the fire.

"Yer dying with sleep, Peter!" and Robert stretched out a hand and patted his knee.

He smiled sleepily, and Alice lit a candle and brought him across the kitchen to his room. The air was cold, the bed low, and boxes and trunks along the walls. She thumped the pillow a few times and then drew in her breath sharply as a pain stabbed her side. Peter looked at her anxiously and she smiled. "Good-night now, and don't forget yer prayers. And blow out the candle."

He lay for awhile listening to the sea; and later when Alice peeped into the room to see if he had blown out the candle he was fast asleep.

In the morning, instead of the white enamel bed of the orphanage and the noisy chatter of boys, he found himself in a dark little room. Coats with newspapers on the shoulders hung on the door and gulls flew past the window. A bucket clattered and Alice shouted: "Away on, you thief . . . . . . There's that rogue of a gull back again, Robert. I can't leave a pick of hens' mate about the place but she throttles it!"

Robert stamped his feet at the threshold.

"I'll lame her one of these fine days! That's the same girl that lifts the salted fish! Ai, I'll give it to her!" The gull called and dipped low over the house and a fistful of gravel followed in her wake.

Every morning there was the same taunt, but the gulls paid no heed and flocked around unconcernedly. The days were short and cold. The white cottage with its tarred roof overlooked the sea, and in stormy weather the spray flung itself at the windows, swished on the roof, and the gulls forsook the shore.

Slowly Peter fitted into his new life, and he would often sit with Robert on the upturned boat at the side of the house. The boat was propped on flat stones and made a shelter for the hens in wet weather; and one day when Peter himself had crawled under it Robert had seen him and shouted in to him: "Look hard and tell me if ye see any seams of light in her roof." And when Peter had answered "No!" Robert began to praise the great timber that was in her and to tell Peter of the grand fishing they'd have as soon as June arrived.

It was now March, the days dry and blustery, and the sea very blue. Robert's land was ready for the plough and one dry morning he and Peter were early astir. They went out to a last year's potato field which lay grey and uneven under a cold sky.

The plough tore it up without bother. Peter walked in front of the plough and lifted stones out of its way, while behind Alice gathered in her lap potatoes that had lain in the soil all winter. Day by day Peter learned Robert's phrases: "There's no nourishment in land that's easily ploughed," or "The soil here'd kill no horse: it's too dry and sandy," or "It's a hungry bit of land and you have to

204

keep feedin' it with manure." And Peter repeated these to himself and to the boys he met in the evenings or coming from Mass.

When the field was opened Robert began to sow the seed using a bed-sheet looped around his neck as a carrier. He sowed the one way, scattering the grain with his back to the wind for it was blowing fiercely. Peter stood to the side clodding at the gulls and the crows and pouring buckets of seed into the sheet. The small field was at the back of the house and sheltered from the sea by a scraggy line of thorn bushes; they were now stooped and black and from their lower thorns sheep's wool streamed in the wind. To keep himself warm Peter raced and shouted at the birds, and even when Alice called him for his dinner he looked angrily out of the window at the crows waddling over the brown soil and pecking at the seed. "Them's the thieves; they'll have all the corn ate if we don't hurry."

"Aw now, they have to feed like everybody else," Robert winked at Alice.

But Peter rose from his dinner and with his fists full of stones he made out to the field and scattered the gulls and the crows. The next day Robert let him harrow and laughed at the way he sprawkled over the soil. "Aw, Peter, yer not strong enough. But ye'll grow, and next year ye'll be sowing the grain yerself."

Cold days passed and the brown field was swept by a frosty wind. Then came rain and the green shoots appeared above the ground. Buds came in the thorn bushes, but no birds sang in them. And one day when Robert saw Peter searching for nests he nodded his head. "Them bushes are poisoned with the salt water and there's no shelter in them. It's in from the sea the birds build," and he pointed across his fields to the thick hedges and the clumps of trees that rose out of the kindlier land.

Whins came in bloom, the larks rose in the air, and the ewes gave birth to their young. It was time for putting in potatoes. People were in the fields from early morning and in the evenings the dead weeds were burnt and the air was filled with a pleasant smell.

Robert's potato field was small and his own horse opened the drills. The seed potatoes were carried out in crates from the dark barn. Peter forked the manure into the furrows and Alice placed the seed on top with their white teeth towards the sky. The plough moved down and the soil gushed over the seed. In two days they had sown the potatoes; and then Robert made lobster-pots, Peter sitting beside him on the upturned boat learning the craft.

For weeks the wind stayed in the north and there came no rain. The soil turned grey and the young corn ceased growing. At Mass on Sunday they offered up prayers for rain and on the road home Robert joked with the neighbours: "The Man above is tired listening to us. His head is astray with our crankiness. When it does rain we want sunshine and when we have sun we want rain."

But the days continued dry and warm, and Peter had to take the horse to a river a mile off and cart home barrels of water. The sun scorched the land, and the seedlings lengthened their white roots and sought strength and moisture in the darker earth. And in the evenings Robert stood at the gable of the house looking across the land at the sun going down in yellow glory from the naked sky.

Then the wind changed to the south and the air became soft with the promise of rain. Flocks of black cloud blew in from the sea and from their ragged edges rain fell like tails of sand. The soil softened, wet mists lay in the folds of the land, and in the evenings there was the smell of growing things.

The grass thickened and Peter had to take the cow along the sea-road and let it graze from the banks. Alice gave him a switch and when he went into the byre to fetch the cow Robert followed him. "If the policeman passing on his bicycle asks ye why the cow is trespassin' on the public highway tell him yer takin' her to the field. Do ye hear?" And he laughed loudly for he knew there wasn't as much grazing in his field as'd satisfy a goat.

As the cow grazed along the edges of the road Peter ran

down the sloping bank to the shore and searched for crabs; and amongst the hard encrusted seaweed he found whitened corks and rusted tin-tops of bottles, and with these he made a boat with funnels and decks. He lay and watched the tide, like a river in flood, flowing out of the lough to the open sea. And one day when a coal-boat approached he forgot about the cow, so intensely did the boat hold his mind. It cruised about the bar waiting for the tide to turn and carry it up to Portaferry; then as it neared the shore he gazed at the white spurt of water that gushed from its side and at the smoke purling from the funnel. A man in his shirt-sleeves leaned over the rail and flung a bucket with a rope on it into the sea, and then he hauled in and swilled the water along the deck. Peter waited for him to do it again, but the hoot of a lorry startled him and he raced up to the narrow road where the driver abused him for having his cow loose.

Every day, now, he was to be seen with the cow along the road; and the neighbours got to know him and bade him the time of day, as they passed in carts, on bicycles, or on foot. He learned the directions of the wind, and when it blew soft and moist from the south-west and he saw in the distance the clouds pile up on the top of the Mournes he knew it was going to rain. But he never turned home. He sought shelter at the gables of tumbled-down houses or snuggled against grassy banks, knowing that the wind blew strong from the sea and slanted the rain from him. At such times he tore out stones from the bank and prodded the scurrying ants with a twig as they scrambled into their tiny holes. Then he would watch the gulls on the shore all facing windward and he knew they did that to keep their feathers smooth. Sometimes he gathered primroses and put them in a glass jam-pot in the ledge of the window; and once when he was gathering them a lark flew off her nest and he saw her five chocolate eggs, and watched day by day until the young birds had feathered and taken wing.

In the evenings shelduck flew in flocks from the upper reaches of the lough and fed amongst the weedy stones and green glut below the house. He often tried to get near them, but they were always first to fly off and alight again on the other side of the lough. Lazily the gulls would follow, and the shore would be deserted when Peter had gone back to the house. As darkness fell he would stand at the bedroom window, gazing at the windy light of the buoy on the lough's mouth and farther out the winking lights of ships passing through the night.

The summer came, the crops grew and hid the clay in the fields. Robert tarred and painted his boat, spread her brown sail in the sun and patched it in places where the mice had gnawed it. Hens' feathers stuck to the tar, the sun blistered it and Peter burst the blisters with his fingers. The day arrived when she was carried from the side of the house to the shore. Robert taught him how to row and how to feather his oar; and in the evenings he stood proudly at the door, feeling the hardness of his muscles, and looking at the boat lying up on the stones.

In the mornings they were up when the fields were grey with dew, the sea cold and colourless, and the sky dull. The whole world would be asleep but themselves and the sea. They spoke little to each other as Peter pulled towards the line of corks that marked the lobster pots. Robert, standing in the stern, would heave in the pots, cautiously take out the blue lobsters and then rebait with stale fish. The chilly air would fling the sleep from Peter, and resting on the oars he would scan that low, wide land with its white houses, dead and deserted, and nothing astir now but the beasts in the fields and an odd gull swaying in the air. Far out at sea the steamers, lonely and black, seemed to catch a deadness from the morning. But when the sun burst forth and flung a broken quivering light upon the sea, mist rose from the land, whiteness came to gulls, and the cows coughed as they got up from the crushed-warm grass.

"'Tis the best time of the day to be up, Peter. You could thrive on that air; there's great strength in it," and Robert would smoke his pipe as he tied the toes of the lobsters with bits of string. "If you left them boyos too long in the pots they'd find their way out again; and you'd think to look at their ugly mugs that they'd no intelligence. But them big crabs! I don't think they could find their way out of an empty can!"

In again, Alice would have the fire going and bowls of hot tea and eggs on the table. And one morning when they had finished their breakfast Robert told Peter to get the spade, and at low tide they went off to dig in the sand for lug worm. "I'll bring you out to the banks this day and we'll give the whiting a quare scutching. Do you think ye'd be fit to pull her out?"

"I could row her the whole way myself," Peter replied with great eagerness.

After the dinner Robert got ready the hand-lines and Alice filled a can with buttermilk and in another can put bread and scallions.

"This'll help to keep away the hunger till yiz come in again," and she handed the cans to Peter.

"And listen, Alice," said Robert turning at the door, "when Kelly comes round about the lobsters, don't be soft with him. Tell him my orders: a shillin' a-piece for the lobsters or no sale."

She watched them go down to the boat. Peter in front carrying the cans, and Robert with an oar under his arm and the fishing gear in a basket.

They rowed out to the mouth of the lough and when they reached the open sea they hoisted the sail. A few boats were already on the banks and when Robert saw them he said with great pride: "Them boats is too far south for this tide. Wait'll ye see where Robert'll anchor," and his eye scanned the coast. "We'll not be there till the boat's in line with the Mill and the Black Rock," and he pointed to the land and taught Peter the 'marks'.

"Go up to the bow, now, and pitch out the anchor when I tell ye." Robert jabbed at the water with his oars, his eyes fixed on the mainland. "Now!" he shouted.

Out went the anchor, and the rope burned through Peter's hands until the anchor found bottom. The boat swung round and bobbed up and down on the waves. A few gulls floated near and called loudly when the sun shone on them from a blue gap in the clouds.

Robert showed Peter how to bait the hooks, and in a few minutes the lead sinkers on the lines were flung over the side and were racing for the sandy bottom. They hauled in together and Peter laughed with delight when he saw a whiting on each of his hooks.

"And ye tell me ye never fished in yer life before . . . . Well, well, it's hard to believe it. It must be in the blood . . . . . . Ye'll see them other boats comin' over to us when they see how we're killing . . . . . D'ye think ye could find it again?"

Peter faced the land. "Get the Mill and the Black Rock in line with the boat and out with yer anchor!"

Robert laughed loudly at the way Peter answered him and added: "Yer a purty intelligent fella . . . . . Ye must have been born on the sea."

And so they lay out for hours, sometimes Robert smoking or handing round the can of buttermilk and the bread. Peter loved it and only wished now that he could smoke a pipe like Robert. He watched the gannets bursting into the sea and the cormorants with their long necks flying near the surface, but when the Ardglass herring boats appeared in the south he shouted excitedly: "Look, Robert, at the long line of boats."

"Them's the Ardglass men going out in the heel of the evening . . . . . It's a grand sight to see them . . . . . But it's the Dutch boats ye want to see; a lovely sight with their coloured sails. It's like a procession with banners."

Peter listened as he told about other parts of the world, but all the time his eyes were on the herring drifters, watching the distance shorten between them. "Are they tryin' a race, Robert?"

" 'Deed, by my sowl, they might be! But it's not always the first boat gets the most herrin'."

They hauled in the anchor and moved to a fresh mark, and when the sun had set they made for home. The even-

ing was without an air of wind and they had to row,
Robert advising Peter to take it easy as they had a long pull
ahead of them. To the left at the foot of the sky were the
hills of the Isle of Man with a big steamer passing near.

"That boat's goin' to Liverpool from Belfast," said
Robert; and Peter remembered the day he had spelt aloud
the words on the shipping sheds.

"And are there many boats in Liverpool?" he asked.

"Aw, hould yer tongue!" Robert spat over the side.
"They're as thick as the corn in the fields; they choke each
other for space — boats from all parts of the world! That's a
sight! It wasn't the first time Robert was in Liverpool. And
d'ye know that's where I signed on my first boat."

He began to tell how he had left home for Belfast and
sailed for Liverpool. He told of the foreign countries that
he had seen, fights at sea, and how once in a fierce storm he
was flung out of his bunk and had broken his arm.

Peter listened to him in silence.

"What d'ye think of that for a life?" Robert finished.

Peter startled, his eyes were shining, and he gave a nervous little laugh.

Behind them the beam from St. John's Lighthouse was
lengthening in the wading dark. They rowed with long
slow sweeps and soon they rounded the point and came
into their own quiet bay. Alice had the light in the window and its beam made a shivering path upon the sea.

In below the house they landed and when Alice heard
the thump of the oars she came down to meet them She
crossed her hands over her breast when she saw the white
mass of fish.

"Well, yiz did get one or two."

Robert didn't answer her.

"And had you any luck, Peter?"

"Any luck!" And Robert told about the way Peter
fished:

"In the line goes and up it comes — a pair of whiting on
it every time."

Peter smiled and pulled with all his strength when they

211

hauled the boat. There was silence; waves jabbled amongst the stones and a fish flapped in a last leap. Out on the bar the buoy's light shone and a chilly air rose up from the sea. Robert would roll up the sail, Peter bail out with a tin the brackish water, and together they would walk slowly towards the warm light in the doorway. Peter would chop sticks for the morning's fire and then take a last look round at the sheds. Sometimes he would stay out too long and Alice would come to the door: "Peter, are you there? Come on in or ye'll be foundered. There's a draught comes through the mouth of the lough that'd clean corn!"

And when the door was shut for the night, the blinds hooked to the window, the dishes washed and put on the dresser, Robert would take out his pipe, and Peter begin paring a piece of wood that was gradually taking on the shape of a boat. Alice would salt the fish and in the sunny mornings put them on the low hen-house roof and cover them with netting wire.

Week by week their stock of fish increased; the corn ripened early and their potatoes were good. At night when Peter had gone to bed they'd sit close to the fire and talk about him and the year that was ending. "That boy has brought up great luck . . . . . Thanks be to God for him!" And they'd fall silent and feel a deep peace breathing in the house.

The winter was stormy. Robert nailed boards on the outside of the windows to break the force of the tide, the door was shut early, and great fires of coal banked high in the wide grate. If no neighbour had come in for a céilidhe Robert lifted down his old schoolbag and took out his black Reading Book. Its pages were yellow and gave off a damp mouldy smell. Across the flyleaf there was written in scraggy letters: ROBERT GILL, KILCLIEF NATIONAL SCHOOLS, 1880.

"I was a good hand-writer in them days," he said, "but my fingers is now buckled with age."

Peter got the book and was told to read aloud Robert's favourite lesson: *The Locusts . . . . . For twelve miles did they extend from front to rear, and their whizzing and hissing could be heard for six miles on every side of them. The bright sun, though hidden by them, illumined their bodies, and was reflected from their quivering wings; and as they fell heavily earthward, they seemed like the innumerable flakes of a yellow-coloured snow. The poor peasants hastily dug pits and trenches as their enemy came on, in vain they filled them from the wells or with lighted stubble. Heavily and thickly did the locusts fall; they were lavish of their lives: they choked the flame and the water, which destroyed them the while, and the vast living hostile armament still moved on . . .*

"Them's the quare plague for you," Robert commented. "We have the blow-fly here and the cleg, but thanks be to God, we've no locusts. They'd make short work of our wee bit of land."

If Peter balked at a word Robert supplied it without consulting the book for he knew it as well as Alice knew her prayer book. Alice was knitting a blue gansey for Peter and sometimes she'd pause and say "Is there nothing cheerful in that book? I'm tired of them sad stories." Then she'd go on with her work and call Peter over beside her and measure the jersey against his chest. "It's a bit on the short side yet."

"Give him plenty of room in it," Robert would put in, "for he's growin' like a bad weed and I must get him long trousers."

The evening the gansey was finished Robert measured Peter's leg with a string, and the next morning he went off in the cart to Downpatrick. That day Alice was feeding the fowl and Peter saw her sway and fall to the ground. He carried her into the house, sprinkled cold water on her face, and she opened her eyes and slowly smiled at him: "I'm a silly woman to be fallin' on ye like that. Ye mustn't tell Robert on me." But ever afterwards when Peter would gaze at her she'd smile and say: "What's wrong with ye the day, Peter, yer very quiet?" And at Mass on Sundays he noticed how she sat upon the seat and only knelt at the Consecration.

Coming home from Mass Robert and Peter walked

together: Robert with the pipe in his mouth, and Peter with his thumbs stuck in his trousers' belt and his hob-nailed boots striking the road with great vigour.

He grew tall and strong and that spring he was able to hold the plough and put down a barbed wire fence to keep out the sheep. But the rabbits came into the young corn in spite of him, and one evening as they were setting snares Robert said to him: "They aren't as good as the frog."

"What frog?"

"Well, that's a good one," replied Robert, as he hammered a peg into the ground. "And ye tell me ye never heard of the frog. It bates all none of the lads or Alice told you about me and the frog."

He lit his pipe, stuffed his hands in his pockets and began to walk from the sandy banks towards the house. The light was in the window and the wind was stirring in the grass.

"There'll be a few rabbits in them in the morning, for a windy night brings them out on the prowl. Aw, if only we could catch a frog." And then he began to walk slowly. "It was a night like this, only calmer, when I came out my lone to get a rabbit or two. I mind it well, Peter. It was very dark and there wasn't a star to be seen anywhere and there wasn't as much wind in it as'd sway a cobweb. And when I reached the hollow over there I heard a frog croaking, and I crept over on my hands and knees and caught him. Then I takes out a stump of a candle, lights it, and splatters a few drops on the frog's back, sticks my candle on top. What do I do now? Into the first rabbit hole I put my frog and in he hopped with the candle still flaring on top of his back.

"The rabbits must have thought it was the Day of Judgment, for they raced out of the holes, big ones and wee ones, old ones and young ones, fat ones and skinny ones, black ones and brown ones, and out by another hole came the frog and I could see him in the dark and the candle as bright as a torch. He was like a trained dog the way he hopped out of one hole into another. And the rabbits tore round me and I cracked out with my stick and the squeals

214

of them could be heard in the Isle of Man. And then a breeze sprang up and I saw the candle go blind, and I never seen trace of my frog from that day till this. And the next morning I never seen the like of it for rabbits: they lay dead in their hundreds, some of them were paralysed for life, and them that got away took till the sea and for weeks the shores was covered with their carcases. Cablegrams came from Australia asking me to name my price to banish their rabbits. I'd have went right away, but long journeys don't agree with Alice and so we stayed at home."

When he had finished his story Peter waited for him to laugh, but Robert smoked away, and the light of the pipe lit up his eyes and there was a seriousness in them as if he were thinking of something else.

The next day when Robert had taken the horse to the blacksmith's, Peter questioned Alice about the frog.

"Don't heed what Robert tells you. He always blathers when he gets somebody to listen to him. He told me many's a one, but never that one . . . . . The only rabbit he ever brought in was an ould thing a motor ran over one winter's night."

"Well was he at sea, Alice?"

" 'Deed, child, he wrought for whiles in Liverpool and was at sea for ten years. But it'd have taken him forty years to ramble the countries that he says he was in. Don't listen to him." And she went on with her work scrubbing the table and halting now and again to look out the window at the green growth in the fields. She scrubbed vigorously and Peter smiled, remembering the day not long ago when she had fallen at the gable.

But one evening as they were making in from the fishing it was dark and there was a light in one of the bedrooms, and when they came ashore two women were there to meet them. "Alice is bad, Robert," one said, and he hurried up the sloping bank to the house, leaving Peter to moor the boat.

Alice was in bed and she smiled weakly at him when he entered the room. There was a bruise on her forehead where she had fallen in her weakness.

"I'll be all right in the morning," she said, and she raised her hand and it fell limply on the quilt.

In the morning she could see the lovely white clouds of May go sailing across the sky. The gulls flew around the window, and the cold, fresh smell of the sea blew into the room. She could hear Robert calling the hens or throwing out the dregs of the teapot on the causeway. She tried to sit up, but she fell back, and her breathing quickened.

Robert talked to her about little things that livened their lives: "Do you mind the time, Alice, that the ould gypsy said you'd lose something soon? . . . . . Do you mind the time we had to fut it the whole was home from Crossgar? . . . . ." Alice looked at him and shut her eyes. "Ah, Robert, my memory is wearin' as thin as an ould shoe."

Peter would come into the room and sit on the edge of the bed, and she'd stroke his hand. "Stay with me for a wee while, I be lonely when I hear no stir about the house."

The priest came. Two days afterwards she was brought to the Downpatrick Infirmary, and one morning about three o'clock a policeman on his bicycle rapped loudly at Robert's door and when he hurried out of bed to open it he knew that Alice was dead.

For days a gloom hung over the house; Robert was quiet in himself, and at night he would sit in the light of the fire. He sold the cow, for there'd be nobody to look after her or milk her when they'd be at the fishing.

But even at the fishing he was quiet and full of unrest, and as he pared his tobacco he'd say: "I declare to God the tobacco they make nowadays is not what it used to be," and he would hold out a chunk of it to Peter. "Smell that! D'ye not get an ould stale reek of it?" And before sundown he would order Peter to lift the anchor.

"But we've another hour or two yet," Peter would answer.

"Do as yer bid. We must get in before dark. Lying out here like an ould plank that has nowhere to go!"

But one evening a head wind blew strong and they had to pull hard against it. It was pitch dark when they reached the little bay below the house. No light from the window warmed the sea, and looking up at it from the boat Robert said brokenly: "It's a lonesome looking place without a light . . . . . The house is dead!" And Peter saw something of the man's mind and remembered the first night he had stepped across the threshold and how Alice had lit the lamp on the wall.

Now it was changed. The house was chilly with no fire reddening the grate. Crusts discoloured by tea lay on the table and dirty dishes were pushed to the side. The floor was unswept and ashes were high in the grate.

Robert bent to a few sticks and began chopping.

"Sit down, Robert, and rest yerself and I'll light the fire."

"And d'ye think I'm not fit to light my own fire?" he answered crossly. "Fill the kettle with water if ye want a job and see that the hens are all in."

Robert stuck a lighted candle to an upturned bowl, placed it on the table, and sat down to the tea. He buttered a piece of bread for Peter. "Eat up now, for I like to see a growin' lad eat his fill . . . . . Ye'll have to make yer own in the mornin' for I'm going to Downpatrick."

And Robert went to his bed and lay awake, his mind disordered. He thought of Alice and prayed for her soul; he thought of Peter. "A brave lad, but if I show him he's too useful he'll override me. I must be firm with him."

In the other room Peter was standing at the window. A high moon had arrived in the sky and where it shone on the water he could see the rise and fall of the waves. Down on the beach was the boat, and a glint came from the bailing tin that lay beside it. Out at sea a big steamer passed with her port-holes all alight, and he watched them until they were swallowed up by the night.

In the morning he was up first and Robert was not astir. He lit the fire. It was past nine o'clock when Robert came into the kitchen, pulling his braces over his shoulders.

"Why didn't you call me, boy? Didn't ye know I was for Downpatrick?"

"I thought maybe ye'd changed yer mind."

"And how'd I have changed my mind?"

Peter didn't answer him. He put a few sticks below the kettle and the water sizzled.

Robert got down on his knees, pulled out his boots from below the table, and knocked them hard against the stone floor.

"Get the horse in the cart and I'll wet the tea . . . . . Will ye have a pair of eggs?"

"I won't have any eggs."

"And why won't you have an egg?"

"I don't want one, that's all."

Peter went out. When he came in again, Robert had bowls of tea on the table and two boiled eggs on Peter's plate. They supped the tea loudly and a contentment filled Robert when he saw Peter eating the eggs.

A hen came in through the open door, looked sideways at the table, and snatched a crust from the floor.

"Whisht on out o' that," Robert rattled his boots at it. "Ye'd think they never seen mate in their lives; it must be the sea air gives them the appetite."

Peter said nothing.

"I'll be back as soon as I can," Robert shouted from the cart. "What's this now the size of boots ye take?" And then he added quickly and in a sharper tone, "Weed a few drills to-day; that yellow weed will have the purties destroyed," and he looked at his growing potatoes and the yellow weed thick amongst them. Soon he turned his back to the sea and made inland; once he looked back and saw Peter standing against the gable.

It was late in the afternoon when he reached Downpatrick, and it was sunset when he was ready to leave, a bag of yellow meal in the cart, a young lamb with its feet tied, bacon and candles, a few badly-tied parcels, and a pair of heavy boots for Peter. It was still bright but the rain was falling and, sitting in his cart, he sought shelter under a big chestnut tree. The heavy drops rattled down through the leaves and he pulled up the ears of his coat and threw an empty sack over the young lamb. He hated the long journey before him and recalled the day they had brought Peter along the same road and how Alice had pinned her shawl about his shoulders. "God be good to her but she was the kindly craythure!"

The rain slackened and he moved off. He felt cold. Steam arose from the horse's back and rainwater lay near the tailboard, straw floating on it. The brown paper parcels were sodden. He shut his eyes and dozed.

The headlights of a motor wakened him and he drew the horse to the side and lit the lamp. The cart jolted in the puddles on the road. He shrugged his shoulders. He'd soon be home; the fire would be reddened for him, the kettle on the boil, and the lamp in the window. He urged on the horse and presently came within the sound of the sea. The waves rolled in slowly and broke with a tired splash. . . . . .

Peter leaned over the rail of the boat that was taking him to Liverpool. It was dark and cold, the deck wet, and all the passengers gone below except himself and an old seaman who walked quietly up and down. Out from the ship's side the waves swirled white and beyond them was darkness, and beyond that again lighthouse beams swept the sky.

Peter hailed the seaman: "Could you tell me where Strangford Lough would lie?"

The seaman stood beside him. "There's the Copeland Light aft and there's St. John's Lighthouse; midway between them would be Strangford – a treacherous lough!" and he paced the deck again.

Peter peered into the darkness towards a land that he could not see.

Flocks of thoughts crowded his mind; the lobsters and the fishing . . . . . the cow on the road . . . . the corn growing in the fields . . . . . the reading about the locusts . . . . . and the death of Alice . . . . .

A cold sorrow swept over him and tears formed in his eyes. He gripped the iron-rail and tried to stifle his grief.

Below someone laughed, a door opened, and a thick smell of tobacco floated out to him. And he thought of Robert jolting home in the cart to a hearth cold for his return. He shuddered. A piercing sense of utter worthlessness crept into his soul, the tears flowed thickly down his cheeks, and he could no longer see the lighthouse beams that wavered across the land.

Father Christmas

"WILL YOU do what I ask you?" his wife said again, wiping the crumbs off the newspaper which served as a tablecloth. "Wear your hard hat and you'll get the job."

He didn't answer her or raise his head. He was seated on the dilapidated sofa lacing his boots, and behind him tumbled two of his children, each chewing a crust of bread. His wife paused, a hand on her hip. She glanced at the sleety rain falling into the backyard, turned round, and threw the crumbs into the fire.

"You'll wear it, John — won't you?"

Again he didn't answer though his mind was already made up. He strode into the scullery and while he washed himself she took an overcoat from a nail behind the kitchen door, brushed it vigorously, gouging out the specks of dirt with the nose of the brush. She put it over the back of a chair and went upstairs for his hard hat.

"I'm a holy show in that article," he said, when she was handing him the hat and helping him into the overcoat. "I'll be a nice ornament among the other applicants! I wish you'd leave me alone!"

"You look respectable anyhow. I could take a fancy for you all over again," and she kissed him playfully on the side of the cheek.

"If I don't get the job you needn't blame me. I've done all you asked — every mortal thing."

"You'll get it all right — never you fear. I know what I'm talking about."

He hurried out of the street in case some of the neighbours would ask him if he were going to a funeral,

221

and when he had taken his place in the line of young men who were all applying for the job of Father Christmas in the Big Store he was still conscious of the bowler hat perched on top of his head. He was a timid little man and he tried to crouch closer to the wall and make himself inconspicuous amongst that group of grey-capped men. The rain continued to fall as they waited for the door to open and he watched the drops clinging to the peaks of their caps, swelling and falling to the ground.

"If he had a beard we could all go home," he heard someone say, and he felt his ears reddening, aware that the remark was cast at him. But later when he was following the Manager up the brass-lipped stairs, after he had got the job, he dwelt on the wisdom of his wife and knew that the hat had endowed him with an air of shabby respectability.

"Are you married?" the Manager had asked him, looking at the nervous way he turned the hat in his hand. "And have you any children?" He had answered everything with a meek smile and the Manager told him to stand aside until he had interviewed, as a matter of form, the rest of the applicants.

And then the interviews were quickly over, and when the Manager and John were mounting the stairs he saw a piece of caramel paper sticking to the Manager's heel. Down a long aisle they passed with rows of counters at each side and shoppers gathered round them. And though it was daylight outside, the electric lights were lit, and through the glare there arose a buzz of talk, the rattle of money, and the warm smell of new clothes and perfume and confectionery – all of it entering John's mind in a confused and dreamy fashion for his eye was fastened on the caramel paper as he followed respectfully after the Manager. Presently they emerged on a short flight of stairs where a notice – PRIVATE – on trestles straddled across it. The Manager lifted it ostentatiously to the side, ushered John forward with a sweep of his arm, and replaced the notice with mechanical importance.

"Just a minute," said John, and he plucked the caramel

paper from the Manager's heel, crumpled it between his fingers, and put it in his pocket.

They entered the quiet seclusion of a small room that had a choking smell of dust and cardboard boxes. The Manager mounted a step-ladder, and taking a large box from the top shelf looked at something written on the side, slapped the dust off it against his knee, and broke the string.

"Here," he said, throwing down the box. "You'll get a red cloak in that and a white beard." He sat on the top rung of the ladder and held a false face on the tip of his finger: "Somehow I don't think you'll need this. You'll do as you are. Just put on the beard and whiskers."

"Whatever you say," smiled John, for he always tried to please people.

Another box fell at his feet: "You'll get a pair of top boots in that!" The Manager folded the step-ladder, and daintily picking pieces of fluff from his sleeves he outlined John's duties for the day and emphasised that after closing-time he'd have to make up parcels for the following day's sale.

Left alone John breathed freely, took off his overcoat and hung it at the back of the door, and for some reason whenever he crossed the floor he did so on his tiptoes. He lifted the red cloak that was trimmed with fur, held it in his outstretched arms to admire it, and squeezed the life out of a moth that was struggling in one of the folds. Chips of tinsel glinted on the shoulders of the cloak and he was ready to flick them off when he decided it was more Christmassy-looking to let them remain on. He pulled on the cloak, crossed on tiptoes to a looking-glass on the wall and winked and grimaced at himself, sometimes putting up the collar of the cloak to enjoy the warm touch of the fur on the back of his neck. He attached the beard and the whiskers, spitting out one or two hairs that had strayed into his mouth.

"The very I-T," he said, and caught the beard in his fist and waggled it at his reflection in the mirror. "Hello, Santa!" he smiled, and thought of his children and how they would laugh to see him togged up in this regalia. "I must tell her to bring them down some day," and he gave a twirl on his toes, making a heap of paper rustle in the corner.

He took off his boots, looked reflectively at the broken sole of each and pressed his thumb into the wet leather: "Pasteboard – nothing else!" he said in disgust, and threw them on the heap of brown paper. He reached for the top boots that were trimmed with fur. They looked a bit on the small side. With some difficulty he squeezed his feet into them. He walked across the floor, examining the boots at each step; they were very tight for him, but he wasn't one to complain, and, after all, the job was only for the Christmas season and they'd be sure to stretch with the wearing.

When he was fully dressed he made his way down the stairs, lifted his leg over the trestle with the name PRIVATE and presented himself on one of the busy floors. A shopgirl, hesitating before striking the cash-register, smiled over at him. His face burned. Then a little girl plucked her mother's skirt and called, "Oh, Mammy, there's Daddy Christmas!" With his hands in his wide sleeves he stood in a state of nervous perplexity till the shop-girl, scratching her head with the tip of her pencil, shouted jauntily: "First Floor, Santa Claus, right on down the stairs!" He stumbled on the stairs because of the tight boots and when he halted to regain his composure he felt the blood hammering in his temples and he wished now that he hadn't listened to his wife and worn his hard hat. She was always nagging at him, night, noon and morning, and he doing his damned best!

On the first floor the Manager beckoned him to a miniature house – a house painted in imitation brick, snow on the eaves, a door which he could enter by stooping low, and a chimney large enough to contain his head and shoulders, and inside the house stacks of boxes neatly piled, some in blue paper and others in pink.

The Manager produced a hand-bell. "You stand here," said the Manager, placing himself at the door of the house. "Ring your bell a few times – like this. Then shout in a loud, commanding voice: 'Roll up now! Blue for the Boys, and Pink for the Girls'." And he explained that when business was slack, he was to mount the ladder, descend the chimney, and bring up the parcels in that manner, but if there was a crowd he was just to open the door and shake hands with each child before presenting the boxes. They were all the same price – a shilling each.

For the first ten minutes or so John's voice was weak and self-conscious and the Manager, standing a short distance away, ordered him to raise his voice a little louder: "You must attract attention – that's what you're paid for. Try it once again."

"Blue for the Boys, and Pink for the Girls!" shouted John, and he imagined all the buyers at the neighbouring counters had paused to listen to him. "Blue for the Boys, and Pink for the Girls!" he repeated, his eye on the Manager who was judging him from a distance. The Manager smiled his approval and then shook an imaginary bell in the air. John suddenly remembered about the bell in his hand and he shook it vigorously, but a shop-girl tightened up her face at him and he folded his fingers over the skirt of the bell in order to muffle the sound. He gained more confidence, but as his nervousness decreased he became aware of the tight boots imprisoning his feet, and occasionally he would disappear into his little house and catching the sole of each in turn he would stretch them across his knee.

But the children gave him no peace, and with his head held genially to the side, if the Manager were watching him, he would smile broadly and listen with affected interest to each child's demand.

"Please, Santa Claus, bring me a tricycle at Christmas and a doll's pram for Angela."

"I'll do that! Everything you want," said Father Christmas expansively, and he patted the little boy on the

225

head with gentle dignity before handing him a blue parcel. But when he raised his eyes to the boy's mother she froze him with a look.

"I didn't think you would have any tricycles this year," she said. "I thought you were only making wooden trains."

"Oh, yes! No, yes, Not at all! Yes, of course, I'll get you a nice wooden train," Father Christmas turned to the boy in his confusion. "If you keep good I'll have a lovely train for you."

"I don't want an oul train. I want a tricycle," the boy whimpered, clutching his blue-papered parcel.

"I couldn't make any tricycles this year," consoled Father Christmas. "My reindeers was sick and three of them died on me."

The boy's mother smiled and took him by the hand. "Now, pet, didn't I tell you Santa had no tricycles? You better shout up the chimney for something else — a nice game or a wooden train."

"I don't want an oul game — I want a tricycle," he cried, and jigged his feet.

"You'll get a warm ear if you're not careful. Come on now and none of your nonsense. And Daddy Christmas after giving you a nice box, all for yourself."

Forcibly she led the boy away and John, standing with his hands in his sleeves, felt the prickles of sweat on his forehead and resolved to promise nothing to the children until he had got the cue from the parents.

As the day progressed he climbed up the ladder and down the chimney, emerging again with his arms laden with parcels. His feet tortured him and when he glanced at the boots every wrinkle in the leather was smoothed away. He couldn't continue like this all day; it would drive him mad.

"Roll up!" he bawled. "Roll up! Blue for the Pinks and Boys for the Girls! Roll up, I say. Blue for the Pinks and Boys for the Girls." Then he stopped and repeated the same mistake before catching himself up. And once more he clanged the bell with subdued ferocity till its sound drowned the jingle of the cash-registers and the shop-girls had to shout to be heard.

At one o'clock he wearily climbed the stairs to the quiet room, where dinner was brought to him on a tray. He took off his boots and gazed sympathetically at his crushed toes. He massaged them tenderly, and when he had finished his dinner he pared his corns with a razor blade he had bought at one of the counters. He now squeezed his bare feet into the boots, walked across the room, and sat down again, his face twisted with despair. "Why do I always give in to that woman," he said aloud to himself. "I've no strength – no power to stand up and shout in her face: 'No, no, no! I'll go my own way in my own time!'" He'd let her know tonight the agony he suffered, and his poor feet gathered up all day like a rheumatic fist.

Calmed after this outburst, and reassuring himself that the job was only for three weeks, he gave a whistle of forced satisfaction, brushed the corn-pairings off the chair, and went off to stand outside the little house with its imitation snow on the chimney.

The afternoon was the busiest time, and he was glad to be able to stand at the door like a human being and hand out the parcels, instead of ascending and descending the ladder like a trained monkey. When the children crowded too close to him he kept them at arm's length in case they'd trample on his feet. But he always managed to smile as he watched them shaking their boxes or tearing holes in the paper in an effort to guess what was inside. And the parents smiled too when they looked at him wagging his finger at the little girls and promising them dolls at Christmas if they would go to bed early, eat their porridge and stop biting their nails. But before closing time a woman was back holding an untidy parcel. "That's supposed to be for a boy," she said peevishly.

"There's a rubber doll in it and my wee boy has cried his eyes out ever since."

"I'm just new to the job," Father Christmas apologised.

"It'll never occur again." And he tossed the parcel into the house and handed the woman a new one.

At the end of his day he had gathered from the floor a glove with a hole in one finger, three handkerchiefs, a necklace of blue beads, and a child's handbag containing a halfpenny and three tram-tickets. When he was handing them to the Manager he wondered if he should complain about the boots, but the tired look on the Manager's face and his reminder about staying behind to make up parcels discouraged him.

For the last time he climbed the stairs, took off his boots and flung them from him, and as he prepared the boxes he padded about the cool floor in his bare feet, and to ensure that he wouldn't make a mistake he arranged, at one side of the room, the contents for the girls' boxes: dolls, shops, pages of transfers, story books, and crayons; and at the opposite side of the room the toys for the boys: ludo, snakes and ladders, blow football, soldiers, cowboy outfits, and wooden whistles. And as he parcelled them neatly and made loops in the twine for the children's fingers he decided once again to tell his wife to bring his own kids along and he'd have special parcels prepared for them.

On his way out of the Store the floors were silent and deserted, the counters humped with canvas covers, and the little house looking strangely real now under a solitary light. A mouse nibbling at something on the floor scurried off between an alleyway in the counters, and on the ground floor two women were sweeping up the dust and gossiping loudly.

The caretaker let him out by a side door, and as he walked off in the rain through the lamp-lighted streets he put up the collar of his coat and avoided the puddles as best he could. A sullen resentment seized his heart and he began to drag from the corners of his mind the things that irritated him. He thought they should have given him his tea before he left, or even a bun and a glass of milk, and he thought of his home and maybe the fine tea his wife would have for him, and a good fire in the grate and the kids in bed. He walked more quickly. He passed boys eating chip potatoes out of a newspaper, and he stole a glance at Joe Raffo's chip-shop and the cloud of steam rolling through the open door into the cold air. The smell maddened him. He plunged his hands into his pockets and fiddled with a button, bits of hard crumbs, and a sticky bit of caramel paper. He took out the caramel paper and threw it on the wet street.

He felt cheated and discontented with everything; and the more he thought of the job the more he blamed his wife for all the agony he had suffered throughout the day. She couldn't leave him alone – not for one solitary minute could she let him have a thought of his own or come to a decision of his own. She must be for ever interfering, barging in, and poking into his business. He was a damned fool to listen to her and to don a ridiculous hard hat for such a miserable job. Father Christmas and his everlasting smile! He'd smile less if he had to wear a pair of boots three sizes too small for him. It was a young fella they wanted for the job – somebody accustomed to standing for hours at a street corner and measuring the length of his spits on the kerb. And then the ladder! That was the bloody limit! Up and down, down and up, like a squirrel in a cage, instead of giving you a stick and a chair where you could sit and really look like an old man. When he'd get home he'd let his wife know what she let him in for. It would lead to a row between them, and when that happened she'd go about for days flinging his meals on the table and belting the kids for sweet damn-all. He'd have to tell her – it was no use suffering devil's torture and saying nothing about it. But then, it's more likely than not she'd put on her hat and coat and go down to the Manager in the morning and complain about the boots, and then he might lose the job, bad and all as it was. Och, he'd say nothing – sure, bad temper never got you anywhere!

He stepped into a puddle to avoid a man's umbrella and when he felt the cold splash of water up the leg of his trousers his anger surged back again. He'd tell her all. He'd soon take the wind out of her sails and her self-praise about the hat! He'd tell her everything.

He hurried up the street and at the door of his house he let down the collar of his coat and shook the rain off his hat. He listened for a minute and heard the children shouting. He knocked, and the three of them pounded to the door to open it.

"It's Daddy," they shouted, but he brushed past them without speaking.

His wife was washing the floor in the kitchen and as she wrung the cloth into the bucket and brushed back her hair with the back of her hand she looked at him with a bright smile.

"You got it all right?"

"Why aren't the children in bed?"

"I didn't expect you home so soon."

"Did you think I was a bus conductor!"

She noticed the hard ring in his voice. She rubbed the soap on the scrubber and hurried to finish her work, making great whorls and sweeps with the cloth. She took off her dirty apron, and as she washed and dried her hands in the scullery she glanced in at him seated on the sofa, his head resting on his hands, the three children waiting for him to speak to them. "It was the hat," she said to herself. "It was the had did the trick."

"Come on now and up to bed quickly," and she clapped her hands at the children.

"But you have to wash our legs in the bucket."

"You'll do all right for tonight. Your poor father's hungry after his hard day's work." And as she pulled off a jersey she held it in her hand and gave the fire a poke under the kettle. John stared into the fire and when he raised his foot there was a damp imprint left on the tiles. She handed him a pair of warm socks from the line and a pair of old slippers that she had made for him out of pasteboard and a piece of velours.

"I've a nice bit of steak for your tea," she said. "I'll put on the pan when I get these ones into their beds."

He rubbed his feet and pulled on the warm socks. It was good that she hadn't the steak fried and lying as dry as a stick in the oven. When all was said and done, she had some sense in her head.

The children began to shout up the chimney telling Santa Claus what they wanted for Christmas, and when they knelt to say their prayers they had to thank God for sending their Daddy a good job. John smiled for the first time since he came into the house and he took the youngest on his knee. "You'll get a doll and a pram for Christmas," he said, "and Johnny will get a wooden train with real wheels and Pat — what will we get him?" And he remembered putting a cowboy's outfit into one of the boxes. "A cowboy's outfit — hat and gun."

His wife had put the pan on the fire and already the steak was frizzling. "Don't let that pan burn till I come down again. I'll not be a minute."

He heard her put the kids to bed, and in a few minutes she was down again, a fresh blouse on her and a clean apron.

She poured out his tea and after he had taken a few mouthfuls he began to tell her about the crowd of applicants and about the fellow who shouted: "We'd better all go home," when he had seen him in the hat.

"He was jealous — that's what was wrong with him!" she said. "A good clout on the ear he needed."

He told her about the Manager, the handbell, the blue and pink parcels, the little house, and the red cloak he had to wear. Then he paused, took a drink of tea, cut a piece of bread into three bits, and went on eating slowly.

"It's well you took my advice and wore the hat," she said brightly. "I knew what I was talking about. And you look so — so manly in it." She remembered about the damp stain on the floor, and she lifted his boots off the fender and looked at the broken soles. "They're done," she said, "that's the first call in your wages at the end of the week."

He got up from the table and sat near the fire. She handed him his pipe filled with tobacco, and as she washed the dishes in the scullery she would listen to the little pouts he made while he smoked. Now and again she glanced in at him, at the contented look on his face and the steam arising from his boots on the fender.

She took off her apron, tidied her hair at the looking-glass, and powdered her face. She stole across the floor to him as he sat staring into the fire. Quietly she took the pipe from his lips and put it on the mantelpiece. She smiled at him and he smiled back, and as she stooped to kiss him he knew that he would say nothing to her now about the tight boots.

Mother and Daughter

THE OLD lady in the private ward had expected her married daughter since two o'clock and since it was now nearing four her scrap of patience had begun to shrink. Propped up in bed with a woollen lavender cap on her head like a tea-cozy she stared aggressively at the closed door and saw in its dull glass panels the blurred figures of nurses passing to and from the public ward. She could hear their bantering voices raised in laughter and she grew more annoyed and tried not to listen to them. They didn't give her much of their time, she reflected; indeed, she could be dead and gone for hours before they'd discover it. No one gave her a moment's notice, a moment's consideration. She supposed private ward meant privacy – it also meant neglect where she was concerned! And wasn't she old, and wasn't she paying through the nose for this private room, a room furnished like a Victorian hotel. And then there was the bell-push looped round the rail of the bed which she was to ring if she wanted anything. Oh, she liked that part of it! How often had she rung and rung and no one had paid any heed to it. And it wasn't that the bell was out of order for the seldom time they did answer it they did so immediately.

But today you'd think they had gone on strike for she was sure she had a calloused finger from ringing the same bell. She was sure too her temperature and blood pressure were rising steadily.

She turned around and eyed the bell, and to appease her annoyance she pressed it again and heard it cheer itself hoarse in some part of the building. But no one answered it. Laughter came again from the public ward, and she wondered what they had to laugh at and maybe some poor patients needing a little rest or, God help them, lying at death's door. Come to think of it she herself would have been much better off in the public ward instead of being cooped up all alone like a Victorian dowager. For one thing she'd have had loads of company and loads of attention, and strange people traipsing in and out, and so many of them on visiting days there wouldn't be enough chairs for them to sit on and they'd have to perch on the edge of the bed or stand leaning over the bedrails. Her daughter wanted her to go there in the first instance and it was a pity she didn't heed her.

But what on earth was keeping her so late today after promising she'd be here at two. Oh, the same girl never hurried except when it suited her! Selfish, selfish – that summed her up.

She sighed resignedly and glanced at the chart hanging over the aluminum rail at the foot of the bed. She saw the black peaks and hollows on it like an outline of the Rockies and wondered what it all meant.

The door was knocked and a nurse slipped in.

"Did you ring, Mrs. Collins?"

"On and off for the past three hours."

"And what may I bring you or do for you?"

"You're all doing for me if you'd like to know! But I'll lodge a complaint to the doctor in the morning."

"There are other patients in the hospital, too, Mrs. Collins."

"I don't want any impertinence, any back answers, either from you or anyone else. I'm in a private ward and I'm not paying dear money to be scolded or abused. All I ask is a little attention, a little consideration – half of what's given to the patients in the public ward would suffice."

"We're doing our best for all, Mrs. Collins. We're short-handed."

"You may be short of hearing too, but you're not short-tongued. Would you please hand me my knitting from the top drawer there."

"Let me prop you up on the pillows properly, and get you ready for your daughter."

"I'll require that if she comes. What sort of a day is it outside?"

"It's snowing steadily and the roofs are covered white."

"Snowing! Why wasn't I told so that I needn't expect my daughter. That's another instance of the silent cruelties of this place."

"It only came on a short while ago."

"You've an answer for everything, my girl. Perhaps you'd refill my hot water bottle before my poor feet are frozen stiff."

"With pleasure, Mrs. Collins," and the nurse fished it out from under the bedclothes and held it in her arms as she would a baby. "I'll be back in a minute," and she smiled and hurried from the room.

Mrs. Collins eyed the hand of the clock on the dressing table. She'd time that lassie.

Five minutes passed, and then ten.

She'd give her two minutes more before she'd poke the bell. Who ever heard of a quart of warm water taking ten minutes to boil!

I suppose she'll tell me the gas is on low pressure or the electric has failed because of the snow.

She lay back on the pillow and drew her feet up from the cold regions of the bed. She shivered. She'd get that blade to take her temperature when she'd come back! She stared at the clock and then gripped the bell-push and gave the button a prolonged squeeze.

At last someone stood outside the door and she could distinguish the white uniform of the nurse. She was talking to someone. Perhaps one of the young student doctors. The impudence of that one! The bottle would be cold by the time she had finished her tête-a-tête.

The door opened and the nurse came in backwards.

"I thought you'd never come and my poor feet frozen."

235

"Was I long, Mrs. Collins?" the nurse said brightly as she stowed the bottle beneath the blankets.

"It's a pity I'm not a young man and not an old woman. I'd get full value out of my private ward, I'm thinking."

"You needn't expect your daughter today. By the look of it that snow's on for the whole evening."

"Indeed I'll expect her! My daughter has a sense of duty. From an early age she was taught to have consideration for others."

"If your daughter's wise she'll stay at home," and the nurse stood at the window and gazed down at the snow obliterating the cars tracks that led from the gate. "I wouldn't be at all surprised if the buses cease to run."

"You're very comforting, I must say."

"If you turn your head, Mrs. Collins, you can see the snow on the roofs. It must be an inch or so deep, for the outline of the slates is blotted out."

"If you give me the hand mirror I might be able to see the snow without getting a crick in my neck."

The nurse lifted the mirror from the dressing table, blew her breath on it, and wiped it with the corner of her apron.

"Well now, Mrs. Collins, what do you see?"

"I can see nothing except an old woman who's badly failed since coming to this inhospitable place."

"Indeed, you're looking well."

"If you had seen me 20 years ago you would have seen a very beautiful young woman. Anyone would tell you that who knew me."

"I'm sure."

"The way you say it you're not so sure."

"You're still handsome. One hasn't to go back 20 years to find that out."

"Why don't you sit down, nurse, and relax for a minute or two."

"You never saw a nurse sitting except at meal times. We're always on the go."

"If you are it's not to this room you do be going. It's little attention I get from any of you."

"If you needed attention we'd be in and out 20 times an hour."

"So I'm not sick at all – is that the next of it!"

"Oh, no, Mrs. Collins," the nurse smiled. "You're still far from well. But you're no longer on our danger list."

"If I were no longer on the paying list I'd be happy."

The nurse rearranged a few bedraggled chrysanthemums in a vase at the window and on looking out saw Mrs. Collins' daughter and grandchild coming through the gate.

"I must go now," the nurse said without telling her the good news. "Just ring if you want anything."

Left alone the old lady lifted the mirror and watched the snow falling. Yes, the nurse was probably right. Her daughter wouldn't come, and that snow could be a convenient and plausible excuse. She lay back and shut her eyes, the hand mirror face downward on the eiderdown.

The door was knocked and in walked her married daughter with her six-year-old child. She carried a bunch of pink chrysanthemums that were moist with melted snow, and before greeting her mother she placed them upright in the wash basin.

"Are you asleep, Mother?" she whispered, stooping over the bed to kiss her.

"Sure you know I never sleep. And what possessed you to take Mary out with you on a day like this."

She's in one of her tantrums, the daughter said to herself, and called on God to give her patience during the visit. Slowly she took off the child's cape and hat and draped them over the back of a chair, and sitting beside the bed she told her mother she looked greatly improved since her last visit.

"I may look it, Lizzie, but I don't feel it," and thereupon she launched into a litany of complaints about the nurses' inattention and cold meals served up to her. The daughter sighed and patted the eiderdown, but after listening to another volley of complaints she said quietly, "I wish, Mother, you weren't so querulous. The poor nurses are doing their very best."

"Oh, if that's the mood you're in, my lady, you shouldn't have come out to see a sick and lonely old woman."

"I don't like to hear you complain so much, that's all."

"I'm not complaining, I'm just stating the bare facts."

The child, not interested in their talk, wandered about the room, pulled out drawers in a bureau and was surprised that they contained nothing, only a blue sheet of paper flattened tightly to the bottom. Some of the drawers stuck as she was closing them, and one rather stubborn one she pushed so vigorously that a statuette of Our Lady rocked precariously on top of the bureau.

"Now see what you have done, Mary. Come here beside mother and keep your hands to yourself."

"It's high time you corrected her. She's a little curiosity box."

"Why do your teeth click, grandma, and mine don't?" the child said, staring at her grandmother and the lavender cap on her white head.

"What does the child say?" the old lady asked, leaning forward with a hand to her ear.

"She wants to know if you like her new blue cape."

"She doesn't suit blue. You should have bought her a red one or a black one."

The child, dashed, hid herself at the back of her mother's chair, but after a few minutes they had forgotten about her and she once more roamed about the room.

"John has a bit of a cold," the daughter said, mentioning her husband's name for the first time. "But he'll be up to see you soon."

"I suppose he's overworked these days," the old lady said with false sweetness, aware that sloth was John's predominant passion.

The daughter clasped her hands on her lap and yearned to be out once more in the wide airy spaces of the street. No matter what she said she failed to make contact or break down the tension that divided them. Everything was going wrong: the snow, the long wait for the bus, and

238

then the failure of the visit. She sighed, and as the daylight shrank from the room she switched on the light and drew the curtains.

And then suddenly there was a rumble and stumble on the floor, for the child had opened a press and out spilled bananas, turning black, and oranges and apples.

"Well, well, well, that's a spill! There's no peace with that child. Leave her at home next time you call."

The mother stooped and pressed the burst bags of fruit into the press, and red in the face from exertion and anxiety she sat down and breathed audibly.

"You should give some of that fruit to the nurses. The bananas, I may tell you, are turning black."

"They may turn pink for that matter. I wouldn't give the same nurses the skin of an orange if it were to save their lives."

"The nurses! The nurses! Can you not stop pecking at them sometime. They're an overworked and underpaid body if you'd like to know."

"That's right, stand up for them against your poor tortured old mother."

The child by this time had discovered a small box of Turkish Delight that had fallen at the side of the press and she was poking a finger on the sugared jelly and licking it when her grandmother spotted her.

"My God, look what she has now!" she shouted. "My Turkish Delight, the only sweet that lies at peace on my stomach. Hand them up this instant!"

She took the box and pushed it beneath her pillow, and the child, almost in tears, stood beside her mother and asked if they weren't going home soon.

"In a minute or two, Mary. Be patient, girly."

"You should have left her at home instead of hauling her out through all that snow."

"If I had left her at home you'd have asked why I didn't bring her. Oh, you haven't spoken a kind word to her since we came in."

"I didn't wish to interrupt her plundering expeditions."

"She didn't get much plunder as far as I can see!" the daughter flashed back, and then in an instant regretted it. The old lady closed her eyes, turned her head away, and raised a hand in a gesture of dismissal.

Quietly the daughter put on her own coat and then buttoned on the child's cape.

"Mother."

"Let me sleep, please."

She pulled on her gloves: "Mother, I forgot to tell you that Sally Morgan is getting married." She paused, but her mother didn't stir. "She's getting married to . . . You'll never guess?"

The old lady shrugged her shoulders, but did not speak.

"We're, going now," her daughter went on. "Is there anything special you want and I'll have it sent up to you?"

"Nothing, thanks. My needs are few. But do try to be in better form on your next visit."

"I'll try, Mother," she said, taking the blow. "The snow and the long wait for the buses have put my nerves on edge, I suppose." She stooped and kissed her mother.

The old lady looked fixedly at her: she wanted to ask her whom Sally Morgan was going to marry but she held back, stiffening herself against the impulse to please. But when the goodbyes were said and the door closed she felt her pride uncoiling in a long irregular line of angry discontent. She rang the bell. She wanted the nurse to call them back. She rang again and again but no one answered her.

Meanwhile her daughter had reached the outside gate, glad to be out in the free falling snow. She held Mary's hand tightly, but the child disengaged it, and while waiting for the bus watched the flakes turning her cape white.

They boarded the bus and the child knelt up on the seat, wiped the mist from the window with her gloved hand and looked out at the streets that were as white as the bed in the hospital.

"Why was grandma cross?" she asked.

"She wasn't cross, child. Your poor grandma is sick."

"And what made her sick?"

"She's growing old."

"And what made her old."

"Turn round and sit on the seat like a good girl."

The child turned around from the window and sat on the seat, watching the flakes of snow melt on her blue cape and dribble on to the floor.

At the centre of the city they had to change buses and stand in a queue. Beside them was a cafe and when the door opened the warm burnt smell of coffee rushed out into the cold air.

"Come, Mary," the mother said, and taking the child's hand she led her into the cafe and sat at a round table near the window.

"And now, Mary, what would you like to eat?"

"Sweets, Mammy. Turkish Delight like grandma's."

"We'll see."

The mother rose from the table, crossed to the counter, and carried back two cups of tea, a few biscuits, and a small box of Turkish Delight.

The child smiled, took the box, and pushed the inside out like a matchbox. Lying closely side by side were cubes of coloured jellies dusted with fine sugar.

"You take one first, Mammy," the child said.

The mother smiled, and to hide the warm tears of joy that rose up beyond her control, she lowered her head near the box and rhymed:

Eena, meena, mina, mow,
Catch a sweetie by the toe,
If he squeals let him go,
Out you must go.

She prized out a cube with her fingers and put it in her mouth. The child smiled, but seeing the tears in her mother's eyes she said:

"You're crying, Mammy."

"The cold is making my eyes watery – that's all."

"But it doesn't make my eyes watery," she said, lifting out a sweet and putting it in her mouth. She smiled and looked at the large window that was misted over except for drops of water wriggling down the pane and leaving clear tracks behind them.

Is she thinking of her grandma and the hospital? the mother wondered, staring at her child.

The child swallowed the remains of her sweet and smiled:

"Look, Mammy, the window's crying. Look at all its tears."

Steeplejacks

THE BRICKWORKS at the edge of the town had been closed down for many years and wind and rain had made wrecks of the old kilns and drying sheds. Nearby in the deep pit lay a pond of greenish water and across it on sunny days there stretched the shadow of the tall brick chimney with its lightning-conductor, a chimney that was a landmark for miles around.

One day it was rumoured that the brickworks was to be reopened and the rumour became a fact when Tim Rooney, a famous steeplejack, arrived one morning with three assistants to repoint and renovate the tall chimney. After much manoeuvring and hammering, the sectional ladder was placed upright against the face of the chimney, and from the top of it Tim gazed down at his three workmates who were shading their eyes against the sun and staring up at him. From the broad lip of the chimney he hauled out abandoned jackdaws' nests and flung the bundles of sticks into the air, and after putting his hammers in a straw basket that was suspended from a pulley-block he plucked at the rope and signalled to his men to lower away. He watched the basket move to the ground in short, irregular jerks, and before descending the ladder himself he looked across the fields to the houses at the edge of the town where smoke rose untroubled from the chimney pots and freshly washed shirts hung limp from the lines in the backyards. The sight of the clothes made him thirsty and he licked his dry lips and resting his hands on the topmost rung of the ladder, now warm under the sun, he began to descend with slow and definite rhythm.

"Well," he said on reaching the ground and clapping the red dust from his hands, "there's a grand view from the top. Three counties lie below you," he exaggerated, "and you can gaze down the throats of all the chimney pots in the streets beyond. Well, John," he addressed the youngest of the group, a lad of 18, "what about that jaunt you're to make to the top? When you're married you'll be able to boast to your children how you climbed to the top of the tallest chimney in the town."

John's gaze travelled slowly to the top of the chimney but he didn't move or speak.

"He boasted all week he'd climb it," said George, the eldest of the group.

"Nobody's forcing him if he doesn't want to go," Tim declared, unwilling to encourage him. "We'll take our lunch first."

"I'm not afraid," John answered and spat on his hands. "It'd be better if I'd climb on a fasting stomach. I'll go before we take our lunch."

"It would be better for us all if you would," George mocked. "You'll be seasick before you're halfway up."

"I was never seasick in my life."

"Hard for you! The biggest boat you were ever in was a swing-boat in the children's playground."

"Here goes!" John answered, fastened his belt and cartwheeled toward the base of the chimney. He gripped the side of the ladder with one hand, bowed gracefully, and said, "You're now about to witness an exhibition of how a chimney should be climbed. There's nothing in it, gentlemen, as long as you keep your head. Nothing in it."

"Hear! Hear!" George applauded and eyed him humorously. Tim said nothing.

The lad climbed some rungs rapidly and then with slow caution ascended another four. His toe dislodged a piece of mortar and he heard it clink against the ladder on its way to the ground. He paused, frightened. Above him he saw the ladder converge at the top like railway lines. He had a long way to go yet, and on looking down to measure his distance from the ground he saw, in one swaying moment, the old drying sheds buckle and stretch like an accordion. He held grimly to the ladder and allowed his head to clear. Sweat oozed in blobs on his forehead and his hands became clammy. In front of him he saw tiny hairs of moss growing like moles between the bricks and he noticed with rising terror that some of the bricks were cracked. He closed his eyes, swallowed with difficulty, and made an attempt to descend. His foot missed the lower rung and his trouser-leg caught on it and rolled back, and for a moment he felt the free air on his bare leg. He drew his two feet together, twined his arms round a rung of the ladder and remained still.

A tizzing sound trembled through the sides of the ladder. They were hammering on it, signalling to him to come down. He was afraid to move or to look up or look down. He heard Tim call up to him, but what advice was given he couldn't make out. The gray rope at the side of the ladder tautened and presently the basket halted beside him, but when he put a hand on it it swung away from him and in an instant he gripped the rung above his head and closed his eyes to shut out the drunken tilting of the chimney.

"Hold tightly, John, like a good lad," Tim shouted, his voice near at hand. "Hold tightly and don't look down."

Tim was now directly below him: "Don't be afeared," he was saying, "give me your right foot. Let it loose and I'll guide it. That's the stuff. Now give me the left foot. Hold tight with your hands and leave the feet to me. . . . Here we go again. Put the right foot down and now the left beside it. That's the way it's done. That's the ticket! We'll make a steeplejack out of you yet, never fear. Off we go again. First the right and now the left."

"Are we nearly there?" John asked without turning his head.

"We haven't far to go. Keep looking up and you'll be safe in port before you know where you are."

Tim hurried down the last few rungs; John followed him and on reaching the ground his workmates clapped

245

loudly.

"It's not as easy as it looks," he breathed, his face a green colour and his eyes large with fright. "Was I up far?"

"You were near the top."

"I was like hell."

"I warned you you'd be seasick but you wouldn't heed me."

"Give over," Tim said. "We all have to learn. For a first attempt he didn't do badly."

"Never again," John said and sat on the ground which swayed like the deck of a ship.

Tim patted him on the shoulder: "Breathe in the air deeply and you'll be as right as rain in no time."

They helped him to his feet and gave him a drink of water from a can that lay in the long grass out of the sun. They spread newspapers in the cool shade of the hedge, opened their lunchboxes, and took out their thermos flasks. In front of them across the sunny field the windows of the houses were all open and the smoke from the chimneys lay in a smother above the roofs.

"It's so still here," Tim said, "it'd be a nice place for a cemetery. But you'll not be going there for a while yet, John."

John smiled like a convalescent and his hand trembled as he took the cup of tea that Tim poured out for him. He drank it slowly, and when he had finished he lay back on the grass and felt his nausea slip away from him. For awhile he listened to the man talking, and then closing his eyes he tried to relax. He dozed over, but the smell from the men's pipes made him feel sickish and he sat up and rubbed his forehead. Above the hedge towered the chimney and as he stared at it he saw a young boy halfway up the ladder.

"Tim, look!" and he turned pale and felt his head grow light.

Tim peered through the leaves in the hedge and saw the boy nearing the top of the chimney.

"For the love of God, men, don't budge, don't breathe,"

he ordered. "There's a young lad at the top of the ladder. Keep still and don't frighten him."

The two men turned and watched the boy lever himself on to the lip of the chimney and sit dangling his legs as if he were seated on a roadside wall.

"We mustn't show ourselves," Tim urged, "mustn't let him know we see him, If he has the head to climb up, he'll have the head to get down."

Suddenly the boy ceased dangling his legs and crawled on his knees round the lip of the chimney. He did the complete circle and on reaching the top of the ladder he turned his back to descend. He twined his arms round the topmost rung and clung to it without moving. The men watched and waited, bending the branches of the hedge to see better.

"He's staying there because he can't get down," John said. "I know what it's like – he's afraid to move. We must do something. Tim. Go up after him; help him the way you helped me."

"Take it cool; that boy will get down all right. I know what I'm talking about."

"He's stuck. He's afraid to move – anyone can see that! I'm going for the fire brigade; they'll get him down," John said, springing to his feet.

"Don't make a fool of yourself. Stay where you are. That boy has a head for heights, I tell you. He'll manage by himself if we leave him alone and not startle him."

The boy still clung to the top rung, but made no attempt to descend.

"I can't bear to look at him any longer," John said, and before his workmates could stop him he was running along the hedge to the town.

At that moment, slowly and steadily, the boy began to descend, sometimes halting to look around him.

"That's the way, my boy," Tim breathed to himself, "that's the way to do it. But for the love of God, don't look down. Come on, another rung. You're just half way. Come on, what are you hesitating for!"

From their look-out behind the hedge they watched intently every movement that he made. They saw him halt, rub each hand in turn on his jersey, look up, and once more begin to ascend.

"Did you ever see the like of that for cheek since God made you? There's the makings of a great steeplejack in that boy," George said.

"He has the head all right, but I wish I had my hands on him before John fetches the fire brigade," Tim said. "I should have left someone on watch when we were at our lunch."

The boy had now reached the top of the ladder and after struggling on to the lip of the chimney he stood up on it, walked round to the lightning-conductor and gripped it like a Roman soldier with his spear. At that moment a woman came out of the end house across the fields and taking damp clothes from her washing basket she hung them on the line. The, shading her eyes, she called to left and right: "Jackie, Jackie, Jackie." She didn't see him crouched at the top of the chimney, and when she had gone back to the house he descended the ladder rapidly and raced across the fields.

"Thanks be to God he's safe anyway," Tim said and rose to his feet. "Never again will I leave the ladder without a watchman."

He walked across the field to the end house and on reaching the open door he called to the woman as she moved about the dark kitchen and asked if he could have a word with her son.

"I hope he hasn't been up to any mischief, Mister," she said, coming to the door.

"Nothing much. I was wondering if you'd like him to be a steeplejack."

"A steeplejack! What on earth's that?"

"My job — pointing and renovating mill chimneys."

The woman smiled: "Is it our Jackie! He hasn't the heart of a rabbit, Mister, and that's the truth."

"I can tell you he climbed to the top of the brickyard

chimney when we'd our backs turned."

"He wouldn't do the like of that, Mister!" she said and stared at him incredulously.

"He did, indeed. Ask him yourself."

She beckoned Jackie beside her and scrutinised the red dust on his jersey and trousers.

"Where were you?" she shouted and gripped his shoulder.

"Over in the brickfields, Mother."

"What were you doing?"

"Looking around and playing."

"Playing at what?"

Jackie lowered his head but didn't answer.

"You climbed the ladder to the top of the chimney," Tim challenged him.

"Speak up to the man, Jackie, where's your manners!"

Jackie plucked at a loose thread on his jersey.

"You walked round the lip of the chimney and put your hand on the lightning conductor," Tim pressed.

"Merciful God!" the mother exclaimed and sat down on a chair. "Wait till I get my breath back. My boyo, but you're a heartscald. You'd some poor body's blessing about you when you weren't killed stone dead."

"He has a head for heights. You should let him follow his gift. He's a born climber, a born steeplejack."

"He'll not be able to climb into bed when I'm done with him. . . . And wait till his father hears about it. . . . It's the last chimney he'll climb in this life. . . . Oh, you'll be in your good safe school tomorrow if you're fit to go. . . . I'm thankful to you, Mister, for if I'd seen him at the top of the chimney the sight'd never have left my eyes."

The bell of the fire brigade could be heard approaching the edge of the town.

"I'll have to go," Tim said. "But when the lad's the age keep my job in mind for him. There's good money in it."

He hurriedly took his leave and headed across the field to the hedge where his two workmates awaited him.

The Schooner

IT WAS August and very warm; Terence Devlin, a boy of eight, was leaving the city with his father for a holiday on the Island of Rathlin. It was early morning when they walked to the station where porters were rim-rolling milk cans along the empty platform. At Ballymoney they had to change and wait for a long time for the narrow-gauge train to take them to Ballycastle. That train was very small and the people seemed too big for it; steam dribbled from all parts of the engine and Terence held on tightly to his father for he feared that it would explode at any moment. The wooden seats in the carriage were rough and hacked with names, and they hurt the backs of his knees. In the floor boards there were wide slits and through them could be seen the sharp stones which lay between the sleepers. The train shook violently and Terence's teeth rattled in his head and the suit-case fell off the rack on to the floor.

"I hope you'll not be sea-sick in the train," his father smiled to him, and put away the paper he was trying to read. When the train slowed down he would shout out to his son the names of flowers and mosses that grew on the rocky embankments. But to amuse himself Terence dropped cigarette-cards between the floor boards and spelt out words that were pencilled on the ceiling. His father told him to try and sleep and not be straining his eyes reading words that were written by bad boys: "It's the like of those things that bring a bad name on the country. I hope, Terence, you'll never scribble in a railway carriage."

After that Terence dozed off and when he awoke he was in Ballycastle. There was the smell of turf and the air was heavy with heat. Down past a siding they walked where the wooden sleepers were sticky with oil and smelt sharply of tar.

They stopped at a shop and Terence bought ice-cream, a wooden spade, and a red bucket with black letters: *A Present from Ballycastle.*

They took the long road to the sea. Men with twisted towels round their necks passed them. Blinds were pulled down in the big houses and on the lawns old ladies sat on deck-chairs under the shade of red umbrellas. Terence shook a pebble from his sandal, and Mr. Devlin walked on, fanning himself with his hat. The big chestnut trees that lined the road were stiff with heat, but under the leaves flakes of shadow quivered. The tarred road crackled as a motor raced by, then a drove of cattle came up, their hooves sticking in the tar, their dung-caked sides as dry as the bark of a tree.

"If we get weather like this, Terence, we'll not know ourselves on the way back."

While Mr. Devlin went to inquire about the boat Terence leaned over a sun-warmed wall and saw below him boys and girls playing tennis. Boys hung blazers on the net-posts, hitched up their belts, and through the sun-sifted air came the cord-rattle of tennis balls hitting the net and nearby a lazy plunge of waves falling on a curve of sand. Idly he picked moss out of the crevices in the wall, and then a finger flicked his ear and he turned to see his father smiling down at him: "We'll go over to the quay now, the boat's going to the island shortly."

Alongside the quay lay a boat, a brown sail wrapped round the mast and old motor tyres hanging over the sides. The out-going tide had left pools of water on the quay, and strands of seaweed had entangled themselves under the mooring rings. At the end of the quay three boys were fishing for fry and behind them sat glass jamjars filled with shining water and green moss. Terence yearned to take off his sandals and dabble his scorched feet in the pools, but already his father was handing the suit-case to a man in the boat and he joined him to see the cargo being taken aboard: two bags of flour, a tea-chest filled with loaves and covered with sacking, a coil of barbed wire and two panes of glass.

There were five islanders, some tall and awkward-looking, standing loosely as if they were ashamed of their height. Terence and his father sat in the stern; the tyres were pulled in, and one of the crew lifted an oar and pushed the boat out from the quay. The gunwale was warm and blobs of resin had oozed out of the wood. The sky was clear, the sea smooth and a fierce sun striking into it.

Ballast stones were dropped overboard and Terence saw the water fizzle white and felt splashes of salt on his lips. Four oars were fixed between the thole-pins and dipped into the water simultaneously; drops dripped from the blades, whorls were left by the thrust of the oars, and looking back Terence watched for a long time the wrinkled patches of water fade into the smooth sea. He could still hear the dull thud of waves on the sand and he wondered in what part of the ocean the waves were hatched. He was going to ask his father, but he was now pointing out Fair Head to him and telling him a story about beautiful children who had been turned into swans and how for many lonely years they had wandered about this sea.

Far out from the Head two steamers were very black and seemed to float in the sky. Gulls flew close to the boat, their reflections clear in the smooth water; puffins stood up and flapped their wings, or to escape the boat they arose in a flock and flittered the top of the water with their feet. But for all the rowing the island seemed to draw no nearer. It lay spread out in front of them, its white cliffs like a row of teeth, and to the right its black cliffs polished by the sun.

"Now, men," said Mr. Devlin, "I could give one of you a spell," and he took an oar, splashed awkwardly, and broke the rhythmic dip-and-lift which had fascinated Terence.

"Don't dip the blade so deep," said one of the islanders,

and with great patience he showed Mr. Devlin how to feather his oar. In no time the sweat was gleaming on Mr. Devlin's forehead, and soon he had to take off his coat and waistcoat.

"It's tough work when yer not used to it," said a little brown-faced man who was rowing near the bow.

Mr. Devlin grunted and turned around to look at the island: "I'm damned if we're moving at all. I thought we'd row over in ten minutes."

"No, nor in ten times ten minutes. 'Tis a long pull – eight miles across."

Mr. Devlin puffed loudly and his oar left no whirling holes in the water. Presently he gave up: "Gentlemen, I think I've worked my passage," and he sat in the stern and his hands fell limply on his lap.

Later Mr. Devlin began to ask questions about the island, and the boatmen answered him, and in his own mind he began to plan what walks he would take during his fortnight's holiday. Terence picked out the white houses that lay in the scoops of the hills and the square-towered church and graveyard that edged the coast. Now the boat was passing between two quays, and a clump of men with their hands in their pockets gazed at the boat as she came in. There was a strong smell of rotting seaweed rising from the bay. White ducks were dozing on the grass above tide-mark; along the strand a man in his shirt-sleeves was carrying two cans of water, and a barefooted boy was throwing a stick into the water for a black dog to retrieve it.

Terence and his father made their way up the stony quay, past a rusty winch and a broken boat with green-scummed water. The houses were low and slated, and one of them with two sentry-box porches had its name in Gaelic letters printed on a thin board.

"This is our ticket," said Mr. Devlin, and they walked up a gravel path towards it.

A tall woman in black opened the door: "Welcome to the island," she said. "We didn't see the boat comin' in or faith we'd have sent Paddy down to meet it. . . . Come on in. Annie's bakin' and the place is a bit throughother."

They were in a warm kitchen with a shining range, and Annie was turning farls of bread on a griddle and hurried to greet them: "Ye must be famished with the hunger. I'll not be long gettin' the things on the table."

The two women were dressed alike: black blouses with high collars, grey hair topped with big combs, but Annie had on a spotted apron, and two broad rings were grooved so tightly on her finger that the flesh was swollen at each side.

"Lizzie," she said quietly, "take their things up to the room," and she stood beside Terence, holding his cap and stroking his fair hair.

A door opened on the opposite side of the kitchen and Paddy slouched in, his sleeves rolled up, a rough-haired terrier at his heels. The dog began to bark at the strangers and Paddy swiped at him with his hat: "Chu, you brute! Chu, Bumper, and have some manners!"

He shook hands with Terence and Mr. Devlin, and then sat beside them on the sofa, idly picking clay from his fingers with his thumb nail. Annie moved from the table to the griddle: she was very quiet, shadow-like, her elastic-sided boots making no noise, her eyes withdrawn and brooding.

The kitchen was big: a wag-at-the-wall ticked loudly, and in the deep window that faced the sea there was a white spool, a yellow tape, and a calendar with its leaves curled and a red outline of a fish on all the Friday dates.

"Ye got a lovely day for crossin', so ye did," put in Paddy. "It was a long pull, but ye had the tide with ye."

"There wasn't a ripple. I never saw the sea so calm," asnwered Mr. Devlin.

Annie scraped the griddle noisily with a knife and swept the scrapings in to her hand with a goose's wing. Paddy crossed and re-crossed his legs.

"The sea was like oil," continued Mr. Devlin, trying to make conversation. "And it was covered with birds."

Annie dropped the knife, and then quietly opened the back door and went out.

Paddy got to his feet, glancing at the door: "Calm weather is scarce in these parts. There wasn't an air of wind the past two days." He stuffed a piece of twisted paper between the bars of the grate and lit his pipe. "Weather like this would do no good; the soil's as dry as snuff."

Annie came in and Paddy added hurriedly: "And, Mr. Devlin, while you're here you must get a night or two's fishin'. The sea's thick with fish." He hitched his belt: "I'll leave ye now till you get your tay. I've a field of purties I have to weed."

Bumper slid out from under the table, but when he saw Lizzie enter with an old raincoat he wagged his tail.

Lizzie smiled at Terence and turned to the dog: "Bumper, are ye goin' to Ballycarry?" The dog jumped into the air three times, ran under the stairs and came out with a basket in his mouth.

Terence laughed and said to his father: "Could I go to Ballycarry?"

Lizzie folded her arms: "Ah, child, it's too far. It's away up in the mountains, but if you come here next year you'll be a big boy and I'll take you and Bumper up to Ballycarry."

Kneeling on the sofa he watched through the window: Bumper walked in front, the basket in his mouth; Lizzie followed, a gleaming can hooked to her elbow. They passed behind a limestone wall, her head bobbing up and down; then the road swept alongside a hill, dipped into a hollow and they were lost from sight.

For the next two days while his father tramped the island gathering specimens of wild flowers Terence played about the house waiting for the time when Bumper and Lizzie were to set out for Ballycarry. On the third day he was strolling about like that when he saw the door of a little lean-to lying open. Cautiously he went in and found Annie sharpening a knife on a hone. She didn't hear him. The sun was shining through a small window and the shadow of a buch flickered against the pane. It was cool and quiet, and broken cobwebs dangled from the bare slates. There was no sound except the rasp of the knife. He was going to go out when he saw on a shelf a model schooner with brown sails, brass hooks and rings, and underneath the tail-shaped stern the painted name: *Windswept.*

"Oh," he said, "who owns the lovely boat?"

Annie started at the voice and turning round she saw him tapping the deck and moving the sails backwards and forwards. Silently she stared at him. He stroked the hull with the palm of his hand and toyed with the helm.

"Who owns it?" he asked again, his eyes wide with anticipated joy.

For a moment she was rigid, then she relaxed, and a look of brooding doubt spread across her face. Again he tapped the deck, and her expression changed to one of patient sadness.

"You can play with it," she said, almost in a whisper. "You can play with it, and Paddy will show you how to trim the sails."

In a minute he was out and off to the shore. Paddy met him: "Where are you goin' with that? You can't have that!" he said in great surprise.

"Annie lent it to me. She said I could play with it and you could fix the sails for me."

"Wait now a minute. Don't go away." And Paddy hurried up to the little lean-to. Annie was standing in the shadow of the doorway and came to meet him. Both raised their hands and waved to Terence to go on. Paddy followed him, thinking how long the little schooner had remained on its stand and how for many years Annie had polished it: "It's curious the changes that come over people – changes ye'd never dream of." And he rubbed the back of his neck with his hand.

He sat on the beach stones above the little bay, took the schooner on his lap and showed Terence how to use the helm: "Turn it to the left when you're sailin' her with her bow pointin' to the house."

Terence took off his sandals and placed the schooner in the water. All her sails tightened in the breeze and her brass rings glinted in the sun. Annie saw it from the door: the rust-brown sails, the wet-gleaming hull, and the silver flakes of water skimming from the bow. Paddy walked along the strand, then a disturbing thought whorled in his mind, for he wondered was the ship watertight after her years on the stand? He called to Terence to bring it up to him, and with his ear to the hull he turned the boat up and down; he could hear nothing except a slight sccd-rattle of a chip of wood inside her.

"She's as tight as a pig-skin – a lovely boat! She's the girl can whip along in a thin breeze. . . . Take good care of her."

All that day Terence played with the boat, and in the evening after his supper Annie, with a thin shawl on her shoulders, came down to the shore to bring him home. The sun had gone down and the water was darkened by a chilly breeze.

He shouted: "Look now!" as the boat tore across the bay and a knife-curve of water rolled white at her bow.

"Come, Terence, it's gettin' late. What'll your father say if you're not in bed when he comes back from fishin'?"

She waited on the shore road for him, and presently he came floundering up the loose stones of the beach with the schooner hugged to his breast. He was out of breath and full of joy. Then he saw that her eyes were wet.

"What's wrong?" he asked.

"I was just thinkin'," she answered clumsily and tried to draw his attention to a shower of moths that flickered over a field of beans.

"But why were you crying?" he persisted.

"I was thinking of the boat. It was my husband made it."

"And will he make one for me?" Terence asked eagerly.

"Indeed, he'd make you one."

"And when will he make it? Where is he?" he kept repeating. "Where is he?"

She stood still on the road: "When he comes back, please God, he'll make you one."

"And when will he be back?"

"It's getting cold. We must hurry now," she evaded.

There was great heat in the kitchen from the humming range. The curtains were drawn and the oil lamp lighted. Terence was allowed to look at the book of flowers that his father had already gathered and sometimes Annie would bend over him, take from her apron pocket a sugar lump and put in in his mouth. He loved this time of the evening with no one in the kitchen but the two of them, and even Annie, herself, looked forward to this hour before his bedtime. He was great company. Sometimes he would thread her needle and she would sit and watch him, her hands loosely on her lap. She would give him milk to drink and he would sit near the range feeling the heat on his knees and hearing outside the unhurried breath of the waves. Then when he would nod his head in sleep she would light a candle and bring him to his room. She used to allow him to keep the schooner under the dressing-table, but one evening when she heard him coughing she stole upstairs and found him asleep on the floor beside the schooner.

The next day she feared he would have a cold, but he set off with his father to swim and later she coaxed him to sit with her in the sunny field at the back of the house. The foot of the field had a crop of blossomed potatoes and Paddy was spraying them with bluestone and from where they sat they could hear the spray rattling like hail on the leaves and see the blue sheen of it as it dried in the sun. Butterflies pirouetted over the field and Terence caught one and placed it on the palm of his hand. The powder from its wings clung to his fingers and he put the butterfly on the ground and it began to struggle up a blade of grass.

"It'll never fly again," Annie said to him as she looked over the calm sea. "The powder on its wings means as much to it as wind for the sails of a boat."

The remark hurt him and he watched with growing sorrow the blade of grass bending under the weight of the ungainly butterfly and how brilliantly white its helpless wings shone in the sun.

Paddy came up to them for a drink from the can of milk, his eyebrows and clothes covered with a fine blue dust. One foot crushed the butterfly, and Terence was going to cry out when he noticed that Annie was engrossed in her knitting and didn't see what had happened. Presently she got up and went inside to get ready the tea, leaving her rug and knitting in the field.

"Do you know what you've done?" said Terence to Paddy. "You've tramped on a butterfly and killed it."

"And sure what sin is there in that?" replied Paddy, noticing how his lips quivered. "Sure they only live for a day and some of them don't live as long as that – the swallows and thrushes snap them in two while you'd wink."

Paddy lay back and pulled his hat over his face. Terence took off his sandals and felt the soft grass on his bare feet. He closed his eyes from the glare of the sun and thoughts of cool things stirred within his mind – moss floating in a jamjar, drops on the blade of an oar, and rain washing the powder from a butterfly's wings. He sat up and on gazing at the sea he saw that a schooner with all her canvas out was passing up the sound.

"Oh, Paddy, look at the lovely schooner like Annie's!"

Paddy took the hat from his eyes and stared at the ship: "It's not often you see them about now. They're a grand sight. That one is only drifting up there on the first of flood – there's no wind for her."

"I'll run and tell Annie."

"Come back here and let her make the tay," and he rose to his feet. "Come on with me and spray the spuds."

Terence hesitated: "Let me tell her!"

"You'll not!" Paddy said sharply. "Do what I say!"

Reluctantly Terence came over to him, and slowly they walked down to the barrel of spray, Paddy looking now and again at the schooner and calculating how long it would take her to drift out of the sound, knowing also that she would surely drift back again if the wind did not rise during the night.

He got Terence to pick up the flinty pieces of limestone that lay between the drills and to search under all the leaves for the Queen of the butterflies. "And you'll know her," says Paddy, "by her wings, for she has one wing of pure gold and one of shining silver, and if you find her you'll be able to sell her for hundreds of pounds." And while Terence searched, Paddy sprayed until the schooner had nearly passed up the sound. Then clapping the dust from his hands he went to the top of the field and gathered up the rug and the knitting.

When they came in Lizzie and Bumper had arrived from Ballycarry, and Bumper lay at the open door in the sun snapping at the flies. The cement floor was cold under Terence's feet and Annie made him sit down at once and put on his sandals.

As the evening grew old the warmth left the earth and the potato-blossoms closed up and drooped their heads. In the kitchen a warm silence crept into all the corners and a trapped fly buzzed madly in a web.

During the night a rainy storm blew against the house, and in the morning when Terence wakened he saw his father standing at the window: "Terence, boy, it's like a winter's morning. The summer's finished and tomorrow, if the boat can leave, you'll be on your way back again."

Two conflicting thoughts encumbered the boy's mind: a desire that the storm would last a long time so that no boat could leave; a desire that the storm would die at once so that he could get sailing the schooner before he left. At breakfast he heard Paddy assure his father that the storm would last no time and that it would blow itself out before night.

When Annie was making the beds Terence went with her and from the window they looked out upon the bay. Ducks and hens sheltered under the boats that were hauled up on the grass. The wind flayed the water into jagged peaks; waves tores between the two quays, crashed on the strand, and sent jabbling fingers amongst the stones on the beach. Gulls rose from the stones and tipped the waves before they broke. Tangles of brown sea-wrack curved the bay and clumps of it floated in a solid mass.

"Oh, look!" Terence would call out as a big wave struck the quay and burst in snowy spray. Annie would cross to the window and share for a moment the vigorous joy of wind-torn water.

When she had the beds made Terence shyly plucked her apron: "Could I have the boat?"

"Terry, you have no sense — one wave would smash the riggin' and leave it like a butterfly that had lost its wings," and she stroked his head and smiled at him meekly.

"Well, could I have it after awhile if the wind goes away?"

"We'll see."

In the afternoon the wind had fallen, and late that evening when the wind was exhausted and only a glimmer of it flicked across the bay Terence pleaded again for the boat.

Annie laughed at him: "At this time! Ye'd be frozen down on the shore."

"Ah, please, I'll be going away in the morning."

"But sure you'll be back next year and you can sail it till your heart's content."

"Just one more for the last," he kept pleading.

Paddy was dozing on the sofa, and Lizzie was trying to read a paper in the light from the fire, but did not raise her head.

Terence asked again.

"All right," said Annie, and getting the key she went out for the schooner. "Just sail her once. Darkness will soon be here."

The chilly water took his breath away as he set the rudder and let the boat slide from his hand. As he ran along the cold strand he could see the sails black against the light from the water. He sailed her back across the bay again and then heard Annie call to him from the lighted doorway.

"I'm going now," he shouted, waiting for the boat to come to shore. But then something happened. The schooner stopped, tangled in a clump of floating wrack. He waited for her to free herself. Then he noticed she was slewing round. He clenched his hands and involuntarily pressed his feet into the sand. The sails flapped, caught the wind, and she headed out between the two quays towards the open sea. He began to cry. He ran to the first quay. He skinned his legs as he climbed on to it from the strand. Annie called to him again, but he didn't hear her. He lifted a boat-hook that lay on the quay and peered at the waves that slopped in amongst the stone steps. Once he thought he saw something pass at great speed, but he wasn't sure. Backwards and forwards he ran from one quay to the other like a dog that had lost his master. Desperately he searched, lifting up sand-soaked tins and flinging them into the water. His throat was scorched. He heard Annie call to him from the shore: "Terence, Terence, are you there?"

He went back to look for his sandals. The incoming tide had almost covered them. Annie came down to him over the beach stones: "Where did you get to?"

He couldn't answer. When she came close to him she saw him without the boat and heard him sobbing.

"Where's the boat?" she asked.

Through his tears he told her how he had fixed the rudder and how the boat had caught in wrack and had turned round. She stood beside him and squeezed his head against her breast: "Don't cry, Terence. Don't take it so ill." A deep shivering convulsed her and she squeezed him with great possessiveness and stroked his hair.

Paddy and Lizzie were seated at the fire and looked questioningly at Annie when they saw Terence's scratched legs and the tears in his eyes.

"He lost the boat," said Annie, "and he's broken-hearted." An awkward silence fell. Lizzie poked the fire and Paddy fumbled in his pockets.

"Wash your face and legs and don't let your father see

you in that state," and she made much noise under the stairs getting a basin and a towel. Lizzie and Paddy said nothing.

"Don't cry; sure that could happen to anyone?" she said, drying his face and legs.

"It was the rudder. . . . I fixed it right and it caught in seaweed on the way over and turned round."

"They're a misfortunate thing to put on any model boat," put in Paddy.

Annie stared at him, and he went out and walked about until the lamp had been lowered in the kitchen and all had gone to bed.

In the morning it was raining heavily and some sheep that were to be taken to the mainland stood on the quay bleating and calling to others that were being driven along the strand. Dogs were barking, and drenched men with no overcoats shouted to one another. Mr. Devlin heard them as he washed, and he hurried Terence out of bed and carried down the suit-case to the kitchen.

"There'll be a bit of a jabble on the sea," said Paddy as they sat down to their breakfast. "It's raining badly and I have an ould bit of a sail you can spread on your knees."

He looked out of the door: "Yiv plenty of time – eat yer fill. They're carrying the sheep to the boat but I'll not bring my three down till yer nearly ready."

Through the open door they could hear the melancholy bleat of sheep and see a loose web of rain wind-trailed across the bay.

Annie was quiet: "You'll send Terence back next year for all his holidays. Paddy, there, could meet the train at Ballycastle."

"Would you like that?" said Mr. Devlin.

Terence nodded his head. He wanted to talk about the schooner, but he knew if he opened his mouth no words would come.

Paddy carried the suit-case to the boat, Lizzie and Bumper followed. In the porch Annie held Terence's hand: "It won't be long till next summer and if God spares

263

us all you'll be back again."

He couldn't look up at her and he noticed that stains of salt water had whitened the toes of his sandals.

"Goodbye," she said and watched them go down the gravel path.

They clambered into the wet-soaked boat and a man rubbed a seat for them with a wisp of straw. When Paddy had tied the legs of his sheep he carried them aboard and sat beside Terence and Mr. Devlin. The sail was unrolled from the mast and blobs of rain-water fell from its folds; it filled in the breeze and the driving rain rattled on it like countless bird-pecks. Lizzie stood on the quay with her arms folded and Bumper ran around shaking the rain from himself. From the porch Annie waved to Terence; the tears came to his eyes and he pretended to look for something under the seat. The water slid past the boat, her bows crunched into the waves, and Terence raised his head and scanned the shore for the schooner. But he could see nothing, only black rocks with waves jumping over them. Slanting clouds heaved up against the hills and stitched the valleys with rain. The houses were falling behind and soon there would be nothing to mark them except the big telegraph pole above the post-office.

The wet sheep lay on yellow straw, steam was rising from them, and now and again with the pitch of the boat they tried to scramble to their feet. The rain wormed down the bit of sail that was spread across Terence's knees, and Paddy tried to light his pipe by pulling the edge of the sail over his head.

Terence now searched the sea, and his gaze was so prolonged and intense that Mr. Devlin nudged Paddy: "He's looking for the boat."

"Ach, God knows where she is by this time," replied Paddy.

"Would it cost much to replace it?"

"Ach, Mr. Devlin, it's not the cost that matters — it's what it meant to Annie," and he bent confidentially to Mr. Devlin. "It was her husband that made it thirty years ago.

It was a model of his own ship and since he went away she cleaned and polished it. It held raw memories for her!"

"Where is he now?" Mr. Devlin asked.

"He never came back. They were married in June and early in September of the same year he went away and she never saw him again."

"Were they . . . happy?"

"Happy! . . . He was a ship's carpenter — a fine lump of a fella — and made every stick of furniture that went into their house. They lived at Ballycarry on the east side of the island. We still have the house, but she never goes there now. . . . She still thinks he'll come back."

"And will he, do you think?"

Paddy shook his head: "He'll not, poor fella. I think he's drowned."

Terence's eyes were on the sea, but sometimes when a sheep would move he would stretch out his hand and pat its wet head. Paddy spoke in a low voice, but Terence wasn't listening to him.

"They spent three happy months together on the island," continued Paddy. "His ship was bound for Canada for a load of grain. It left the Clyde and it was to pick him up passing the island. He was on the look-out for it and when it came into the sound they sent a small boat ashore for him. But at night the wind had fallen and the schooner was becalmed."

Mr. Devlin noticed that his suit-case was lying flat and the rain was creeping into it, but he did not move and inclined his head nearer to Paddy's.

"Annie kept her light in the window and at dawn she was down on the shore looking out at the great schooner. She waved, knowing he'd see her. The next day the ship was still there. It was a day like the one you met coming to the island — terribly warm. But during the night a wind sprung up and she saw her lights moving out of the sound. . . . That was the last she saw."

"And what happened?"

"The boat nor crew were never heard tell of. . . . She

always felt that he was alive and that he'd come back. . . .
She's got very old waiting. . . . For awhile she used to
walk about the house at night, opening and shutting doors.
But she got over that."

"It's a great pity Terence lost the little schooner on her.
She shouldn't have lent it to him."

"Ah, Mr. Devlin, she has a great liking for your son —
great liking. And you'll have to send him back next summer. The loss of the wee schooner may do good, for it's
gone now and she won't be cleaning it and thinking. . . .
There was times I wish somebody had stolen it."

They were both silent. Three big waves hit the boat and
sent the spray flying over them.

"Man, Terence," said Paddy, "if the wee schooner met
fellas like that they'd make short work of her. But, maybe,
she's ashore somewhere below the white rocks."

"And will you look for her?"

"I will, I will," said Paddy, trying to relight his damp
pipe. But the abstracted way he answered made Terence
feel that the schooner meant nothing to Paddy; he knew he
would never see it again and that he'd have no schooner to
play with when he'd come back next year.

The Circus Pony

THE FOUR children were in the sitting-room, warmly sheltered from the cold wind that was sweeping up in gusts from the lough. Now and again it flung handfuls of hailstones against the window-panes and bumped like a mattress against the gable of the house. Kevin, a boy of ten, was standing at one of the windows gazing out at the dry hailstones as they bounced on the lawn and combed through the chilled trees in the orchard. And with each shower that passed he saw the hailstones gather in the hoof-marks in the fields and lie white as snow on the road that switch-backed across the hedgy countryside.

For awhile he scanned the road for he wanted to be first in seeing his father's car coming from the town and be the first out of the room as it drove into the stabled yard at the back of the house.

His father was to be home before five, and already five had chimed from the marble clock on the mantelpiece, and soon the blue of the sky would darken down for the coming of night and the lights in the farm-houses would shine out across the cold fields.

Of his three sisters Eileen, the eldest, was practising her pieces at the piano, playing softly, and paying no heed to anything else. Rita, with her black fringe broken in places like a comb, was stretched out on the hearthrug with a book propped between her elbows, and Kevin sensed that she was slyly watching him, determined that he wouldn't be first out of the room to greet the car. Joan, the youngest, was kneeling at the sofa with her dolls and scolding her teddybear for having fallen forward with outstretched arms and head touching its legs. "If you don't sit up straight and have manners like the rest of the children you'll have to go to bed," she said. "Do you hear? Now be a good teddy" – and straightening the brass bell on his ribboned neck she stood him soldierly against the sofa and propped dolls at each side to comfort him.

Rita, with one side of her face red and swollen by the fire, glanced at Joan, with unspoken cynicism, and closed her eyes.

"You played with dolls yourself, Rita," Kevin said, "so you needn't sneer."

"I'm not sneering. I'm reading, so mind your own business, Mister Smarty."

Kevin shrugged his shoulders and turned to the window again. He tapped with his fingers on the window-ledge, beating time to the tune of the piano. Once more he gazed across the fields to the road but seeing its whiteness still unmarked by carlines he knew his father hadn't passed yet. The blue sky was empty of cloud, the fields white except for black patches under the hedges near the roadside. He breathed mist upon the window-pane and as he drew a little man on it with his finger something moving below on the road caught his eye. He put his hands in his pockets and humming to himself he withdrew from the window with a lazy, casual walk. But his manner didn't deceive Rita and she bounced to her feet and rushed to the door shouting: "Daddy's here!"

"Come back at once!" Eileen ordered as Rita and Kevin struggled for possession of the door-knob. But Rita ignored her, shouldered Kevin aside and was first out to meet the car as it drove up with its roof white with hailstones.

Usually they all fought to get opening the car door but this evening they held back, fascinated by what was standing up in the trailer attached to the car. It was a black pony, not much bigger than a goat, and it was twitching its ears from the melting hailstones that tickled it. The two yard-dogs were barking furiously and jumping up at the side of the trailer, the children gathering at each side of it, patting the pony's head and picking off the straw and hailstones that were entangled in its mane.

"She's mine, Daddy! She's for me!" Kevin was exclaiming as Joan scampered off to tell her mother to come quick.

"She's not a lady," the father said as he clouted the two dogs aside and unhitched the tail-board. And there, cradled in yellow straw, stood the whole pony with spills of steam hanging from each nostril. "He's so small he could hide in a potato bag," the father said, piloting the pony on to the wet yard. The pony stood with patient unconcern, the children hugging his damp cold neck, and the dogs sniffing at the long tail blown sideways by the wind.

"He's for me, isn't he Daddy?"

"He's for all of you if you behave yourselves."

"He's one of the ponies we saw in Cinderella", Joan said.

"He's not one of Cinderella's ponies, stupid," Rita corrected. "They were all white and he's all black."

The mother hadn't come out yet to see the new arrival so the pony was led through the back door and down to the warm kitchen, the children skipping with delight on hearing his tiny hooves tinkle on the tiles.

"Glory be to God what have you here!" the mother said, her hands white with flour. "Where on earth did you pick up that toy?"

"No toy at all," the father answered, and lifting the pony's long tail he used it to dust the window-sill. "He can be used for many things, and I believe he can do tricks to no end. He's so clever he can almost tell what you're thinking!"

"I know what I'll be thinking if you don't take him out of my kitchen and let me get the tea ready in some sort of Christian decency," and she patted the pony leaving a floury mark on his forelock.

"He can sleep in my room in the corner, can't he Mammy?" Kevin was asking but before she had time to reply the father was leading the pony out to the yard again. And leaning into the back of the car he produced another surprise for them: a leather saddle complete with stirrups; and as he strapped it on the pony Kevin and Rita pushed one another and shouted: "Me first, Daddy. Oh, please, please!" Without a word the father lifted Joan on to its back, and as he led it by the bridle her mother waved out to her from the kitchen window.

Soon they all had rides on it except Eileen and when it came to her turn she refused to take it.

"I'm too heavy," she protested as Kevin and Rita tugged at her arms.

"She's afraid! Eileen's afraid," they chanted.

"I'm not afraid."

"Then why don't you go for a ride?"

"I don't want to."

"Come on, Eileen," enticed the father, patting the saddle. "He's as quiet as a rabbit. He'll not throw you."

"I'd only hurt him," she said, disengaging Kevin's hand as he dragged her forward.

To encourage her her father threw his leg over the pony's back and lifted his feet to keep them from trailing the ground. "Come on, Eileen. Look how he can carry me." But Eileen could not bear to look at him and she turned and fled into the house, and her father realising he had distressed her slid off its back and led the pony to the stable door.

"Daddy," Kevin pleaded, "get him to do some tricks before he goes to bed."

"Oh, do, do!" Rita said.

"Some other day but not now. He's tired after his journey and we can't stay out here in the cold all evening."

"Just get him to do one."

He didn't listen to them. He lit the hurricane lamp and led the pony out of the draughty yard and into the warm stable. Dolly, the mare, turned her head slowly and glanced sideways at the pony. Beside her great bulk he looked like a strange, undeveloped foal, a foal that could pass under her belly without touching her. He pressed against her front leg and pulled hay from the manger, their shadows staggering on the wall in the light from the lamp. The children eyed him in joyous stillness.

"There's a cheek for you!" the father laughed. "He's only a visitor – only here on a holiday and he's ready to eat us out of house and home. You'd think he owned the place."

"Oh, is he not ours for ever, Daddy! Can we not keep him? Can we not buy him?"

"Nothing could buy him. His circus would collapse without him. He has to go back before Easter."

"But why can't we buy him. Why, Daddy, why?" Kevin said, plucking his father's sleeve to attract his attention.

"Hurry in out of the cold," the father said and bolted the stable door.

It seemed suddenly darker outside, the lamplight flashing on the wet concrete, more stars in the sky and one trembling in the water-trough under the pump in the middle of the yard. An aeroplane zoomed overhead but none of the children looked up to pick out its red and green lights that winked from the wing-tips.

At the tea-table the father related how he had managed to get the pony on loan and how, without fail, he would have to be sent back at Easter to join his travelling circus. Shaking a finger at Kevin he warned him never to take the pony out onto the road. They could ride him of course up and down to the gate and around the sloping field as soon as the fresh grass began to rise.

He explained how he was to be combed and brushed, how foddered and bedded, and what polish to use on his saddle. He mentioned everything except what mattered most: how you got the pony to do his tricks.

"Tomorrow you'll show us – won't you, Daddy?"

"I'll see," the father smiled. "He mightn't like to do tricks except for payment. If he broke his leg doing a trick, what'd we do?"

"Tell them the truth and don't torment them any longer," the mother said. She waited but he didn't answer her. "It's my firm belief you don't know at all," she added.

"The owner told me he's the cleverest pony in Ireland. He can do everything but talk."

The mother shook her head and turned to Kevin: "Go to bed, son. If the pony can do tricks you'll be the one to make him. No one else could do it but you."

"That settles it," the father said. "We'll leave all his capers and performances in Kevin's hands. Here and now we appoint him chief ringmaster."

When Kevin was in bed Rita came into his room and got in beside him for a few minutes; and they lay and talked about the pony and arranged to call him Dandy. No other name would suit, and if Eileen wanted to change it they wouldn't allow her. He would be called Dandy – and that was that!

Next morning Kevin awoke early. A light covering of snow had fallen during the night and his room dazzled in the reflected whiteness. As he dressed he looked down at the yard to where drips from the eaves drew a dark line on the snow beneath. The pump with its neck maned with snow looked like a stiff little pony drinking at the water-trough; and there were even drips from its mouth tracing little circles on the water, little circles that looped together for a moment and then disappeared. That's how Dandy would drink, Kevin thought; and he wished at that instant to be taking him out just to see how his hooves would print a black letter 'n' all over the surface of the snow.

The latch of the back-door clicked and his father crossed the yard with a bucket, and the two dogs came bounding from the hay-shed and over to the stable-door where they sniffed at the yellow straw that stuck out between the jambs. And in a few minutes the thin snow was patterned crazily with their paw-marks and Kevin knew that before he had his breakfast taken the whole snow would be completely melted from the yard.

He hurried out to school, running ahead of Rita and

Joan. He was bursting to tell about the pony, and the boys gathered round him in the playground to hear about it. It was a prize circus pony, he told them, and it could do tricks to no end. What kind of tricks could it do? Oh, all kinds: it could catch the handle of the pump in its mouth and pump up the water. What else could it do? Kevin hesitated, drawing up from his memory tricks he had seen ponies do in Christmas circuses in Belfast. It could beg for bread, he told them, and it could give you its right hoof like a dog gives you its paw. It could walk round on its hind-legs and it could lie down and pretend to be dead. It could add up sums like 2 and 3, and 6 and 4, and tap out the answer with its foot. And if you put coloured handkerchiefs in a box and asked it to pick out a red one it would lift it out with its teeth and drop it at your feet.

He allowed three boys to come home with him after school, but when they reached the end of the drive below the house they heard his dogs barking and refused to go any further till he had locked them in.

He ran up the drive, barred the dogs in a shed, and whistled to his three friends who stood swinging on the road-side gate. They immediately threw their schoolbags behind the gatepost and raced up to him, and there in the safe silence of the yard they looked over the half-door of the stable at the black pony. It was, indeed, a wee beauty! And then he pointed to the saddle hanging from a peg in the wall. It took their breath away! — the hard shiny stir-rups and the leather polished like a new chestnut. They would all get rides on it but not today. He wouldn't be allowed to take it out to the fields till the ground warmed. They would have to wait till then.

He let them into the stable, one at a time, to stroke the pony's head and to feel the steel stirrups and the saddle. In hushed voices they called out: "Dandy, Dandy!" and to Kevin's surprise the pony cocked its ears and the mare stamped a hind foot on the straw.

"Get him to lie down and die, Kevin."

"No, no, get him to do a sum."

"Not now," Kevin said. "He doesn't like performing in a stable, and into the bargain he'd only upset the mare."

At that moment Kevin's mother rapped the window sharply and called him for his dinner.

His three friends scampered off, collected their schoolbags at the gate, and agreed among themselves that it was the dinkiest pony in the whole world.

In the succeeding days the sun lengthened his stride up the sky, the withered grass shrivelled from the rising green in the fields, and the mare and the pony were put out to graze. Kevin and his sisters hurried home from school to ride the pony before the sudden fall of evening and since Kevin hadn't yet discovered how the pony could be enticed to do a trick he allowed the two dogs to accompany him – an unexpressed warning to his school friends not to come into the field. From gaps in the hedge they would safely shout up to him: "Kevin, make him do a trick. . . . Make him do a trick. . . . Take in the dogs and give us rides apiece." And as the pony jogged around, now with Kevin on his back, now with Rita, and now with Joan, bursts of enraged impatience would rush from the outcast spectators: "Make him gallop. . . . Ah, he can't run. . . . You'd get a better jaunt on a donkey."

"Come on, Kevin, and we'll hiss the dogs on them," Rita would urge indignantly.

"Pretend you don't hear them," Eileen would advise.

"They'll change their tune when Daddy shows us how he does his tricks. Won't they Eileen?"

"I'm sure they will."

But with each day that passed Dandy displayed no mysterious inclination to do anything out of the ordinary. Kevin's friends ceased coming near the field, and in school they often challenged him to race his prize pony against one of their old donkeys. They never wearied in their taunts and mockery.

He grew to hate the school, and one evening as he followed his father round the stables, beseeching him to get the pony to do a trick, his father shouted at him to give over and give his head peace sometime: "I don't know how he does his tricks and I don't care. You're never satisfied with anything. Away and ride him round the fields and don't bother me any more!"

The next day he didn't go to school. He pretended he was sick. He stayed away for three days. He wanted to forget about the pony's tricks but, when he returned to school, the boys wouldn't allow him to forget. They mimicked him with cruel exaggeration: "When it begs for bread give it a loaf with jam on it. . . . It's the cutest pony in Ireland. . . . It can do sums that'd puzzle the master."

But the following day, St. Patrick's Day, the miracle happened. Rita and Joan were playing near the orchard, fixing a swing to an ash-bough when they heard in the distance the sound of the Lough Neagh Flute Band, that was marching to the opening of a new sports ground near the chapel. They threw down their ropes, raced to the gate, closed it, and stood up on the bars to await the band.

Kevin was on the topmost bar and by turning his head he saw the band as it came along. The band-leader, out in front in his blue uniform and white gloves, was twirling a pole with a silver knob that caught the sun; and the sound of the flutes and the big drum swamped the noise of the marching feet of the bandsmen and the stumbling feet of the boys who straggled at each side of the road.

The sticks drubbed with furious rapidity on the kettle-drums, and their sounds ribbed out and belaboured the air with a frantic tizzing and frangling that forced Joan to draw back in fear.

The band came abreast of the gate and Kevin looked down at it, seeing the fingers hopping madly on the flutes, and the tiny cards of music with their printed notes like wriggling tadpoles. A boy with spectacles clashed cymbals together, the kettle-drums rolled out once more, and the air pranced with vigorous delight. The band passed the gate, but Joan who was peering fearfully through the hedge screamed out: "Look! Look what Dandy's doing!"

Near the roadside hedge Dandy was parading round in a

circle, nodding his head, lifting his forefeet with exaggerated precision and increasing his pace to the roll of the drums. And then at the sudden cessation of the kettle-drums and at the deep incoming beat from the big drum he rose up on his hind-legs pirouetted and boxed the air.

The roadside hedge was now lined with heads at all levels, laughing and cheering the pony. And the bandsmen marched on, and their leader tossed up his tasselled pole, twirled it dexterously to the cheers behind him and strode ahead with ceremonial pomposity. Dandy followed the band on the inside of the hedge but at the end of the field where a fence blocked his way he halted with one foreleg raised like an equestrian statue, his ears pricked towards the dwindling sound of music.

Tearing across the fields to him came the three children shrieking with delight.

In school the next day everyone was talking about him and of the strange acts he had performed for the Lough Neagh Flute Band, and after school six or seven boys bolted down their dinner and set off to see for themselves the tricks of this wonderful pony. When they arrived at the field the two dogs were nowhere to be seen and the boys scrambled through holes in the hedge and raced up to Kevin and Rita. Eileen was in the field, too, holding Joan by the hand.

In front of the pony's head Kevin stood with an empty milk can and a stick. He was hammering at the bottom of it, but the pony, with the vacant saddle on its back, was showing no interest in the unrythmical sound. Kevin's friends drew closer to him and pulling pencils from their pockets they held them to their mouths like a flute, ran their fingers along them and began to whistle. Kevin flogged away at the can with his stick. The pony shook itself, turned his back on them and began to graze.

"Dandy!" Kevin shouted, and he jerked the reins till the pony faced them again.

"Ach, he's stupid," one of the boys said with disgust.

"He's the cutest and cleverest pony in Ireland."

"Everybody knows it," Kevin said.

"Make him give you his paw."

"Make him lie down and die."

"Make him do some damned thing and not keep us standing here all day."

"Nobody's asking you to stand here all day!" Rita said pertly.

"Give us a ride on him."

"We're not allowed to," Rita said, tossing her head.

The boys laughed and elbowed one another, and one of them lifted a lump of sod and threw it at the pony.

"Just for that we'll not get him to do any tricks!" Kevin said.

"You don't know how! You don't know how!" they chanted.

"Don't I! I could get him to do thousands of tricks!"

"Get him to do them! Get him to do even one!"

"Go on home out of this," Eileen said, noticing that Kevin was nearly in tears.

"We'll go when we're ready. You think because you're at a convent school you can order us about," one said, and they giggled and stumbled against her. "I'll get the dogs and they'll fix you!" she said, and on hearing this they fled down the field and on to the road where they hung about, shouting and jeering through holes in the hedge.

Rita lifted Kevin's stick, marched over to the pony and mounted him smartly. She tapped him with the stick and he suddenly took fright and galloped down the sloping field. She was bounced about without grace or rhythm. She tried not to scream, and as she was joggled off she held on to the reins and was dragged along the ground.

She heard a volley of cheers from the road and she scrambled to her feet and lashed out at the pony with her stick. And suddenly the pony rose up stiffly on its hind legs, grimaced horribly, the silver bit in its mouth and grass between its teeth.

"Rita! Rita!" Eileen yelled as she and Kevin ran down to her. Eileen snatched the stick and broke it in two, the pony still pirouetting, and breathing with a fearful choking sound.

"Now you see how you get him to do his tricks! You see it now!" Eileen said in a broken voice. "It's horrible, horrible," she cried, waiting for the pony to cease its painful caperings.

"There, Dandy! That'll do! Down, please, down!" she said soothingly, and at that moment she saw the fear of punishment in its dark eyes, saw the cruelty that produced circus joys.

At last, exhausted, the pony placed its forefeet on the ground. Its sides heaved rapidly and little patches like snow gathered at the corners of its mouth. It stood still, subdued, motionless with expectant fear.

Rita was crying and rubbing her knee, and Joan was helping her to pick the pieces of crushed grass from her frock.

Kevin stared dumbly, now at the pony, and now at the broken stick lying at Eileen's feet. He was thinking of something, something that puzzled him. But what it was he did not know.